THE ART TEACHER

PAUL READ

Legend Press Ltd, 175-185 Gray's Inn Road, London, WC1X 8UE
info@legend-paperbooks.co.uk | www.legendpress.co.uk

Print ISBN 978-1-7850795-7-3
Ebook ISBN 978-1-7850795-8-0
Set in Times. Printed in the United Kingdom by TJ International.
Cover design by Simon Levy www.simonlevyassociates.co.uk

After gaining a first in Fine Art at the Kent Institute of Art and Design at Canterbury, **Paul Read** moved to London, finding employment at Foyles bookshop before becoming a teacher. He has worked in several inner-city schools as an Art, English and supply teacher, both in England and Italy. He received a distinction from City University London for his creative writing MA.

A few years ago, Paul was involved in a hit-and-run incident which put him in a wheelchair for several months and was where he wrote the first draft of *The Art Teacher*. He lives with Patricia and their two children.

Follow him on Twitter:
@paulreadauthor

For Patricia

Mi vuoi sposare?

PART ONE

ONE

Patrick Owen had managed seven years at Highfields Secondary School without punching a pupil in the face.

The week he found his patience tested beyond its usual limit started, much like any other, with Patrick swallowing a pint of sugared coffee and rising from his emails to watch the morning madness from his classroom window. Outside, pupils streamed into the playground past the teacher on gate duty – Jill McFarley from Maths was today's tearful Cerberus – and a sea of blue jumpers and swinging bags accompanied the high-pitched recounting of the previous night's soap plots. A cold, bright dawn. The last week before Christmas.

Billy Matthews was tagging the word 'KILLA' against the Science block while Sherry Dixon tugged up her top to show Hussein Sagar a new tattoo. Frankie Griffiths was being punched in the gut by Daniel Malaise, who didn't even bother to take the cigarette out of his mouth. It looked like a comradely, playful beating. Perhaps it was Frankie's birthday.

The registration bell tolled.

A few members of Patrick's tutor group were already outside his classroom, picking paint off the wall by the Art storeroom and casting aspersions on one another's sexuality, but most of them, being fourteen, were still in bed. Those present – strangely proportioned man-boys, flirting timidly with girls wearing false nails so long they couldn't hold paintbrushes – talked about television shows he didn't watch and bands he'd never heard. It was this cultural gap, Patrick suspected, which, more than anything, made him so invisible to youth. He didn't know the names of many footballers, let alone their equally famous girlfriends, and would certainly never consider appearing in a pair of tracksuit trousers with the word 'Juicy' stitched across the arse.

His form class had learned it was easier, in the long-run, to enter the classroom quietly, to channel their natural irreverence into non-verbal art forms. Therefore, once the register had been taken, Patrick wasn't surprised to find the still life arrangements in the table centres covered in Euro 2016 football stickers and half-inflated condoms. He couldn't bring himself to be angry about it. It was too early, and he'd need every last kilojoule of energy for later.

Patrick powered up the humming overhead projector and an image of the *Mona Lisa* filled the pull-down screen covering his old whiteboard.

'You all know this painting of course…'

A hand sliced up. That was a good sign. They normally just called out.

'Yes, Gaia.'

'It's shit. She don't have eyebrows.'

He was vaguely aware of girls passing notes between them on a back table. Sebastian was streaking something horrible from his fingertip under his desk.

'Moving on.' He presented to them an Expressionistic classic of inner turmoil. No teenager ever failed to associate with Edvard Munch's *The Scream*.

'It's shit too,' opined Matthew, the purplish trace of a black eye worn like a trophy. 'He don't have no eyebrows either.'

'Why did you choose Art again?' Patrick snapped.

'Music had too many people, innit.'

With an exhalation too deep for his lungs, Patrick persevered. 'These are examples of overly familiar artworks from popular media. We are entirely dislocated from their times, their initial power. You dislike them because they've been, perhaps, over-promoted. Try to imagine it's the first time you've seen them and...'

'It *is* the first time I've seen them,' wailed Sonja.

'Me too,' said Simon.

'The first time you've seen THE *MONA LISA*?'

The class stared at him in horror as he ordered them, with a despairing shake of the head, to finish their work from last week.

This class could be well behaved sometimes, but it was the last lesson of the day and they were full of E-numbers and holiday spirit. For half an hour he condoned the exasperating antics of young adults who should have known better, of children who acted deliberately like children in front of the adult, until he finally deigned to raise his voice. The rapping and bratting ceased for a few minutes, much to the relief of the headache he'd acquired after his Year Nine group's endless carousel of paper aeroplanes, tie peanutting, epileptic seizures and nosebleeds.

Patrick gazed out his window, his reflection and the view morphing into a double exposure against the apocalyptic vision of the neighbouring Union City estate. It dominated the landscape with its three square miles of stark Brutalism and asymmetric blocking, the school itself built out of the same visually objectionable concrete, as though little more than a penal-looking addendum. Many of the pupils knew no other kind of architecture; though the catchment area officially included the elegant Edwardian terraces of the lower-middle class on the other side of the school, most Highfields kids were of the free school dinner demographic.

The lesson entered its last fifteen minutes and Patrick was just about to reward the class with a few minutes of unlistenable horror courtesy of a mainstream radio station when Denis Roberts appeared through the door, making teenage noises into his iPhone.

Denis was one of the more problematic members of his Year Eleven Art group. He was a well-built boy, had grown twenty centimetres outwards and upwards over the year, and now sported a thickening moustache and passable sideburns. As a child, he'd had an operation to repair a cleft lip and the scar remained, running angrily up the left side of a flat philtrum to his nostrils.

'…You shoulda seen him… I banged him *up*, bruv. Listen, give us a call laters, yeah,' he said, 'I gotta be doing Art or someshit now.' He walked slowly, with exaggerated torso bobbing and a smoothing of his eyebrow, to his seat.

'Stay where you are,' Patrick demanded, walking briskly towards him. Such was Denis' over-confidence, he allowed the teacher to scythe his phone from his grasp. 'I'll take that, thank you. Wait outside.'

The boy threw his shoulders back, bunched his mouth into a kiss and balled his fists.

Denis was not going to wait outside.

A few kids snickered in anxious response, thrilled that one of them dared to stand up to the grown-up, his rules, his routines.

'Sophia,' the Art teacher ordered, still calm, still measured in his tones. 'Could you call for rapid response please?'

Sophia sheepishly left her seat at the front of the class and brushed past Denis, who continued to puff out his chest. Sophia was the best kid in the class, honest, quiet, dependable, and far from brainless. She knew to whom she should remain loyal. Two minutes later, following Denis' numerous variations on 'Why'd you do it?' and 'You're so bait, man,' Sophia returned with news that the day's designated senior teacher was 'on their way'. Rapid response wasn't coming.

'Stop disturbing the class, Denis. I'll speak to you at the end of the day.'

'It *is* the end of the day. You're jacking my phone. That's racist, man.'

'Denis, we're the *same* colour.'

'That's racist, man.'

12

'Denis, really... What's the point of bursting in here and disturbing everyone's learning?'

'What's the point of you, you old fart?'

The class laughed. It was true. Right now, he felt unfathomably ancient.

He heard someone at the back mutter, 'Owen got owned.'

Kids today communicated with words he simply didn't understand. It was the same mangling, freeform approach they took to walking, of all things. Denis was doing it now: a lounging gangsta gait. Why was walking in the upright manner which homo sapiens had historically preferred now deemed so embarrassing? Patrick felt it was surely something to do with the unnecessary exposure of boxer shorts. 'Underwear,' he kept telling them. 'It's called UNDERWEAR. You wear them UNDER.'

Patrick thought the class had been hard to control before, but after the projector screen chose this moment to fly up into its housing with a drum-rolled whipcrack and reveal a crudely-drawn, ejaculating penis and two curly-pubed bollocks, he had no chance.

He looked at the clock. Only five minutes left of this torture for today.

As the rest of the class cried with laughter, Denis perched himself on the teacher's desk and announced, 'I'm gonna wait here until the end of the lesson, and then you're gonna gimme back my phone.' Patrick was sorely tempted to cast his phone to the floor and stamp on the fucking device, but in the grand scheme of things none of this mattered; he knew how petty he looked. The fact that Denis was never without his phone, yet managed to leave his pencil at home every single day shouldn't really have got to him as much as it did. He began wiping the cock and balls off his board. Four minutes to go.

Down the corridor, he spied Charlotte, his head of department. He called out for her, then watched her try to pretend she hadn't heard before eventually, slowly, walking in the direction of his classroom. She hovered with impatience at his door.

'Ms Purchase, I caught this boy using his mobile and confiscated it. Now he's causing all sorts of trouble,' Patrick explained.

His head of department was able to transmit, through a facial expression which remained both remote and indifferent, that she was far, far too busy to deal with this.

At twenty-nine, Charlotte was six years younger than Patrick but it was her innate, as opposed to financial, superiority which irked him most. She was the sort of woman who wouldn't walk through a door unless it was already held open. Fortunately for her, being heir to two Highgate houses and symmetrically pleasing Italianate looks, she was also the sort of woman most men held doors open for, so was used to getting her way.

Patrick, wishing he hadn't bothered in the first place, once more repeated the school's code of conduct to Denis.

'You're joking me, man,' the boy scoffed. 'Don't be dry.'

Patrick noticed the plastic compass in Denis' left hand, with which he'd idly carved what looked like an AK47 into the Art teacher's desk. Sadly, this was the first decent drawing the boy had managed all year.

'May I have his phone?' Charlotte asked.

Relived and grateful, Patrick handed it over. Then watched in astonishment as Charlotte gave it back to the boy.

'Look, young man, just don't get it out again, okay?' she cooed, undermining her colleague in fangless fashion.

Patrick watched her face, the vacant excuse for nervous happiness it presented, and wondered who the bigger idiot really was. Once upon a time, they'd both taken Fine Art degrees.

She walked off, indomitable, victory-flushed. Denis looked pretty triumphant too, his lips curled in a combination of apathetic impudence and a superiority Patrick couldn't understand how a mere fifteen-year-old could possess. He had a cluster of small whiteheads around his mouth, a new, fourth, slice in his right eyebrow.

Patrick shot a glance out the window, where a few of Denis' little gang waited in a shattered bus stop. How he'd got mixed up in that group – older boys, mostly expelled or past-pupils who'd made a habit of truanting and intimidation during their own tenures – Patrick didn't know. They were always there at the end of the day, smoking and shouting obscenities at the sixth form girls. One of them was supporting a gimpy leg with an inverted golf club.

Thirty seconds to go.

Patrick tried to smooth matters over with a lie: 'You know, you've got talent in this subject. If you could just…' But praise only works on children who aren't already as egocentric as their Premier League idols. 'Listen, Denis,' Patrick said in response to another giant huff, 'I know you're not keen on the subject but others are, they don't want to be constantly distracted. You've all got a GCSE to take.'

'Man, I ain't got no talent, you know that.'

Ah, the fabled double negative. 'You mean, you haven't got…'

The bell went.

Denis jabbed a sovereign-ringed finger into Patrick's chest. 'Apologise for jacking my phone,' he demanded.

The class were still in their seats, despite the bell, watching the drama unfold.

'What's the magic word?' Patrick asked, attempting to inject a kind of levity into the lesson finale.

'*Bender*. Apologise for jacking my phone.'

How Patrick even found the strength to sigh these days was beyond him.

'Denis, I don't have to…'

'It ain't nice to snatch. You gonna apologise?' Menace reddened his eyes.

'You can go now.' Desperately, he addressed the class. Still, no one moved. They knew there was more to come.

'Everyone thinks you're gay, sir. D'you know that?'

Patrick turned to face the boy again. 'I couldn't care less. Goodbye.'

'You got a wifey?'

A slow smirk crept across Denis' face as Patrick prickled. Denis had sensed something, a nerve grazed, a mask slipped. 'Did she dump you because you're such a loser, sir?' This was followed by an enquiring look, serious, deadpan.

Despite himself, the teacher let fury win. 'Get out!'

'I'm just asking, innit. Keep your hair on.' Denis raised his eyes towards Patrick's hair, as if denigrating the style Patrick sported, though it was of a style little different to Denis' own. Patrick wore his hair short because he was thinning, Denis did so to separate himself from the fingerless-gloved Emos who played a card game known as Arsehole in the Design Technology rooms at breaktime. 'I mean, you went to university and everything to get this job, did you? And you think you're not a loser?'

'And what about you, Denis? What do you expect to amount to?'

He hadn't meant to say that, and certainly not with such venom. It had come from within him, unauthorised. Denis took half a step away from his teacher, his bruised look of disbelief echoing the gasps from the room. Teachers weren't meant to say things like that. You could wind them up, and up, and up, but they were never supposed to come back at you. Still, what *would* Denis become? Patrick dreaded to think.

The atmosphere in the room was leaden. Still, no one moved.

'I won't ask again. Get out.'

'And I won't either. Apologise.'

Denis spat on the classroom linoleum – it glistened in the muddied sunlight cast from the estate-shadowed panorama – then walked right up to his teacher. The boy was employing a primal trick, moving into another's personal space, making

16

himself bigger in the presence of a rival. There were more gasps from the assembled students, but muted now.

Patrick put a hand out to repel the boy, the flat of his hand on Denis' breastbone. The two of them glared at each other.

'Get *out*.' Patrick put defiance, a trained authority, into the words, but Denis continued to stare, his eyes screwed into black holes. Fingers curled by the boy's sides, gunslinger style.

'You can't touch me,' Denis hissed, shrugging Patrick's hand off. 'You ain't *allowed*.'

Patrick felt his desk meet the back of his legs. He'd been backing away without realising. His fists were so clenched they hurt. If the boy dared take another step towards him, made to move, speak, breathe, Patrick doubted he'd find the strength not to knock his block off.

They both stood in silence.

Fear, or the embers of professionalism, kept Patrick's arms pinned to his side.

'Sorry,' he whispered.

'What?' The boy theatrically cupped his hand to an ear. 'I didn't hear you.'

Marginally louder, though the class had all heard the first time, Patrick repeated himself. 'Sorry.'

With eerie and surreal calm, Denis took a step back and swaggered towards the door.

One by one, and visibly disappointed, the class stood and followed the boy out into the growling corridor.

TWO

The sound of his own footsteps echoed around him as he sped through pages of tabloid and the crabgrass sprouting in fractured concrete. Any other time, he would have feared what his frantic scurrying must have looked like to the estate's residents. But no one was out. No one ever was after dark, except the gangs.

The earth had long since tilted on its axis, retiring the sun, as Patrick half-ran to the bus stop. He'd recently toyed with buying a cheap car but the roads around Highfields were a congested nightmare and the headteacher's Beemer had been found with its tyres screwdrivered on more than one occasion.

This small section of the estate, the only part of it he ever dared penetrate, was a gridded mess of Escher-like confusion, the majority of Union City stretching vast and dark and mildewed to his left. Shadows flitted under raised walkways, sparked metallic-smelling joints. He'd always been conscious of the potential embarrassment of meeting pupils but today he was apprehensive, to put it mildly, about running into Denis. He kept thinking of that parting sneer, the coldness of it, the emptiness.

A trio of youths rounded the corner ahead and he held his breath as they parted for him, neckchains glinting blades under the sodium smearing of streetlamps. He thought he heard one of them whisper, 'Mr Owen...'

Running from the darkness onto the main road, he saw

his bus approaching. With fifty metres between him and the bus stop, the bus slowed and ejected a solitary passenger. The driver flicked on the indicator, hissed the doors closed. Twenty metres. Patrick threw himself towards the bus as it anticipated a gap in the traffic then, breathless, banged on the doors to attract the driver's attention. Reluctantly, the doors reopened. A tired mother eyed him as the bus sighed on. An addict with pinpricks for pupils. Posters above the windows beseeched kids to join the army, to apply for college, to buy the latest video game. The only advert not aimed at children was an old one. 'Use Your Head' it said, above a photo of a young trainee standing before a class of eager learners. 'Teach.'

Patrick regarded the recruitment poster's carefree, lying stagecraft in numb agony for a moment before a kid – probably Year Seven or Eight – in an over-ironed Highfields uniform jogged down the stairs. Patrick attempted to shift to one side in his seat, turn his body to the window, but he'd already been noticed.

'Alright, sir.'

Who was it? He never could remember their names.

The kid lingered by the door, waiting for his stop, then began rummaging in his school bag before tearing out a drawing and wordlessly holding it out to Patrick.

It was a drawing of a dragon, his tail engulfed in scribbled fire.

'Oh, that's *lovely*.' It was terrible.

The bus hiccoughed to a halt.

'See you, sir.'

'Your drawing.' Patrick attempted to pass it back to him.

'You keep it, sir.' The kid beamed proudly and stepped off the bus.

Patrick, a faint feeling of victory and pride rising like a bubble through his chest, turned at the sound of what seemed to be his own voice.

'Oh, that's *lovely*.'

A group of boys in Highfields uniforms were huddled round a mobile phone, sniggering. One of them re-pressed a button.

'Oh, that's *lovely*,' went the recorded voice.

'This is *so* my ringtone,' one of them declared.

Patrick screwed his headphones into his ears to drown out their laughter.

Patrick lived at number six 'The Heights', a block of flats built in the fifties as cheap replacements for the Blitz-damaged dwellings which had once stood, like their survivors opposite, tall and boastful of relief laurels and alabaster covings. The Heights weren't cheap any longer of course but Patrick knew the residents of the larger Georgian properties in the area – clear-skinned toffs in bespoke winter wear who avoided his eyes on Sunday mornings – still considered them to be. All that mattered to Patrick was that he lived far enough away from Highfields to avoid bumping into his pupils in the pub.

He put the picture the kid on the bus gave him on the mantelpiece, looked at it properly – it wasn't a dragon, he now realised, but a soaring phoenix, mockingly reborn from the flames – then slumped at the kitchen table and uncorked a bottle of wine, staring at his red, ballooned face in the convex bulge of a glass he didn't even rinse out before refilling. His eyes were two puffy, brown lozenges of exhaustion, his chin weak and tapering towards triangular.

For a long time, until quite recently, Patrick knew he'd got away with looking younger than his years. But no longer. His body was stepping up its war against youth, that irreversible submission to the ageing process every living creature must endure. In the evenings, the mirror showed his face as a net of worry lines and, upon waking, revealed it to be pressed into channels and creases by an unforgiving pillow. Gradually, he knew, the look he sported in the evening would move back in time through the day and the morning wrinkles would last until the afternoon. One day soon, at the day's centre, the two faces would marry.

Teaching wasn't entirely to blame. Time, and its accompanying intimations of mortality, was taking its toll. The eyes which passed over him in nightclubs. The blockbusters starring millionaires younger than him. Everywhere he looked, Patrick saw ugly and incontestable vanitas symbols.

He thought of Denis. The unfolded whiteness of his skin, the unstained teeth, and felt more terror than he'd ever felt in his life.

The telephone shrieked on the desk.

This was it. The call. All he'd done was touch the boy's bloody shoulder, for God's sake. And now the headteacher was demanding to know why Denis' mother had threatened to have the school razed to the ground, the teachers lynched and the parent-governor body shot against the playground wall. There was nowhere to run; Denis had once again got him with his back to his desk.

He reached out and lifted the receiver.

'Hello?'

A brief pause. 'Patrick. Hi.'

There were times when he wondered whether it was merely his wife's voice he'd desired, that oddly dichotomous mix of Catalan and American, the curt nature of her Barcelonan Ts and the lazy drawl of the West Coast. He once told her he'd never stop loving that accent and now, looking back through the prism of the years, that voice, he was sad to admit, hadn't faded in his affections. Though thousands of miles away, she was as clear and familiar as though she were in the same room.

'Ana. How are you?'

She launched into a story without pause. Something about the colour of the sand, the price of steaks, and how these seemingly disparate subjects were linked by the confusing colloquialisms and contortions of South American Spanish. He dreaded the moment she asked about his life, and when

21

she did he merely replied, no longer buoyed by the wine, 'Oh, okay...' She was under the Argentinian sun, living, while he reposed on a futon in a rented London apartment six decades past its peak, aware of the fact that, two hours earlier, he'd nearly been beaten up by a child in front of a room full of other children. 'And how is...?'

'He's fine. He misses you.'

Patrick found himself in the spare room, his eyes skimming over the reasons he'd moved to this flat in the first place. The Lightning McQueen duvet cover. The Darth Vader money box. Danny's weekend home, before the extended holiday that took him away.

'Does he want to Skype with me?' Patrick asked.

'He's with Mum at the moment.'

'Right. So...?'

A leaden pause. 'So *what's the point of me ringing exactly*?' she asked with sarcasm.

He drained the rest of the glass. An argument was brewing and he needed fortification. 'Yep.'

'I received a letter from your solicitor this morning...'

It hadn't been right between Patrick and Ana for some time, but the killing of routine is never painless and he'd been inconsolable the morning she told him she was taking their son with her to Buenos Aires. He regained enough control to say, 'Look, I didn't want to get the solicitor involved but... He's my son too. I don't want to have to catch a plane every time...'

'But you must understand that there was nothing left in London for me.'

'You think there's anything left here for *me*?'

Another silence.

He surveyed the communal garden no one ever tended, the inky steeple of the neighbouring church, shelled and awaiting its second life as luxury accommodation. In a nearby block of flats a girl played a silent violin at her window, stabbing her bow arm up and down at firm and practiced angles. It might have been an Edward Hopper painting.

'So when are you back?' She'd only been supposed to stay with her mother for a month. It had been two already.

She hesitated. 'Soon. The minute I get a job offer, I guess.' If her leaving had been the death of their relationship, this new lie felt like its internment. 'How's work with you?'

'It's been better. Busy, you know.' He chose platitudes and the expected response.

'At that dodgy place still?'

He chuckled without mirth. 'At that dodgy place still.'

'Nothing else lined up?'

'I went for an interview at another school a few months ago, but no luck. Everyone wants cheap, new blood. I've been doing this a while. I'm expensive.'

At this, Ana seemed to realise the cost of the call. Patrick was aware of an urgency in her voice as she attempted to wind up the conversation.

'Look, I want to sort this amicably…' she started.

'Me too.'

'I wish we didn't have to…'

'I know.'

'Bye,' she said.

'Ana, I….'

He listened to the silence from the other side of the world for a long time before turning off the phone. The violin's high-pitched and frenetic melody was audible now, hitchhiking on the wind, and he opened the window to eavesdrop on a sound which reminded him of days when perseverance and talent had seemed enough.

Patrick remembered the exact moment he knew something had slipped through his fingers.

Walking home from Highfields the previous spring, he'd seen twenty boys from Year Eleven fighting an avaricious game of football on a small recreational patch near the school, one side in white shirts, the other bare-chested. It was an unusually hot day – or so it seemed to him in retrospect – and, as he walked behind the makeshift goalposts, he'd fancied he felt a fraction of his pupils' exuberance, the sensation of the oncoming summer, the genesis of adulthood. The joyous, competitive nature with which skinny centre forwards thundered over the churned, makeshift pitch seemed to belie the nearness of the exam season.

He'd gone home that day and slumped in his kitchen with his favourite guitar, the flame-maple Les Paul he'd had flown over from Japan. A tune had been running through his head for the afternoon and he'd wanted to pin it down. He attempted a few standard chords, groping around in his musical memory and, deciding the tune had been based around D minor, dropped the sixth string two frets. As he strummed, a different melody emerged and, slowing it and playing only minor notes, he intensified its mournful quality, as one might compose a nursery tune. It wasn't technically innovative but he gave it a title – 'Sixteen' – in honour of his own carefree teenage years, the hair grown, the girls loved, the nights wasted. He wanted to immerse himself in the bittersweet vertigo of youth having passed.

After playing with the new melody for a while he found, to his disappointment, that it refused to grow and, after the first four bars, became stuck in a musical cul-de-sac. This happened sometimes and he knew he only had to rest the idea and come back to it later, but it had now become impossible to unlock the original melody he'd conjured during the day. The longer he tried, the more unplayable it became. Like the mismatch of ambition and the harsh light of reality, what he'd heard in his head and what came from his fingers were not the same.

Music had once been Patrick's life but now it seemed as though his teaching qualification, a fallback career encouraged by a well-meaning Ana during the early days of their relationship, was all he had. He'd often wondered whether his status would be raised with his kids if he dared tell them about his old life, the star he nearly became. But failure wasn't saluted, or attractive. Failure wasn't even conceivable to those football-punting teenagers on the grass, in their perpetual summer.

At the time, Patrick didn't look upon it as an omen. Not being able to excavate the symphony in his head wasn't evidence he'd lost his ear for music entirely. But he knew something had changed inside him.

He was still standing inside his absent son's bedroom, empty glass in one hand, humming telephone in the other. There was a photo of Danny and Patrick on the cupboard door, taken at the Hyde Park Winter Wonderland last Christmas. He was almost four now. Did he even look the same? And to whom was he offloading his cartoon, pillow fight-violence, his pigeon-chasing skills (did they have pigeons in Argentina?), his sweet tooth demands? Ana's parents? Ana's lover? Ana's *lovers*? Patrick missed him, missed treating him, and the presents had been building up in the corner of the bedroom. He knew he'd see him soon enough, but probably not before Christmas. Yes, it was cruel of Ana, but she wasn't a cruel person. She'd be back with him. He was convinced of that. They'd both be back.

The violinist had stopped – he couldn't be sure when – but she was still standing in her window. She wore a dressing gown which had fallen open to reveal one half of a black bra and she looked at Patrick as if trying to place him from somewhere. A moment flickered between them. A common, human understanding amid the urban chaos.

He waved.

She gave him the finger before drawing the curtains.

THREE

All the kids knew Patrick's classroom was haunted.

Patrick knew something else: the lighting was screwed. And the electricity didn't play ball either. Sometimes the whiteboard turned itself off for no reason. Sometimes the glue guns blew up without warning.

Tuesday morning, the lights flickered halfway through his Year Seven lesson.

'It's Dave!' a kid shouted.

Three years ago, a BTEC pupil left Highfields under mysterious circumstances. Of course, the rumour was that he'd died. He hadn't, but calling the 'ghost' Dave was appealingly stupid; after all, ghosts were supposed to be named romantic, resonant things like The Lady in the Well or The White Huntsman. Such was Dave's fame, even the Sevens were in on the act now.

The lights flickered back on and Patrick growled at the class to keep them in line. Sometimes 'Dave' putting the spooks up them worked wonders. Control was restored.

His computer thrummed in the background as the children drew their arrangements of bottles, books and dying plants. Patrick paced the room with hands clasped behind his back like some old, learned professor, informing them about balance in their paintings, how cool colours receded, warm colours came forward, the way both could be used, in far corners or foregrounds, to move the eye around a piece. They either looked at him blankly, or pretended he wasn't

26

talking. Unperturbed, he explained how backgrounds should be soft and uncluttered, with light, delicate colour-blending. He explained stability, rhythm, depth and calm. All things he used to have in his life, he thought ruefully, before the palette changed and everything became conflict, distance; a canvas hanging off-centre from a broken nail.

Halfway through his little unheard lecture, a loud fart ripped through the room, closely followed by the horrific aroma of Weetabix and puberty, which hung in the air like some foul atomic fallout. Laughter followed, and the predictable grasping at throats as though Agent Orange had been unleashed. It died down eventually, until Trevor Holbein fell off his stool and the hysterics began again.

At breaktime, Patrick shuffled down to the staffroom to avoid Charlotte and settled himself on one of the uncomfortable waiting room-style chairs by the window. The Christmas tree in the corner was last year's and its decorations were staff donations, the tinsel arranged with some cunning to disguise the fact it was no more than a piece of string in certain places.

He was supposed to be on break duty but, frankly, it was an English winter outside. No direct, natural sunlight hit your face all day, and when it did, as you navigated the fights in the litter-strewn playground with cold hands thrust deep into pockets, it burned like liquid nitrogen.

'Hi, Patrick.' A figure flopped down beside him, Tupperware box smelling faintly of choucroute and tomatoes.

Christophe was a French teacher, dark-haired but pale from lack of sun, with a smearing of grey stubble over the bottom of his face. He claimed to be a Communist, and wore a red star on mufti days, but was too tall and too overweight to look genuinely proletariat; his girth merely supported Patrick's long-held suspicion that he wasn't as stressed as his blue-arsed colleagues.

'Hi, Chris. How's it going?'

'Simon in 9A squashed his chewing gum into Shaun's

27

hair,' the Languages teacher said, forking a slice of sausage. 'Why do they do this shit?' Like all educators across the world, Patrick and Christophe tried not to talk about children when they didn't have to, but, like all educators across the world, failed miserably. 'How are you?'

'Tired. Harriet's still off "sick". I doubt we'll see her again until the new year.'

Harriet Dylan, a cynical, fiftysomething bastion of old-school laziness, had croaked her continued unavailability down the office phone with exaggerated infirmity that morning, claiming 'one of them twenty-four hour bugs.' It had been a fortnight now. Her patience, like their department's budget, had run dry long ago.

'You've got yellow paint on your tie.'

'Thanks.' Patrick rubbed at the stain with the heel of his palm before realising it was just a part of his tie's pattern.

Christophe was a failed comedian, but it wasn't the 'comedian' part that Patrick had warmed to, it was the 'failed'. Successful people bored Patrick. He'd never been to see any of Christophe's gigs – he hadn't known him long enough – but knew he must have been pretty awful. There are, after all, two types of people in this world: those who find themselves funnier than they are and those who don't know quite how funny they can be. The latter type of person was understated, unamused by their own jokes, often confounded when people found them uproarious. Natural comedians. Christophe's jokes, bless him, often created awkward silences or, worse, heckles.

Other teachers buzzed around them, collecting sheets from cabinets. Absence forms. Health and safety slips. Detention letters. The PE department were in their usual seats, doing sod all, and an aggregation of teaching assistants huddled round a computer at the other end, each furnished with enough coffee to kill a person over seventy.

He realised Christophe was looking at him as though awaiting a response.

28

'I'm fine,' Patrick said, then, assuming he needed to justify his disposition, added, 'I heard from Ana yesterday.'

'Shit. How is she?'

Patrick relayed the latest. Briefly, the routine of their breaktime chat, the salted meats in Christophe's plastic box, the watching of the clock, calmed him. Eighteen lessons to go before the holiday.

'How do you feel about the situation?'

Patrick practiced his nonchalant shrug while looking at the carpet, possibly the only square foot in the whole school unstained by gum. The gesture came across as it was intended; he hadn't worked out how to take the break-up yet.

Christophe crunched the lid back on his lunchbox and sighed, massaging arthritic wrists; his forefingers curled vaguely away from their neighbours as though broken. 'Who you got next?'

'Year Eleven. More's the pity.'

'Denis?'

'Denis.'

Patrick had spent the morning dreading the latest confrontation with Denis Roberts. Hopefully the boy had forgotten about the teacher's insult the day before. If not, Patrick knew there was only one course of action open: he would steadfastly refuse to admit yesterday had ever happened. It was a tactic he'd learned from wrongdoers at school, who, with limitless fervency and indignation, denied all manner of misconduct, even when he'd seen them do something idiotic with his own eyes. Maybe, if Patrick refuted it strenuously enough, he might even convince himself he hadn't done anything wrong.

'I had 11E period one. He turned up halfway through.' Christophe chuckled to himself as he stood, confidently, unhurried. 'He was good as gold, actually.' Though Christophe's English was impeccable, his Gallic accent was strong. He spoke from the front of his mouth, the last syllable of every word stressed, as though he couldn't bear them to end.

'Really?' Patrick turned, almost relieved.

'Yeah, right up to the point when he threw Stacey Cunningham's work out the window.'

'Excellent. So he's excluded?'

Christophe looked at him sadly. 'A verbal admonishment. You think I *want* a golf club through my head?'

Patrick took a moment to calm and steady himself before the class came in. The usual pre-match pep talk: deep breaths, face slapping.

Denis was near the back of the group as the class shuffled in and took their seats. He sat down, unshouldered his bag, folded his arms; his dead eyes, locked on Patrick, gave nothing away.

Patrick did his best to appear unfazed and, indeed, the lesson started as usual; his class completely ignored him as he attempted to show examples of previous pupils' work on the whiteboard. They laughed at the monobrow on a copy of a Frieda Kahlo painting, even though he explained that, due in part to her inability to conceive children, Frieda always exaggerated her features to uglify herself, externalising her conflict by making herself appear more masculine.

'Looks like your mum, Gerald,' said Mohammad.

Patrick announced they were to continue with their self-portraits. Ten minutes in, Denis, normally one of the more vocal classroom components, still hadn't spoken – no threats, no swearing, no phone calls to Dominos Pizza – but neither had he stopped looking at his Art teacher.

Patrick had moved Denis to the front table in an attempt to even out a pretty disastrous seating plan a while back, and the boy had soon contaminated a pupil called Matthew Keane. Formerly one of the best-behaved kids in the class, he was a perfect example of ill-at-ease teenage gangliness, chest flat and unmuscled, jaw bearded with acne. The result of this mixing of oil and water was, in hindsight, obvious; it was more likely Matthew would end up a reprobate than Denis an angel.

Denis didn't move his head when Matthew asked him, 'How do you make brown, dickhead?' and neither did Patrick bother to admonish Matthew, deeming his description of Denis perfectly accurate.

'The three primary colours,' Patrick replied. Had this boy no rudimentary knowledge of colour theory? Of course not: Charlotte had been his teacher last year.

'That's what I've done, but it looks well dirty.' Matthew's voice was so shrill it was almost a whimper.

'Just use the brown then,' Patrick snapped, indicating the poster paints racked together at the rear of the classroom. Matthew slouched over and squeezed out half the tube into his palette. 'Only take what you're going to use,' Patrick added mechanically. Almost every sentence that left his mouth these days had been uttered before.

Still Denis sat there. Had someone been training a camera on the boy, and were to play it back at high speed, they would find him perfectly still against a tornado of movement, like a time-lapsed predator in a nature documentary. Patrick had been avoiding speaking to him in case it was the provocation Denis had been looking for, but other members of the class were cottoning on to Denis' singularly sinister focus.

'Um, Denis,' he mumbled. 'You going to paint anything today?'

Patrick jumped as Denis shot out of his seat, then watched him with a mixture of relief and concern as the boy marched to his folder and pulled out his latest masterpiece. He took the paper back to the table and began painting over his handiwork in thick black paint. To his credit, he was careful to use the right amount of water and avoided streaks. When finished, he went to the drying rack and laid it down, then took another piece from his folder and began the process afresh.

Reluctantly, Patrick went over. 'Denis, this is your GCSE. You can't systematically ruin every single piece of work in this manner.'

The boy turned to him, looked him directly in the eyes.

31

'What level was this, sir?' he asked.

'You're currently working at an E.'

'That's racist.' Denis carried on.

Patrick allowed himself dangerous thoughts. Maybe standing up to Denis yesterday had taught him, a boy excluded seven times for fighting, some respect. Maybe he, a male Art teacher, that most lowly and mocked of specialists, had managed to sort matters out through the boy's own tribal idioms of the raised voice and offensive language. Maybe the incident was already forgotten. Maybe he'd got away with it.

Outside the window, on the patchy grass in front of the school fence where TATIANA IS A FAT SLAG was burned in weed killer, Denis' gang waited.

Denis stood to place his latest newly destroyed exhibit in the drying rack and, on his return to his seat, brushed his hand across the bare leg of the girl sitting immediately beside him. Far from act offended, Jenna Moris smiled at him.

Patrick had often overheard girls commenting upon Denis' 'buffness', despite signs of acne and a general air of contempt for humankind. The cleft lip wasn't something that spoiled his looks; it barely registered as an imperfection. In any case, he doubted many pupils knew its true origins, and he probably touted it as a fight scar. But it was odd that Denis was touchy-feely with Jenna Moris, of all pupils, a pretty and *sensible* brunette who remained on the borderland of Patrick's senses, never excelling, never causing trouble, getting on with her work. Admittedly, Jenna had lately taken to wearing a skirt shorter than the regulation length, canvassing the attention of testosterone-surged boys, but to even consider romantic attachment to Denis Roberts? Surely not.

And then he translated the look on her face. It wasn't a smile that existed behind the eyes. It was fear.

The hand was still on her leg. Jenna sat, staring ahead. Tiny muscles bunched under her jawline, beneath the smile, as she began to twist subtly away. His fingertips rose up the thigh, then slipped into forbidden territory. As she made desperate eye contact with the teacher, Denis released her.

Patrick could only ask, 'You two okay?'

'Sure, sir,' Denis said

Patrick knew no teacher could let something like that go, so swiftly moved her to another table – it was easier than getting the boy to move. She went willingly.

Denis scowled at Patrick, then banged a fist down, hard, on the table, silencing the class. The anger was terrifying, but Patrick couldn't help but be envious of Denis' classroom management skills. He was only fifteen, yet built entirely of a brute anger which demanded authority. He crossed his arms and resumed the silent eyeballing of his teacher.

Patrick attempted to act naturally as he paced the room, putting as much distance between himself and Denis as possible. 'Sophia… Lovely work. Lauren… Excellent. Josh… Fewer naked ladies, perhaps?'

There were some pupils, from time to time, who gave a damn. Like Serene, the quiet Palestinian whose work was awful last year, her English worse, but who appeared to learn at a superhuman rate and possessed a work ethic that put the rest of the class to shame. Or Cosmo, who when asked how he thought Degas had created his unique brushstrokes, had simply replied, 'It is pain, only pain.' He knew it was probably a mangled translation but, by comparison, Denis was nothing but a Vandal. Or maybe he'd simply been trying to say 'paint'.

The end of the lesson arrived and Patrick asked for a volunteer to help pack away. The usual swots extended their arms amid the squabbling and swearing. As did Denis.

It was an obvious challenge. Dare he refuse him? Denis had never offered help before.

'Okay. Denis, thank you.'

Patrick watched the boy as he went around the room collecting mirrors and paper. At his own table, Denis almost knocked a pot of water across Matthew Keane's work. It wobbled, then righted itself. Nothing was ruined, no one got wet, but Matthew saw fit to shout, 'Watch it, Harey.'

Maybe Matthew had decided to place a public challenge for his crown, or maybe it was a joke gone disastrously wrong, but this insult was far from sophisticated, even by schoolboy standards. The classroom fell silent.

Denis carried on collecting the work as if nothing had happened. Was it possible Denis really hadn't heard him? Patrick didn't think so: in those eyes, just for a second, he saw cold, smug malice. The grin of a Napoleon. A bad seed. The boy scratched lightly, perhaps involuntarily, at his cleft lip scar.

'Um, Jenna,' Patrick said. 'Can I see you after class please?'

When Patrick dismissed the group he watched Denis as he retrieved his bag from under his stool then straightened to face his teacher. Patrick braced himself, his deltoids as tense as masonry. One by one, the class left behind him.

Just Patrick, Denis and Jenna remained.

'Denis, I said you could leave.'

'I know.'

Patrick walked out of his room, into the corridor, then beckoned for them to follow. He felt safer there, with the CCTV.

'So what was that? You were touching her leg.'

'It's fine, sir,' she said.

'See?' Denis declared. 'It's cool.'

Jenna's eyes never left the ground, but Patrick could tell she was tearful.

'It's inappropriate...' Patrick began.

Denis took a step towards the teacher. 'You wanna know what's inappropriate? You'll see inappropriate. But not in front of a woman, innit. You and me. You'll see how inappropriate I can be.'

'What the hell does that mean?' Patrick asked, but it was to the back of Denis' head as the boy strode into the corridor and was lost amongst the sea of blue jumpers. Jenna followed.

Thirty seconds later, there came an enormous, prehistoric roar from the stairwell. His recently evicted Elevens were no doubt 'rushing' the younger years en route to their tutor rooms and the echoed screams of delight and panic sang like Saturday terraces across the whole floor. He edged towards the stairs to investigate but saw only a mass of heads.

Patrick was just about to retreat into his classroom when a different noise assaulted him above all the others. An animal in pain.

He ran down one set of stairs. Two. The sound seemed to remain the same volume the nearer he got to the source; the animal's whimpers were dying down.

There was a huddle of bodies around a boy lying in the turn of the stairs, cradling his arm. The boy was Matthew Keane.

'What's the matter?' Patrick asked. 'Who did this?' And as soon as he spoke, he knew.

Matthew was cradling his arm, Patrick suspected, not to ease the pain, but to keep it in place. The boy was as white as paper, and it was this, and the sweat, and the tears, rather than any other physical evidence, which told Patrick the arm was horribly dislocated at the shoulder.

'Was it…?'

'It was no one. I fell.'

'I saw,' said some spotty kid without a single inch of his uniform tucked in the right place. 'He stacked it.'

'Yeah, he stacked it,' said another.

The gathered crowd all nodded. They were all lying. Patrick looked around. No CCTV here, of course.

Patrick asked to have a look but Matthew shuffled away, shaking his head from side to side. The teacher took out his phone to call an ambulance.

'Already done it,' several children announced in unison.

'I reckon we should get him in the recovery position,' said a lone voice. Another boy hunkered down next to Matthew and whispered, 'Stay with us, bruv. Hang in there.'

'Don't touch him.' The booming voice came from behind them. One of the new deputy heads (they changed quicker than Charlotte's boyfriends, and a few of them even had been) was barrelling through the crowds.

The stairwell was soon closed off and Patrick was moved on to deal with the hysterical crowds, Chinese-whispering the incident into delectable untruths.

'He got shanked.'

'His neck's broken.'

'He shat himself.'

Finally, the mournful wail of an ambulance cut through the madness and the ghoulish crowds headed outside. Patrick headed up to the comparative peace of his classroom to watch through the window.

The ambulance was swarmed, rock star-style, as the paramedics struggled to convey the stretcher towards it. All pairs of eyes were on the boy. All but one.

Denis Roberts, hands in his pockets, was standing under the walkway connecting the library to the English department. His eyes weren't on the ambulance, or Matthew.

Neck craned, he watched only Patrick. His parting words seemed to play across his features like some kind of television drama voiceover: 'You and me. I'll show you how inappropriate I can be.'

Slowly, to make sure his teacher couldn't possibly mistake the gesture, the boy sliced a calm and steady forefinger across his own throat.

FOUR

The phone in the Art office rang at the end of the day.

'Shall I get that?' Patrick asked after three trills, once it'd become obvious Charlotte, the nearest to the phone, wasn't going to.

Generally, Patrick could hear the excuses forming in her throat before she fashioned them into words, preliminary sighs and clicks, the gobbledegook of academic dissatisfaction. 'Is that the external line, or the other one?' she eventually asked.

They both sat there looking at the phone until it rang off. In the playground outside, Luke Dylan in 8H was trying to make Mr Daniels jump by rapping, in the old sense of the word, against the Science lab window. Terry Valentine in 10G peddled poppers behind the tuckshop. The phone rang again.

Patrick leaned over and plucked it from the cradle.

'There's a Ms Sarah Ellis here to see you,' a nameless office entity stated. 'Shall I send her up?'

'Who?' The surname was unfamiliar to Patrick, and he had no appointment scheduled. Reception was strict about people just showing up, ever since Martin Bingham's father strolled into one of the ICT suites and struck Mr Baker across the chin with a keyboard.

There was muffled chatter on the end of the line. The voice returned: 'Jenna Moris's mother.'

Patrick groaned inwardly. 'Yeah, go on.' He replaced the phone.

'Problem?' Charlotte asked.

'No. Nothing.' Patrick had yet to report the incident he'd witnessed earlier. He'd told himself he hadn't found the time to do so, that maybe Denis and Jenna were an item after all, that maybe it wasn't his business. But, when it came down to it, Patrick was ashamed to admit he simply didn't want any kind of confrontation with the boy.

He wandered over to the pile of still life artefacts in the corner of the office. A plastic skull. The top half of a department store mannequin. A coil of blue rope. Their Australian technician had been in the middle of sorting it all out before he was given the heave-ho for 'inappropriate use of the darkroom'; the blonde sixth former concerned was already hiding the first bulgings of her pregnancy with looser clothing.

Absentmindedly, Patrick ran his hand over the Les Paul guitar half-buried under the collection. There was a thick layer of dust upon it.

He caught Charlotte's eye and she looked away, embarrassed.

Jenna's mother was brought to the Art office by the kind of dumpy, fashion-deficient human being who gave women working in school administration a bad image. Sarah Ellis was far more striking. She was dressed in dark blue jeans, a well-fitting light blue jumper and her trainers were incongruous enough to be fashionable. Her hair was mid-length, dark, with a solitary streak of blonde through the front. She wore no earrings, only a light sugaring of make-up and was probably in her mid-thirties. There was a simmering anger behind multicoloured irises which grew darker nearer the pupils.

'Hello,' Patrick said, hoisting over his face the same bogus smile he'd worn for his interview seven long years ago. 'Let's go to my classroom. I think I know why you've…'

'Have you reported it? Jenna says you saw the whole thing.'

'I must be honest: I've been busy. I'm glad you came. The school takes this sort of thing *very* seriously.' He winced at the officious whinny that was his own voice. They arrived at his classroom and he escorted her inside, leaving the door ajar.

The kiln hummed through the rear wall. Though the adjoining room was fitted with an extractor fan, a Sahara of brick dust had built up over the years and, breathed to life by the cloying heat, wisped under the door into his classroom. Harriet and Charlotte generally waited until the end of term to fire the thing up, so the number of asthma attacks Patrick's pupils suffered throughout the year was kept to a minimum. It being the last week before Christmas, the hair-singed smell of flaming brick was prevalent once more, a scent Patrick had come to associate with oncoming freedom.

Sarah Ellis walked into the centre of his room, twirled round to face him.

'So what can we do about that animal?' she asked. 'It's unacceptable. She's too scared to talk to her teachers about it… and she doesn't know I'm up here, so please don't tell her. How dare he lay his fingers on my daughter? It's happened before, she said.'

Patrick made grunting noises of concurrence.

Sarah continued. 'He's a member of a gang. They have to be nowadays, don't they? It's called "The Union Souljas", with a "J" I think. He lives near me actually. We're in Bateman block and his family's in Moore. It's pathetic; all these gangs defending their little corners of a free nation. The whole 'Don't come into our patch and we won't come into yours' sort of thing. It's a big place – it's not called City for no reason – but, I ask you, is it worth beating someone up just because their postcode alters by one number from yours? And it's getting worse…'

He waited for more as she emptied her lungs with a great pout of air.

'Sorry.' She half-smiled; a suggestion of white teeth. 'I've gone off on one, haven't I?

'It's fine.'

Slowly, Patrick became aware of a metamorphosis in Sarah's face. As anger gave way to enquiry, she cocked her head to the side, the half-smile widening.

'The Forsaken?' she asked.

'Sorry?'

'You look familiar. This is going to sound silly but you weren't in…?'

'A long time ago.'

'No way!' Her eyes lit up. She quickly dampened them, recast her face. 'I thought it was you. Owen…' she mused. 'Owen…'

'Please, call me Patrick.'

She searched over his shoulder for a particular memory. 'What was that one you did? The massive one. Oh I *loved* that song.' Her praise seemed honest enough, but he was sure she presented it through a sense of duty, perhaps to forestall further conversation about her daughter. She'd arrived in an apoplectic state and was now just as unruly with her nostalgia. 'What was it called? "Beautiful Heartache", that was it. You guys rocked. What was that? Five years ago?'

'Nine,' he replied, too quickly.

'Wow. Doesn't time go fast? There was some fuss made in the papers about… Oh, I remember now. Your singer's girlfriend and you were having…'

'The band's demise was, as they say, "ignominious".' Patrick attempted a smile.

She nodded, lost in her hazy nostalgia. 'I kind of stopped listening to that sort of stuff, I guess. More important things got my attention.'

'Yes, well. Tastes change.'

'Oh, I don't mean that in a rude way. I had a child and… I'm sorry, you probably get this all the time from parents don't you?'

'Not really.'

She was only doing what so many people do when they see a vaguely semi-famous face. He knew how genuinely loved music, even the memory of it, could send someone into a tailspin of old emotion, but he also knew how a mere appreciation of someone's back catalogue could be dusted off when face-to-face with its composer. He'd never been her hero – you don't forget your heroes' first names – but Patrick was still mildly thrilled by the recognition.

And then she folded up that personality and cut back to the chase.

'Okay then. What's the school going to do about Denis?'

'I'll speak to Mrs Barnes, his Year Head. From past experience, I think it'll be treated as a criminal matter.'

'Oh.'

'You don't sound too pleased.'

'Will police be involved? I wouldn't want…' The word 'repercussions' remained undeclared. 'I mean… The school will lodge the complaint, yeah? Not Jenna. Or me.'

'We can deal with it here. I'll report what I saw.' He barely realised what he was saying; to bring that suggestion of a smile back to this stranger's face he was willing to risk Denis' fresh wrath. And the hint of information about Denis had whet his appetite. He didn't quite know why, but he felt the need to arm himself with a little more knowledge about the boy and his 'Union Souljas'. 'Tell you what,' he added. 'Do you fancy going for a coffee somewhere? It's not the most exciting of settings here, is it?' He swept the classroom with an arm, almost knocking over a potted plant his Year Eights had been drawing.

'Oh right. Actually, I…'

He couldn't tell for sure if he was blushing or not. It certainly felt like it. There was a smirk in the corner of Sarah's mouth and there existed no doubt that she'd seen through his offer, though had clearly presumed more traditional motives than his real one. It was almost definitely the first time he'd ever hit on anybody by accident before.

41

He extended his hand, attempting to hasten the end of the conversation. 'It was lovely to meet you.' And it had been. She wasn't like the other 'primary care givers' who came to see him; she wasn't trying to punch him for marking her child down, or threatening legal action because he'd failed to prevent them plastering their uniform with oil paint. 'I should get on and speak to Mrs Barnes about, you know, the incident. Right away. I'll let you know how everything goes.'

'Maybe I should give you my number then?' she asked, smiling now. The unabashed smile of someone fifteen years younger.

Patrick looked around, then passed her a scrap of paper from his desk, realising too late that he'd given her Alan Hearn's homework.

Sarah scribbled a number down, appended it with the cross-hairs of affection. X.

She handed it back, her eyes locked on his when they weren't flicking up and down his body. 'I'll leave it to you then. Bye, Mr O... Patrick.' And with that, she sauntered towards the door. 'I'll be waiting for that call.' She smiled over her shoulder, and left.

Patrick stood for a long time staring after her shadow.

Then, slowly, he ambled downstairs to Mrs Barnes' office. At first, he was distracted by the chattering of Senior Leadership behind the door, well-paid Chiefs dreaming up meaningless new ways to keep their main-scale Indians mummified in red tape, but as he stared at the repeatedly recoated paint on her door he found fragmented memories of the day's events slowly dissolving into a vision of Sarah: the contours beneath her blue jumper; her fierce, multicoloured eyes; the dawning smile which reconfirmed that he was, after all, a *Someone*...

A voice called behind him.

'Patrick. You busy?' Christophe wore anxiety on his brow.

'What's the matter?'

'You've been standing outside Mrs Barnes' door for

five minutes. You going to knock, or what, because I've got something to show you.'

Christophe's classroom was half the size of Patrick's. Maps of France were taped to the walls, split into the twenty-two regions, and basic vocab and pupils' own biographies in French coiled in a frieze around the room. There were postcards of Jean-Jacques Rousseau and François-Noël Babeuf above his whiteboard, figures Christophe had previously referred to as '*real* Communists', whatever that meant. He strode over to his desk and yanked open a drawer, producing an impressively large phone from within.

'I confiscated this third period,' he said.

Patrick didn't tell him he'd stopped bothering to impound mobiles, following the repercussions which ensued the last time he'd tried.

'I thought phones were getting smaller, but look at the size of this monster.' Christophe presented Patrick the phone.

'Some genius worked out you could watch porn on them. What am I doing with this?'

'Press this button.'

A video started. A blur of brickwork became a flash of metal stairs, became the granite crunch of feet and expletives, became a kid running. Gold trainers. Grey tracksuit bottoms. Patrick and Christophe watched as the boy collapsed and three pairs of feet crashed upon the whimpering, foetal curl. Laughter squawked off-camera. Two of the boys held the unfortunate victim down and another pulled his trainers off, then his white cap, his black hoodie, kicking him once more across his face.

Patrick winced.

The final image was a smear of asphalt as the footage cut.

'There is a second part.' Christophe's gnarled fingers scrolled through the various menu screens, clearly familiar with the operations of the machine.

'What made you look at this?'

43

Christophe cast the Art teacher a withering glance. 'Property is theft, Patrick.'

'And what do you intend to do?'

'What would *you* do? I have no idea. I've been through most of the footage and recognise none of the boys. It looks like some of it might originate from Union City but, in truth, it could be from anywhere. Most of it's downloaded.'

'It's unpleasant stuff. But no laws exist against possessing it, do they? In truth, a kid with gangland aspirations, who's taken violent images from the net and downloaded them onto his iPhone, isn't going to be a big deal to the police.'

'Probably not.' Christophe seemed to sigh with his entire body. It was a twisted sign of the times that a boy could have a library of videos that included Power Rangers cartoons *and* droog-esque ultra-violence. 'It's not the culture I grew up with, that's for sure.'

'Who does this belong to?' Patrick enquired.

'Look through the photos. Full of selfies.'

'Not sure I should, to be honest with you.' Dusk was already darkening the estate opposite and Patrick imagined malevolent eyes watching them through the classroom window.

'Fine, fine. It belongs to Matthew Keane.'

Knowing Matthew was safely hospitalised, Patrick relaxed. Christophe clicked on a thumbnail named 'UnionSouljas' and passed the phone to him. 'Watch this,' he said.

A cry of 'Northsiders!' rang out from the phone as the gang tramped their way off-camera with a blurring of concrete steps and expensively trainered feet and the shouts of young men at war.

When the blurring stopped, Patrick saw four kids masked in balaclavas huddled on a concrete stairwell. Someone off-camera held up a gun, slapped its magazine into the butt before cocking it. There was something illegible scratched on one side of the gun's chunky handle, gangland runes lending the weapon the impression of battle scars. A boy in a grey and white Palestinian-style scarf, flanked by yet more hooded youths throwing middle fingers at the camera, stepped out from behind the phalanx and burnt a shawl or flag which went up in an instant, twisting into livid flames before wisping into nothing. The boy was Denis Roberts and beside him, drinking from a bottle of beer, spliff in his other hand, stood Matthew Keane. They were unmistakable, even in their disguises.

Patrick wondered what had happened, during whatever time had elapsed since the video was uploaded, to transform those two boys into such rivals. Surely a misplaced insult didn't warrant a broken arm?

The final five seconds comprised of delighted filming of local residents' windows, as an elderly tenant peered out from behind her closed curtains. The fear in her eyes lived on in Patrick's thoughts long after the clip finished.

'You sure you didn't recognise any of these kids, Chris?'

'No. Why? You see someone?'

Patrick swiped the downloads screen away. The browser was still open and curiosity got the better of him.

Noticing his friend's strained silence, Christophe nodded at the glowing screen.

'What you found now?'

Patrick handed the phone over. 'Take a look at this.'

Patrick Owen

From Wikipedia, the free encyclopedia

Birth name	Patrick Richard Owen
Born	5 June 1981 (age 35) Archway, London, England
Genres	Alternative rock
Associated acts	The Forsaken

Patrick Owen (born 5 June 1981 in Archway, London) [1] is an REST IN PIECE SON OF A BITCH English rock guitarist, formerly of the London rock band The Forsaken.[2]

Biography

Patrick Owen grew up in the London borough of Haringey[3] where he attended Bridge Grammar School. Owen went on to study Art at the Medway Institute of Art and Design.[4]

After being kicked off his course due to lack of effort,[5] NO FUCKIN SUPRIES THERE Owen re-located to Brixton where he worked in a bar at the Cock and Bull AHAAAA LOL LOL! on Atlantic Road and met Kris Guard and Adam Roper, with whom he formed The Forsaken.[6] Whilst in The Forsaken, Owen worked as an arranger and songwriter, and co-wrote several of The Forsaken's songs with Roper as well as writing and performing ORAL SEX ON MEN AND a number of B-sides himself.

Prior to the release of the band's massively delayed second album *Nothing*, the band claimed that Owen had been working on a solo album entitled *ArtScape* and that it would be released sometime following the release of the band's album in 2008, and that tracks such as "Ways Of Seeing" and "Nevermind the Pollocks" had been completed.[7] As of 2016, the album has never materialised.

Following extended delays in the band delivering *Nothing* to Parlophone, a posting on the band's MySpace page in September 2008 claimed that "a member of the band has quit amid enormous animosity, did not want to rejoin and the remaining members did not want the bastard back"[8] and that as a result of this, the band had split up after nearly five years together.[9] The album was released using existing studio material and various session musicians in Owen's place. In an interview with *Rolling Stone*, Roper declared that he had been unhappy with Owen's attempts to create a "non-commercial" sound and that one Roper composition in particular, entitled "Find the Ocean", became the subject of "prodigious condemnation" by BUMLORD Owen, who claimed it sounded like "the worst kind of mainstream, sub-Beatles singalong crap [he'd] ever heard in [his] life."[10]

Persistent rumours that Owen had been conducting an affair with Roper's then girlfriend, Ana Carvalho, during the course of the recording of *Nothing*, were eventually confirmed by the marriage of Owen and Carvalho in May 2009.[11]

The couple split in 2015 and have one child.

UNIONSOULJAS FOR EVER MR OWEN SUCKS HAIRY DICKKKKKKSSSS

This page was last modified on 13 December 2016 at 18:39.

FIVE

Patrick arrived home, sat on his sofa and stared at the numbers on the back of Alan Hearn's homework. He drank a glass of wine. He drank another. He typed the numbers into his phone.

'Hello?' the voice answered.

'Ms Ellis?'

'Moris,' his pupil corrected.

'Oh. Is your mother there, please?'

'Who's calling?'

He told her and there was an embarrassed pause, followed by a long, rustling one.

Perhaps, Patrick thought, he would lend Sarah The Forsaken's second album, to show her their music wasn't mere adolescent japery. It still stung him, after the heartache of the way things fell apart, and despite history already ascribing the band little more than one-hit-wonder status, to hear comments like 'I stopped listening to that sort of stuff.' The death threats, the ridicule from his kids, he'd long ago come to terms with.

Eventually, Sarah came on the line.

'Mr Owen,' she said. 'Somewhat after school hours, isn't it?'

He looked at his watch. 'Sorry.'

'So how can I help you?'

He suddenly realised he had no outward reason for the call. Hastily, he made up some guff about speaking to Denis' mother about respecting women and how inappropriate her son's actions were. He proudly decreed Jenna would get no more bother from Denis.

'Okay…' she said. 'Would you still like to meet for that drink some time? If you're not too busy…' Her voice betrayed no nervousness at all. It was as stolidly theatrical as someone who'd been practicing the lines all evening.

He looked at his watch. The wine said, 'Fuck it. Are you free in an hour?'

He waited for her in Leicester Square, amid a fairground cosmos of Christmas colour. A merry-go-round span out orange and amethyst, accompanied by the cheers of children on flying horses, rising, falling, swelling from the carousel. Above him, the trees were bound in sparkling fairy lights and a net of pearls replaced genuine stars. Though it wasn't particularly cold, parents and grandparents alike were armoured against winter as kids swung between them, little gloves flailing on sleeve-tethered strings.

When she arrived, fifteen minutes late, Sarah was Yetied in fur and soaring boots, with a demi-cloche hat angled not-quite horizontally atop a nest of wavy brown hair. He was too embarrassed, and she too unfamiliar to him, to remark on how beautiful she looked; all he could stammer out was, 'Nice coat.'

'It's fake,' she explained, pulling at the collar.

They walked towards St. Martin's Lane, their conversation pretty much lost to the racket of Christmas anthems blaring from every restaurant, and they slipped into The Coliseum between the swearing taxis and rickshaws. *Madame Butterfly* – indeed opera in general – was a suitably middle-class pursuit and conformed to Patrick's idea of a first date. There was no cunning psychology behind treating a woman from the estate to several flutes of champagne, but once the curtains swished closed after 'Con Onor Muore' she was visibly addicted to the occasion. He didn't tell her he'd been saving up 'prestige package' coupons from *The Metro* for five months.

Over a candlelit dinner at the only restaurant admitting without a prior booking they discussed the performance, and when she switched from alcohol to water he, out of solidarity, did the same, though it unnerved him that the getting-pissed-and-launching-himself approach which had worked so sublimely in his twenties was out the window. He sobered with every mouthful and, to his relief, found he stopped going through the motions of a date and relaxed. Under pressure, he'd often confused what it took to talk a woman into bed with how to talk her to sleep.

'What does Jenna make of this?' he asked. 'Our meeting?'

'She thinks I'm at the cinema with a friend. Can you imagine what she'd say if she found out about this? I told her you were ringing to discuss another matter.'

'Denis?'

'Yeah. I had to fess up about that. The idea of me being with anyone other than her father would be hard enough for her, but one of her *teachers*...' She checked her watch. 'I ought to be back soon. We have a curfew.'

'There's a curfew in the estate?'

'Me and Jenna have our own. It just isn't safe after a certain time.' She peered at him over the carafe. 'You look tired.'

'It's been a long term.' His exhaustion wasn't something he'd desired to mention. It bored him when Charlotte, first thing Monday morning, assigned the inane fact of her tiredness such importance, alongside how quickly the weekend flew past. He was cutting out dull. He would be dynamic, impressive.

'Doing anything interesting for Christmas?' was all he could think to ask.

She stirred her mange tout. 'Not particularly.'

He was no expert on flirting signals but was sure she maintained eye contact for longer than the standard few seconds, mimicked his body movements. In retaliation, he looked directly at the cherry lipstick with which she'd coated her mouth. 'Me neither.'

He got the impression she held her personality at a distance and, beyond the opera they'd watched and the food they ate, the conversations she instigated concerned, exclusively, his interests. He changed tack before she could press him on The Forsaken. 'So where do you work? You said something about secretarial…?'

'P.A. I'm a P.A.'

'Sounds interesting.'

'It's horrible.' Her smile was so dismissive he could only believe her. 'You must have a large knowledge of art and the exhibitions on, I bet. What have you been to see recently?'

'Nothing for a bit. I went to the RA this summer. I go every year. Have you been?'

She shook her head and gazed with renewed interest at her napkin. 'I went to the Tate Modern a while back. Maybe you can explain it to me. What's it all about?'

'What's it *all* about?'

'Just explain one piece to me. Anything. There were all these, like, oxygen tanks falling out of a van, and a wall of red cows. Most of it could have been made by a blind man. What was with the piano hanging from the ceiling?'

'I'm not sure it's for me to explain. Either you like a piece or you don't. There's really nothing to 'get'. Anyway, most of the stuff there's bollocks. I loved the collection before the rehang. The Cornelia Parker. The Rothko room. I don't know why Serota felt the need to muck about with it.'

'Maybe they worried about people getting used to the layout, or that they weren't coming any more. Change is inevitable.'

Patrick watched her jawbone as she ate, the lips which gently caressed one another. 'Change for change's sake,' he declared.

'I bet it's no different. I bet *you* changed.'

51

Her foot tapped his, probably accidentally, and a spark of desire flickered between the belly-dancing candles on their table. It was then that Patrick knew he would perform his oft-played 'perfect gentleman' role at the end of the night, accompany her back to the tube, offer her cheek a temperate, platonic peck and leave before he gave in to the long pent-up sexual thirst that would, inevitably, humiliate him. He rued his gutlessness and his genitals in equal measure.

She checked the time again. 'Fancy a quick one?'

The Lionswater hotel was exactly as he remembered, a three storey, Victorian building in petroleum-coloured brick. Powerful lights shone upwards between tall windows on the first floor, advertising the hotel's name to the main road, and two naked trees twisted from the earth on either side. Inside, the bar was set in mirrors and golds at odds, he felt, with the high-ceilinged, baroquely corniced charm of its period, and the receptionists wore stiff black and gleaming white and didn't seem to hurry about their duties. He was taken back in time eight years, by the smell of the place, its background jazz. As before, he ordered two glasses of Muscadet. That he could remember what he'd drunk last time didn't surprise him.

The girl who served them was too young to have worked there then but the man at reception might well have and as Patrick caught his eye, raised the glass to his lips, he fantasised that he'd been recognised, that his previous visit to the Lionswater was as famed to the staff as it was to him. It was a depressing fantasy and he was caught off-guard when Sarah returned from the reception with a key swinging from her index finger.

'What we drinking?'

Patrick shrugged. 'Nothing special. Why are you looking at me like that?'

Her lips were screwed tight, quizzical. 'You still think yourself pretty rock 'n' roll, don't you?'

He'd entertained the idea of her coming back to his, but had quickly decided against the notion. Material belongings count, in the end, for little, but what a person chooses to fill their shelves with provides a comforting affirmation of who they aspire to be; unfortunately, he no longer recognised the person who bought the Britpop best-ofs, the Martin Amis first editions, the seventies horror DVDs that stopped being mildly frightening over thirty years ago. On his desk sat a Waterman pen, given to him by a Best Man he hadn't spoken to in five years. And he certainly didn't want to talk about that gold disk in the lounge celebrating half a million sales of The Forsaken's first album. So instead, they sat side by side at a bar in a hotel he'd recommended, squinting under the barrage of halogen bulbs, mirrors, tinsel and baubles, not saying much. She nudged their room key around the bar with a steady finger and he watched her do so with a jester's melancholy. Within three minutes they'd polished off their drinks.

'Shall we go upstairs?' she asked.

The guest rooms were modern, imitation – plain glass chandeliers, gold framed pictures of the hotel's yesteryear – and theirs looked out over the local park, a metal spine of traffic clogging the entire length of road to its left. A potted cyclamen by the window snagged a thread from Sarah's green dress. 'Lovely big room,' she said, drawing the curtains.

Number four was bigger, he knew.

They kissed. Was this risky? There was no law against seeing a child's parent but even if one had existed it would only have added to the illicitness of the situation; hiding their tryst from Jenna was already lending the hours-old relationship a pleasing debauchery. He peeled a bra strap over her shoulder. A constellation of moles on her belly. Soft wisps of hair at the neck's nape. It was to be the first time he'd been with a woman for over a year and his nervousness alarmed him, but he tried not to put too much pressure on his imminent performance. As a conscious result of trying to take control of his inhibitions, their lovemaking, he suspected, would be neither frenzied nor tender; at best, it might carry a disclaimer, the promise of more another day. He hadn't drunk nearly enough.

She pulled back. 'Do you do this sort of thing a lot? I mean, take parents of…'

'Never.' It seemed appropriate to add, 'But in two terms Jenna's no longer my responsibility…'

She winced a smile. Whether it had been mentioning her teenage daughter by name, or the suggestion that such trysts might still be ongoing two terms down the line, the mood had subtly changed.

He looked around the room, searching for some tangible back-up. The radiator was clicking out an irrational time signature.

'Sarah… We can go back downstairs if you like. We don't need to, you know…'

He investigated her face in the semi-dark, her blonde streak standing skunk-like against her darker tresses. She smelt earthy, buttery, the alcohol-strawberry of her lingering perfume now overripe and on the turn. Her cheekbones were prominent and her lips full and, examining the vague puffiness under the eyes and the faint lines traversing them, he wondered how old she was. There was something weary, perhaps even tormented, within her carefully humouring eyes, which, even under the Lionswater's energy-saving wattage, maintained their array of never-before-seen colours. He had that strange sense that he'd known Sarah for years, that they'd already entered an awkward stage in their relationship, and, perhaps unsurprisingly, his thoughts turned to Ana, the one good thing he'd always believed to have come out of the disintegration of both the band and his friendship with Adam. He recalled how similarly beautiful and worried his future wife had looked on the fateful evening they'd stayed at this very hotel.

Sarah's phone rang and she casually retrieved it from her handbag.

54

'...Hi Jen. No I got caught up in some... No. Of course not. Look, I'll be back in half an hour, okay?'

She killed the call, then stood and smoothed down her skirt. 'That was Jenna. I better go.'

Neither of them spoke as she reapplied her makeup in the large wall-mounted mirror.

'You okay?' he finally asked.

There was a long, asexual pause. She peered into him with a calculating expression, as though deciding his entire future.

'You know what? I really didn't like your second album.'

He apologised again, eight years too late. 'I wasn't keen on the remixing they did after I left, but there's some strong stuff on it. A review in the *NME* said...'

'Patrick, shut up.'

'You read it then?' he joked.

'I'm paraphrasing.' At length, she kissed him. 'I have to go. Sorry.'

Patrick was part relieved, part insulted that she rushed home for her daughter's sake and as they walked downstairs he wondered at how he'd got himself into this ridiculous situation, at how fast things had rocketed to this albeit predictable conclusion. He handed the keys to the receptionist before gliding Sarah to the door, and considered initiating an unsentimental kiss for the benefit of the hotelier so he didn't presume either one of them a prostitute. But all Patrick could do was laugh, cold air ripping at his lungs.

'See you.'

Parentheses deepened on either side of lips painted red and dry by the winter. It seemed a genuine smile. 'See you too, Mr Owen.'

SIX

The white emulsion paint, running down the legs of his desk and dripping into an air-conditioned tackiness on the polished wood, had adhered together his Key Stage Three reports and ruined countless mark sheets. It reeked of ammonia, and a looping splash speckled the wall. Two words were scratched into the paint, across the full surface of the desk:

YOU DIE

Patrick was running late and had just enough time to stow his umbrella behind the door before striding back along the corridor. Fellow teachers looked up from desks to scowl at him and in their countenances he saw only desperation, Ofsted paranoia. It was the last week of term, but there was no room for joy here. These people were the pedagogical equivalent of spent matches.

Patrick was led into the boardroom next to the head's office. It was large, bright and boasted a view of the staff car park. The outside world was experiencing the kind of sudden temperature climb which, on a freezing winter's day, so often heralds snow.

He sat at one end of an ovoid table, Mr Hutchinson and PC Thomas the other.

Mr Hutchinson was a mid-height, dumpy man whose soft features might have been prepossessing in his youth but had aged in too kindly a fashion for his role. Despite this, no one had ever seen him smile. His baldness was the baldness of the nineteen-seventies; while electing not to sport a comb-over, he had however thrown caution to the wind and grown whatever nature permitted, affording him monkish sides and a newborn gathering of fluff at the front.

'Take me through what happened,' Mr Hutchinson said. He had a deep and resonant voice and probably made a good baritone.

'Well,' Patrick began, '…Matthew had said something that sounded like "Watch it, Harey" when Denis was collecting materials at the end of the lesson. Denis didn't react, but I'm pretty sure he heard.'

'And after the lesson?'

'Oh, I kept Denis back for some other matter. After I let him go, that's when I heard Matthew crying out.'

'Did you *see* the incident?' the policeman asked, supercilious and mistrustful.

PC Thomas, the on-site constable, was a remarkably lanky and inoffensive-looking man whom Patrick doubted could twist the lid off a jam jar, let alone threaten a Year Seven with jail-time. But he was notoriously trigger-happy, once carting a fourteen-year-old off in irons for throwing a football boot through a window. Generally, he sat reading confiscated comics in his office behind reception, awaiting the call to action. Nine times out of ten he was only required to deal with the triggering of the foyer's security scanners.

'Um. No. But I was the first on the… *scene.*'

'Very little to go on,' the policeman stated. 'But this is serious: you say Matthew insulted Denis' cleft lip… Do you honestly think this 'accident' has something to do with that?'

'It's my theory,' Patrick said.

The headteacher's eyebrows rose. 'We'll speak to Denis, along with the rest of the class. And, once the boy's recovered, we'll get Matthew's story.'

'He didn't seem to be accusing anyone when the paramedics arrived,' PC Thomas chipped in. 'He was in a lot of pain but, in my experience, a kid who's been wronged never keeps quiet about it. Probably just a nasty accident.' He said this with a degree of disappointment.

'We'll sort it as soon as we can,' the head intoned. 'In the meantime, back to the chalk face with you. Registration's in fifteen minutes and not all our kids are as 'armless as Matthew, you know.' Mr Hutchinson had evidently completed his headship training at a university for terminally unfunny cunts, emphasised by the cravat he wore during celebration assemblies.

Patrick remained where he sat. 'How's Matthew doing?'

'Oh, he's alright, I think. The damage is worse than first thought though. They popped the shoulder back in but... Hopefully he'll be right as rain come January.' Mr Hutchinson didn't want his school's attendance figures too skewed. 'He seemed more concerned about his mobile phone, which Mr DuPont confiscated earlier in the day.'

Even if Denis *had* wrenched Matthew's shoulder out of its socket, why were pupils remaining silent on the matter? *All* of them? A chill rippled through Patrick. Might the fact that the 'accident' happened after *his* lesson be significant? Was Denis letting his teacher know that, ultimately, he settled his dues?

'There's one more thing, sir,' he said.

His two examiners stared expectantly back at him.

'I received what could be perceived as a death threat this morning. I wouldn't be surprised if it was also from Denis.'

PC Thomas crossed his arms. Mr Hutchinson unfolded his.

'Go on,' the head said.

'I found paint across my desk. It had the words YOU DIE written in it. Denis once told me, not exactly in so many words, that he was going to... you know.'

'He's threatened you before?'

'There have been... moments. You know. Intimidation. I caught him being inappropriate towards a girl in the class and he told me he'd show me, one day, what "inappropriate" really meant and then, later, he made this lovely gesture to me.' Patrick ran his forefinger against his throat. 'Oh, and someone vandalised my Wikipedia page and told me to Rest In Peace.'

'You have a Wikipedia page?'

'But why would he want to kill you?' the policeman interjected.

'I'm not taking it seriously. Obviously. But I'm pretty sure the mess upstairs was him.'

A few, slow flakes of snow began to spiral outside. The two men opposite him looked at one another, seemed to use clairvoyance to decide whether it was worth getting up off their arses, then both rose in tandem.

'Guess we'd better have a look,' Mr Hutchinson sighed.

They didn't speak on the way up the stairs. Somehow, they had made it clear that Patrick was wasting their time. It was a technique people in power often used, he suspected, to affect the impression of perpetual busyness.

When they arrived, the desk was clear.

It wasn't exactly spotless; the smell of paint still lingered beneath the overpowering reek of cleaning fluid. Some emulsion streaks clung within the grain of the wood like greasepaint in the wrinkles of an old thespian, but otherwise the threat had been completely removed. In the bin beside his desk, his ruined reports lay rejected, the paint still wet.

'This… This isn't how it was,' Patrick protested.

The two men looked over the scene. They probably would have been amused had it not been for the fact that Patrick was very obviously distressed. 'I'll check the CCTV outside your room,' the PC said, pumping his fists together.

'You go with him,' Mr Hutchinson told Patrick.

The lights flickered.

'What was that?' the PC asked Patrick.

'Oh, that was Dave. Don't worry about him.'

They sat in the cramped annex behind reception, three monitors before them showing grey footage of school corridors. Through the glass behind them, the human resources staff typed diligently away at whatever essential bureaucracy it was that kept them in paid employment.

'I'll take it back an hour,' the policeman stated, and stabbed at the buttons on the front of what looked like a sleek, black digibox. They watched the sped-up footage of the corridor, the counter in the top right corner spinning through the minutes until a jerkily-walking figure holding an umbrella approached the classroom door. A Chaplin version of Patrick, arriving for work.

'This is after it happened,' Patrick said, 'but tick it on a bit. We'll see who removed the mess.'

PC Thomas kept fast-forwarding. A few blurs passed the door. Cleaning staff. Colleagues. But no one entered.

Then, ten minutes later, someone flapped open the door and went inside.

'Stop.'

PC Thomas reeled back and paused it on a female figure in school uniform. He zoomed into her with a deftness that gave away the fact he probably did such things quite often.

Patrick scratched his cheek. He hadn't been intentionally growing a beard. 'So that's who cleaned it up. Let's go back again and find who did it in the first place.'

PC Thomas clicked and scrolled. 'You know her?'

Jenna and Patrick sat in Mr Hutchinson's office. Ordinarily, it was a table dynamic reserved for servant and master – indeed, Patrick had previously always been the only other person in the room, sitting directly opposite his boss – so it was odd for Patrick to be squeezed in on the end, as though he was neither on the headteacher's side, nor his pupil's. The room was barely furnished, save for a desk laden with distracting executive playthings, including a six-inch pool table and a silver Newton's cradle. Outside, the kids shrieked their way to registration. Patrick's form were in morning assembly without him, so God only knows what they were getting up to.

'You're covering for Denis. Why?' Mr Hutchinson asked, softly.

Jenna examined her shoes.

'Come on, Jenna,' the head persevered. 'We know it was you who cleaned it up. And we saw you and Denis go in early this morning. So you can stop pretending.'

They'd have had Denis in there with them, except the boy had obviously decided it was too near the end of term to bother with such trifling matters as education. Jenna continued to sit in silence, but it was clear from her worming fingers and sideways anger that she wasn't far from breaking.

It was Patrick's turn. 'Did he threaten you? You can tell us.'

She span and looked at him. He realised, now, that it was the first time she'd done so.

'I did it,' she said.

'You did it?' Patrick said it like a laugh.

'Yes,' she looked back down. Patrick and the head shared a look. The Art teacher was enjoying this, playing the part of PC Thomas. Clearly, he'd missed his detective calling.

Were Jenna and Denis romantically involved? Patrick doubted it, if her expression had been anything to go by when the boy had touched her leg. So what was this all about? Did he really scare her this much?

Patrick dropped his voice, moved slightly closer. 'Why are you covering for him, Jenna? Tell me.' It was easy, natural. The art of teaching was all an act anyway, and so too was this fawning patter he'd seen in a thousand fictional good-cop-bad-cop dynamics.

She rounded on him again. Just for a moment, he saw the same calculating eyes he'd seen in her mother. They drilled at the surface of him, then came to a decision. 'I told you. *I* did it. You saw my mum last night, didn't you? I know you did. You rang the house, and then the next minute she's off out, comes back all smiley and singing those shit songs from, like, ages ago.'

61

Mr Hutchinson was looking at him with Child Protection Issue eyes. The room was silent as Patrick fell back in his seat and fumbled for something to say.

Finally, he spoke. 'You know, some of those songs were actually…'

'Right. Off you go, Jenna,' Mr Hutchinson instructed.

She didn't need to be told twice.

Mr Hutchinson's face was something impenetrable and terrifying. 'Well, there's your answer,' he said, pulling back one of the small orbs of the Newton's cradle and clacking it against its neighbour. The opposite ball sprang out, and so it continued. Click. Click. Click.

Patrick looked towards his headteacher and tried a non-committal smile.

To his great surprise, Mr Hutchinson reciprocated the expression. 'You old dog, Mr Owen…'

The gang waited at the bus stop, Denis hovering at the vanguard, kicking stones and toking what was probably a transcendentally potent spliff. He wore his hoodie up, but Patrick was sure it was him from the rolling, simian bop of his aimless walk. What were they achieving there? If you were going to bunk school, why hang out just outside its gates?

He pulled back from the window in his empty classroom. A ghostly reflection behind his own caused him to jump.

'Bloody hell, Charlotte. You startled me.'

'Sorry. I just needed to use the kiln.' She waded through with some atrocious African masks under her arms. 'The meeting overran, as usual. Didn't mean to startle you.'

'I was just… you know, lost in thought.'

'Actually, I'm glad you're still here. I don't like coming in your room on my own. And the school's almost deserted now. The snow's sending everyone packing.'

He didn't need to say anything. If he just kept quiet she would prattle on by herself.

'It's a spooky room,' she continued. 'Don't you think?

There's something… odd here. Maybe it's because it's the furthest from the front doors, I don't know. The lights – they just can't fix them, can they? And some of those pictures…' She indicated the back wall, where charcoal portraits created by the Year Eights were pinned. 'Their eyes seem to follow me.'

Pointlessly, as if her theory were remotely plausible, he turned to look at them.

'I sometimes think that when I'm not looking, they change position, or swap places. Do I sound mad?'

'You sound like a fucking idiot.' He said it behind a laugh and the dislike washed straight over her.

'Terrible about that Matthew boy…' she said.

He looked back out the window. School was long over. What in hell's name were the gang still doing here? Who were they waiting for? He looked at his desk, the streaks of emulsion clearly visible. He didn't believe Jenna would have responded like that, but then again, how many of his pupils could he honestly say he truly knew? No, it was Denis' caper. It was *his* death threat. Jenna had merely accompanied him. He stepped back when Denis looked up and a blade of ice pricked his spine.

'I don't suppose you were planning to leave soon, were you?' he asked.

'Soon as I've done this.' She placed the clay pieces in the kiln and swung the heavy door closed.

'Could I grab a lift?'

He watched her expression, but to his relief it darkened only a little. Patrick had always assumed she disliked him as much as he disliked her, but she'd probably never really acknowledged to herself that she didn't like him; no doubt, if she stopped to think about it, it would have seemed obvious, but because she so rarely thought about him it had never occurred to her. The extension of a friendly normality – him asking jovially for a lift – was so unheard of it immediately exposed the issue.

'Um. Yeah, if you like.' She was confused, or annoyed, or pleased. It was hard to tell. An excuse hadn't presented itself to her straight away and now it was too late. She didn't dare ask him why he wanted a lift home from her, after all these years, and the obvious bewilderment etched into her nervous smile gave him a small sense of satisfaction.

The feeling left him when he dared look back out the window.

The snow was trying hard to settle, but the wisps dissolved harmlessly into the car park tarmac. Most of the staff had gone, perhaps expecting a proper deluge, and Mr Hutchinson's office was dark. It had always irked Patrick that his office had a view of the car park, as though to keep an eye on the comings and goings of his staff.

Straightaway, it was obvious she had a flat rear tyre.

'Shit.' She ran to her Octavia as though it were a dying pet. The tyre was completely deflated, the wheel trim touching the ground.

'Do you know how to change one?' she asked him.

'Shouldn't be a problem. Do you have a jack?'

'Check the boot.'

Patrick examined the tyre. There was a long slash in the sidewall and it had deflated almost to putty. 'It's been stabbed,' Patrick stated.

'The little fuckers.'

Jack in hand, Patrick got to work.

'Where did you learn to do this?' Charlotte asked.

'Just picked it up,' he said, slackening the wheel nuts. When The Forsaken had been on the road, their camper frequently required similar TLC.

More than a few times, staff members swung past on their way home, but he waved away their offers of help. The longer it took, the better. He lifted the damaged wheel off the hub and stowed it in the boot in place of the new one, which he hoisted up into position only to find the bolts didn't align.

'What the...? Where's this wheel come from?'

'It's always been in the back,' she explained helpfully.

'It's from an entirely different car.'

'Why?'

'*You tell me.*'

She removed her mobile. 'Don't worry. I'll call the AA. You don't need to wait. They'll get me home.'

'I'll take the bus.' Patrick looked around him. There was another route home, which avoided going anywhere near the front of the school, but he'd have to go all the way round the estate and it would look odd if he set off in that direction. Still, an odd look was preferable to a prospective stabbing.

She seemed to sense his sudden discomfort. 'Why did you want me to drive you home anyway? I mean, we live in entirely different parts of the borough. I don't mind, I just wondered.'

'Oh. My bus route was diverted.'

'But you just said...'

'A different bus. I'll get a *different* bus.'

'Patrick? Are you okay?'

She looked at him as though suddenly extremely suspicious. Did she think he'd started fancying her? He felt the grimace crack across his numbing face.

'You know what?' he said, breathing into cupped hands to warm them. 'The AA'll be here in no time. See you tomorrow.'

Patrick ambled through the canteen and out through reception. It was deserted. He knew there were probably staff members still dotted about the building, in classrooms and offices, but he saw what Charlotte meant – it was a foreboding, haunted old place, as only institutional buildings can be. He remembered Ana's three-month neonatal scan at the hospital had been on a Saturday and the empty corridors and darkened exits seemed inherently unnerving.

He closed his mind to his previous life, and walked out through the scanners.

The playground was shadowed and empty, light pooling under the humming lamps. Patrick looked immediately to the empty bus stop outside, then trod slowly as the estate through which he'd have to walk lurked menacingly to his right.

The relief he felt, to be leaving work, the immediacy of the holiday, the empty bus stop, inspired a joy that manifested itself in a brief snatch of tune.

This happened from time to time, but less and less. It was in G, the soporific hum of his old tour bus engine, like most of his compositions. He began humming it as he turned out of the gate. The music chimed in his head, repeating. G to A. A to D. D to E minor. E minor to G. And repeat.

Lyrics came, almost unbidden:

I walked alone
The moon followed me
Home
Amongst the evergreens

He couldn't shake the tune and replayed it, the same four bars, over and over. There were no evergreens round here of course, only the rotting high rises of Union City, but he liked the pristine lie of it, the antidote in his melody. He gave the song a name: 'Danny's Tune'. It wouldn't find its way into any album, or even the ears of another, but he had just made it personal.

He'd been saving. He'd pay for Danny to come over after Christmas. Of course, he'd have to pay for Ana too. To hell with the lawyer's fees.

He whistled his tune as he approached the corner shop. Its windows were shattered to confetti, the aisles strewn with produce, hoardings and overturned standees. A Pakistani woman in her forties was solemnly dabbing a broom at debris while her irate husband, his face slapped into one of abject defeat, attempted to right the destruction. The grammatically abstract adverts – '3 for an £1', 'are apple's our 40p a Kg' – appeared almost heartbreakingly childish.

Patrick heard the man talking to his wife, though he could

understand nothing of the language except a token English word: 'Gangs'.

Patrick traipsed on, faster now, the dual carriageway lurking behind the estate to his left, tiny orange suns of cigarettes burning in the dark amongst a shanty town of dogs and muggers. He fancied he could hear the stanchions creak as lorries strained their way overhead, yet 'Danny's Tune' refused to be drowned out as he entered the alleyway which would lead him into the comparative safety of the main street.

Patrick stopped whistling.

The gang waited ahead. Though they looked like they could have been in their twenties, Patrick knew otherwise. He slowed, but they'd seen him.

One had a crutch, yet seemed perfectly capable of walking properly and all six wore hoods. Two pulled bandanas up over their faces to hide their identities, and it was this that told Patrick they knew who he was. But there was only one boy he definitely recognised.

'Owen!' Denis shouted, delighted, like the surname itself was a joke. Perhaps it was. 'What you doing mincing around here this time of night?'

He swaggered towards him as Patrick stood motionless. Outside of the school corridors, he had no propulsion, no power. The gang behind the boy smirked, shadowed. Patrick took a look around him but saw only darkness.

Patrick knew his own cowardice had doomed him. Asking Charlotte for a lift home, changing her fucking tyre while potential saviours left around them, had only pushed his departure further back into the night. This fate was of his making.

'Denis,' he grunted with grim acceptance. 'Good evening.'

There were titters. He didn't have a particularly posh voice but it sure sounded educated right now.

Denis looked behind him, milked the humour from his crew, then came forward, sluggishly but with intent, as though lining up a pool shot.

'Mr Owen,' and then, facetiously, '*Sir*. I've got something for you.' It was the most sinister sentence Patrick had ever heard in his life.

'Have you?' Patrick stood his ground. Let him come. Under the sodium dark, Denis' face was like ceramic. Only his brow was knotted and sharp with a frown. Let him come.

'Yeah,' the boy said. 'A Christmas present.'

He reached inside an inner pocket.

One step. One more step.

Slowly, the hand began to slide out again. He was laughing in that ghoulish, mirthless manner that had always put the hairs on the back of Patrick's neck up.

'Merry Christmas, sir,' he sniggered, gums pulled back, fake night exposing yellow teeth. Last decade, Patrick considered, he still had his milk ones. 'It's time for you to learn the meaning of inappropriate.'

The hand came out. A flash of something shiny, reflecting a slice of streetlamp.

Patrick uncoiled his fear, and his fist swept up and round and crashed into the side of Denis' head. As he did so, he saw that Denis had brought out of his jacket pocket nothing but an erect middle finger, flashing only an oversized sovereign ring.

Denis, much to everyone's surprise, went down in a grunt of pain. And stayed there.

PART
TWO

ONE

It had been snowing, on and off, since that day.

Despite the snow turning to slush on the pavement and a convergence of grey overhead, Patrick could tell Christophe's tranquil cul-de-sac was as prime an example of the gentry's hinterland as anywhere in London. The notion that Christophe, the self-proclaimed socialist, was every inch a member of the establishment came as something of a shock to Patrick on Boxing Day afternoon.

The Art teacher, clutching his bottle of Rioja, ambled down a short path bisecting a circle of frosted slate chips on a crispy white lawn. Fastened high upon the front wall were movement sensors and above the front door clung security lights and a flashing, wasp-striped alarm box. Notice me, it screamed. We won't get caught napping this time.

The doorbell rang a deep, languid toll.

Christophe's wife opened the door. She was striking but not quite beautiful, with greeny-brown eyes, elegant mid-length dark hair and porcelain-white English skin.

'I'm Angela. Do come in. How nice to meet you, finally. Let me take your coat.'

He slipped off his overcoat and passed over the wine. She thanked him without looking at the label. 'Chris is through there, with Tristan.'

Beyond two vast Persian rugs, an open hall door revealed Christophe on a playmat of roads and petrol stations, surrounded by toy trucks and action figures. Christophe

71

welcomed his friend with a smile, invited him to crouch down and join them, but Patrick, despite being fully educated in the protocol of fathers and sons, felt slightly put out by the boy's scampering disregard. He did his best to try and entertain the little fella, punting a car the youngster's way, only for Tristan to look at him with the kind of suspicious, lingering expression that starts fights in pubs.

'Find us ok?' the Frenchman asked.

'Sorry I'm late.'

A serving hatch was open on the wall above one of three sofas and Angela pushed her charming mannequin's head through. 'Drink?' Behind her, he glimpsed a kitchen that stretched into the next borough.

Patrick fought back a festering jealousy. It was impossible that Christophe's earnings alone paid for this house. Did his belief in state education, or the political principle behind it, actually get him out of bed when he wasn't required, financially, to even bother?

Angela handed both men a glass of wine (Patrick was certain it wasn't from the bottle he'd brought) and relieved her husband of his duties so he could show Patrick round the house, which he did rapidly and inartistically, lingering on aspects he didn't approve of rather than the features he did. Given the chance, it seemed Christophe would have lived somewhere else, and he talked of the 'great summer redecoration' as though it were Stalin's infamous 'Purge'. They paused by the large window on the turn of the stairs and looked out over the vast, perfectly manicured garden, flower beds hoed at deep right-angles beside an obese summer house.

'The price of real estate round here is extortionate,' Christophe announced. 'Even the snow can't afford to settle.'

The look Christophe gave him made Patrick suspect he'd just cracked a joke. 'Your gigs must've been something to behold, Chris.' He tried to keep the envy from his voice; this was almost definitely the largest house he'd ever stepped foot in that wasn't owned by the National Trust.

'We were burgled last year,' Christophe said, following Patrick's stunned gaze. 'My fault – I keep leaving our side gate unlocked. We were lucky though. The police reckon they were disturbed halfway through, by the barking of next door's Retriever. We didn't lose as much as we might've and found quite a lot of our stuff stored in that summer house. For whatever reason, they never came back to collect the Basquiat.'

They ate at the dining table, Tristan holding everyone's attention hostage from his high chair. Naturally, Angela probed Patrick about his 'career'. Naturally, Patrick's heart sank. He dutifully answered her questions anyway, only for her to look through him with the bored gaze of a general practitioner, until he found the opportunity to ask what she did for a living and she replied, quite unapologetically, 'Nothing. My money comes from *daddy*.' Patrick imagined that the subject of Tristan's impending schooling was an ongoing and lively debate inside the DuPont mansionhold.

When the kid started to get bored, Angela carried him off to bed. Outside, the ghostly wattage of a full moon bleached the clouds as the two men edged towards drunkenness. Patrick knew, very soon, he would have to hit his friend with his confession.

'Jenna Moris's mother?' Disbelief swelled Christophe's features, making him look vaguely, joyfully, constipated. 'I thought it must've been a woman. You were... preoccupied the last few days of term. Though I'm not sure if seeing the parent of one of your students is the wisest move you've ever made. It could be... tricky, no?'

'Probably. Definitely. Jenna knows.'

'Shit.'

The politics of courtship still perplexed Patrick. He'd been avoiding Sarah's calls since the Lionswater encounter – in fact, he'd been avoiding pretty much *all calls* – but there was no denying that, when he thought of Sarah,

Patrick felt something he hadn't experienced for a long time: a tugging equidistant between his head and loins. But he also sensed she was trouble. And he was in more than enough of that already.

Patrick settled back into the chair and gulped at his wine. 'You know she lives in Union City.'

'Snob.'

'Those videos we saw…? I had no idea the place was as rough as it is. I kind of wish there was something I could do.'

Christophe shrugged. 'You're already doing it. *In loco parentis* and all that.'

'I'm an Art teacher, not a social worker. There were kids openly brandishing weapons, Chris.'

A security light flashed on above Christophe's patio, wiping away their reflections and revealing the suburbanite infinity of his garden. A startled cat fizzed away into the night.

Patrick continued. 'They act like they rule that estate, those kids. There were people hiding behind their curtains. It actually made me feel quite ill to watch.'

'It's hardly the October Revolution. Probably it's simple boredom. For most children, anyone over a certain age is the enemy. Anyone of an alternative class. You've Oliver Cromwell to thank for that, of course.'

'You've changed your tune, Chris. You were the one who pointed the videos out to me. Why are you suddenly so dismissive?'

'You know how society works, yeah? A small, powerful group controlling a majority of law-abiding citizens? It's as true in London sink estates as it is in Westminster.' Christophe slumped back in his chair, drunkenness bestowing him a sympathetic pomposity. 'Have you raised your fears with your new lady friend?'

'She's not my lady friend… She's… She mentioned something about a curfew, and I'm sure she's not the only one cowering from the gangs. Last week, I walked past a corner shop, completely razed.'

'The last couple of governments have fucked Union City up, amongst… other socioeconomic factors.' The Frenchman rose slightly in his chair, the confident way he poured himself another glass of wine suggesting he believed he'd solved most, if not all, of life's problems. 'I think there's a bigger evil at work. The majority of criminal activity is financially driven. This corner shop. It was the one on Albert Road, was it not? More wine?'

'Please. You know the shop?'

'No. But I read about the incident. The shop was "razed", as you say, because it was selling under the counter, impinging upon a local dealer's ground. Drugs are a lucrative business.' He scowled at the empty wine bottle he was holding.

'You think this gang war is centred around the sale of drugs?'

'Almost definitely.' Christophe looked at his watch, clicked his tongue, then obviously decided he was drunk enough to relent against his better judgement. He held his hands up in front of him. 'For fifteen years I've had rheumatoid arthritis in these damn fingers. At about midday, every day, they start to ache. Three times as bad in weather like this. I've tried everything the doctor's given me: all useless. Cannabis is the only thing that works, believe me, and for some time I've been buying my relief from someone in Union City. Where would the middle classes be without these guys from the estates?' he chuckled. 'I don't go there myself to pick up the stuff – a kind of sub-dealer does – but this guy I get my gear from gets it from someone who gets it from Sean Keane. You won't remember him. He left, or rather was expelled from, Highfields before you joined. He's Matthew's older brother and lives, I think, quite close to your new woman's place. I mean, Sean's a sub-dealer too. They all are. Somewhere, some kid actually grows this shit in his bedroom but… who knows. I'm anonymous in all of this. Or so I like to think. But not innocent exactly; I know the only way to command a monopoly on illegal goods is through violence. Anyway, this goes no further than ourselves?'

Little wonder, Patrick thought, that Christophe was reluctant to chase Matthew and his dodgy phone content down Morality Street. 'Of course.'

'I shouldn't have involved you by showing you those videos. You were in the wrong place at the wrong time.' Christophe opened a drawer in a desk beside him and took out a small tin. As though to cap off his story, he rolled a large rizla full of grass and tobacco then sparked it with a match, curling out silver tendrils of smoke. 'Just because I'm the last link in the chain doesn't mean I can't be shocked by teenage gangsterism.' He took three long, deep lungfuls then passed it over to an embarrassed Patrick.

It was rich, almost berry-sweet, with a metallic aftertaste, and the first pull had no effect upon him. He risked another, and immediately the light-headedness took hold.

'Actually, I *am* involved,' he told Christophe.

Christophe didn't seem to take the conversational hint, merely shook his deadpan expression from side to side and gazed out the window. 'You might be able to help those kids,' Christophe stated. 'But not as a teacher. We both know that. As red tape multiplies, discipline reduces. It's not fucking rocket science. What I want to know is, when do teachers get a chance, once all the acronyms have been cross-checked, to edify the kids with information? To *teach*?'

It was all Patrick could do to nod his head. While Christophe climbed atop his soapbox, Patrick choked back a growing desire to lie on the floor and go to sleep. Christophe seemed larger than usual, fearlessly animalistic, and Patrick was unclear what point the Frenchman was making, or whether he himself might have forgotten.

'Kids aren't scared of the consequences of their actions, because there aren't any. There's an impotence instilled into schools by a single generation of children who've been brought up by children, who believe they're beyond reproach.

Their statements for "behavioural issues" are essentially the sympathies of the medical profession.'

For variety, Patrick shook his head. The carpet still looked mightily inviting.

'I often wonder what older teachers, if they haven't already left education, make of this constant target-setting, this reduction of the teaching of young minds to a business model? I was never hit by a teacher during my schooldays, and yet I remember corporal punishment being a genuine deterrent. It served as a clear barometer of 'crossing the line'. Don't get me wrong, I'm glad the days of institutionalised child abuse are over, but there have been times, I'll admit, as I've stood at my door refusing to let my Nines out until they've picked up every pencil I've watched fly across the room, when I've considered how much easier things would be if I were permitted the odd clip round the ear, as opposed to an hour's detention followed by an "incident report" followed by a "strategy meeting" followed by a... What's funny?'

Patrick's laugh had started quietly before building into a thunderous guffaw he was powerless to stop. Through hiccoughs of stoned laughter, Patrick felt his confidence growing, the truth unshackling. Here was a man who would understand. Here was a man who could hear his confession.

'I punched Denis,' he announced, more with relief than regret.

He'd known it was a stupid thing to say, even before he'd said it.

'You what?'

'Two days before the end of term. I punched Denis. I lost it...'

'Jesus, Patrick.'

The Art teacher described the build-up to the incident as it happened, his head spinning with searing paranoia, his friend's look of judgement. Christophe listened with a mixture of horror and embarrassment, barely making eye contact throughout.

At the part in the story where Denis hit the ground, Christophe asked, 'And… Is he okay?'

'I don't know.'

'You don't know?'

'I didn't wait around to find out. There were more of them than me.'

'They just let you walk off?'

'I think they were as surprised as I was. A couple of them ran over to Denis. But the others simply watched me walk away. Then I started running. I didn't stop. They could have killed me, I suppose, but they didn't seem to know what to do once Denis was down, almost as though their orders ought to have come from him. Fucking hell, Christophe, I can't tell you what a weight off my mind this is, being able to talk to someone about it. I've been living a nightmare for the last week. Too scared to answer the door, to pick up the phone to strange numbers. They could be harmless calls but… I don't know what came over me. I just felt so… threatened. I've done nothing but think about it since. Why *didn't* they come after me? I kind of think I know the answer, and I don't like it. They *know who I am*, of course they do. Or at least Denis does.'

'But what if Denis is… not alright?'

'We'd have heard. Wouldn't we?'

They both searched the empty spaces behind the other, avoiding eye contact. The snow had closed the school prematurely, mercifully, on Thursday morning. And Denis had a history of truanting those last few days of term. They wouldn't have heard anything either way.

'You won't tell anyone?' Patrick asked.

'You put me in a very difficult position.'

'Please, Christophe.'

'As one professional to another…'

Patrick tried another approach. 'You're stoned. Maybe you misheard.' He hadn't meant that to sound like blackmail, but Christophe's own admission was now well and truly cancelled out. 'It's been days already. And who's more likely to be believed? Me or him?' He was convincing nobody now the shaking of his hands had returned, the distant whinnying in his ears.

'You have to teach that boy for another *six months*. There's a Year Eleven parents' evening in the first week back…'

Patrick hauled himself from the chair and, before he knew it, was walking with wavering gait from the room, maybe even from their friendship. 'I can't see me staying in teaching a whole lot longer.'

Christophe kept pace behind him. 'If that's how you want it, I'll try and forget this conversation ever happened. I can keep a secret.'

Patrick turned before he reached the front door. Christophe was visibly sweating.

'Thanks for dinner.'

'Watch yourself,' Christophe said as Patrick headed into the cold, and his words couldn't have been imbued with a more menacing caution if he'd tried.

'Yeah.' Patrick looked around him as the darkness circled. Even wealthy suburbia had its shadows.

'Oh, and Merry Christmas.'

Again, that mysterious mobile number vibrating the phone in his pocket. He imagined the voice on the other end. The twisted half-threat, muffled by a bandana. The insinuations of a bloody revenge. He'd already purchased new locks for his front door and windows.

Patrick entered his street, looked up its entire length then crossed into the light. The silvery shadows rustled. The wind called his surname. A fear as tangible as the one he felt as a boy, petrified of the dark behind the curtains, under his bed, inside his toybox, was reborn. Everywhere the blackness touched, the familiar became terrifying. The security of his own flat was no security at all and he was tempted to turn back, but there was no way to shake off the demons made manifest by children. By *children*.

He slowed as he approached, his heart pitching into his throat. There was definitely a dark figure outside the main door, hunched on the low wall beneath the entry phone. Patrick felt the panic constrict and crawl at the skin of his testicles. It was, by now, a familiar sensation.

He had stopped walking, but hadn't remembered doing so. The stranger raised its head and long hair fell past its shoulder.

The relief coursed through him and he walked on as the shadowed figure locked its pose in his direction, as though in recognition. So, Sarah, unable to get hold of him, had found out where he lived. He had a stalker after all.

He stepped through the gate into the front garden, trying to clear his head of the lingering remnants of fear, to act surprised but unfazed, to string a sentence together.

'Daddy!' a little voice cried.

The figure sat on what was now unmistakably a large rucksack, their hands folded around the shoulders of a beaming child who suddenly broke forward and bear-hugged Patrick's legs.

'And where the hell have you been?' his wife asked, without a trace of humour.

TWO

Ana walked through his door as though taking ownership of the flat.

'This place is a tip,' she declared.

'My wife left me,' Patrick said, following her in.

It had been meant as a joke, sort of, but right now it didn't feel as though they'd split. It wasn't exactly crystal clear what their relationship was, and probably these things never were, but she didn't laugh anyway.

Danny was hyperactive from the flight and the rediscovery of his toys and father. A little blonde ball of energy, he bounced, grinning, round the flat as Patrick watched, dumbstruck with love.

It was true that paternity suited Patrick on occasion. Right now, those miniature limbs, those delicate features, he would protect to the grave. In a few days, perhaps, the old worries might ebb back – the lack of freedom; the overwhelming responsibility; theories of hereditary insecurity – but watching Danny now, he couldn't believe he could ever feel suffocated by the family set-up ever again. This was too precious.

'Are you pleased to see Daddy?' Ana asked, almost grudgingly.

Danny could only nod. He knew words were useless, cheapening things. Then he threw his arms around his father's legs again.

'Drink?' Patrick asked.

'Ribena!' Danny shouted.

Patrick went to his cupboard and scratched his cheek, making a big show of trying to remember his son's favourite drink, then, with a playful wink, pulled out a bottle. He hoped Ana would be touched by this cache of Ribena, but she didn't seem to read too much into it. It was something that would have annoyed him before. She never read anything into anything.

'Don't you think he's hyper enough?' she asked.

He took a beer from the fridge, tossed one to Ana. 'So why didn't you let me know you were coming over?' He tried hard to keep all irritation out of his voice.

'Why don't you answer your phone?' She was looking round the flat, perhaps for signs of other women, or even for signs of herself; old belongings, reminders of who she was or had once been to him.

'We spoke the other day. You never mentioned you were coming.'

She just shrugged and sat herself down on the sofa, watched Danny dancing at his father's ankles. Her mysteriousness was undoubtedly a deliberate ploy to reaffirm that he had no control over them.

'I spoke to your mother,' she said.

'What?'

'She's concerned.'

'It's none of her business.'

'I agree. But she's still easier to speak to than you.'

Sensing an argument, Danny stopped jumping up and down.

Patrick forced a smile. 'Did my mother pay for your flights?'

Ana inspected the bookshelves. Mrs Owen had been flashing plenty of her late husband's money around lately, and would no doubt be expecting a visit from her grandchild at the very least.

Patrick tried to bury his irritation. 'Where are you staying? You're not at my mother's are you?'

82

'Hotel. Not far. I thought Danny might want to stay here.'
'Of course.'

Danny leapt up and down, made up a gibberish song.

'How was Christmas?' she asked.

Patrick sighed and sat down opposite her. 'Mum was asking after you. It was quite an inquisition.'

Ana chuckled. She'd been attending medical school during the early days of their marriage, and her bedside manner throughout Patrick's father's chemotherapy had almost certainly been the reason Ana was so cemented in his mother's affections.

'How's your work, Patrick?' It was a veritable carousel of questions-by-number.

He shrugged and tickled his son, who hurled himself about on the floor with unabashed joy. Ana's smile of sympathy annoyed and anointed him in equal measure.

His wife was intimidatingly beautiful and he wondered, not for the first time, whether the act of punching too high above his weight had been the root cause of their breakup. But, every man's obliged to think that. No sane person would enter a relationship thinking they were above their partner.

'Why don't you stay here? It's late.'

Before she could refute the idea, Patrick grabbed Danny and launched him into the air. 'Shall we check out the new toys in your room, Danny?'

'Yes! Yes!' The boy punched the air as his father carried him through.

Inside Danny's room, Patrick suddenly saw just how tired his son was, how was he was being held awake only by excitement. He opened one present – a soft Spiderman figure – and then encouraged Danny to lie down while he turned on the night light and spoke to him about where he'd got the toy from. There was no lie about Father Christmas here; he wanted his son to know that he was the magical benefactor. Finally, lying down, Danny was asleep in no time.

Patrick looked at him as he slept, as perfect a specimen

of humanity as he could ever hope to see. He tucked him in, then turned off the night light and went back to Ana in the front room. This was almost definitely where it would get awkward.

But Ana had fallen asleep too. He draped a blanket over her, hastily, as though he were doing something perverse, then went to the kitchen window and scanned up and down the dark street. A fox slunk through gardens. A light wind shook Mrs Lingham's conifers.

Outside, the world looked cold and deserted. Victoria Street. Alexandra Road. Holly Park. Town planners in London had a propensity for naming places after women, and, unbidden, the faces of old girlfriends floated past the window in the thin puffs of snow from the guttering. Katy Rowlett, whom Patrick had had to stand on a crate to kiss in the first year of secondary school. Sophie McGee, a college one-night stand who deserved to be so much more. Emma Worthington, the owner of the only heart Patrick had ever definitely broken. And then there was Ana, who refused to be summed up in a sentence, because he had actually loved her. *Still* loved her, surely.

He stayed there longer than necessary, alternatively looking back at the sleeping woman on his sofa, then the hostile world outside, before finally deadlocking the front door and going to bed.

He was woken by the sound of Danny crying out and was fully awake in a second.

Halfway from his bed, he paused. Danny had nightmares, he remembered now. The boy never recalled them in the morning and had probably already slipped back into peaceful slumber. That's if Danny had even made a noise – it was quite probable that Patrick himself had dreamed the sound. He lay back down in bed and stared restlessly at the dark shapes in the corner of his room, his mind alert and excitable, until visibility came. That his family would return to him, no matter how briefly, was a thrill he'd not truly foreseen.

There came a shifting, muffled sound from another room. Patrick's first thought was that it was Ana, but no light had sharpened under the door. Fear held him. His family weren't safe here. He remembered how Denis went down. The unconscious, or dead, body on the alley floor.

Slowly, he slipped out of bed. He kept the light off and stood by the door, listening. How many pairs of feet could he make out through the hallway? Were they a woman's footsteps, or a man's? It was hard to tell. They were light. Tentative. His hand curled round an umbrella and he crept out into the landing.

In the hall he saw nothing, but was aware of rustling from the front room.

Remembering his son's cry, he tore into Danny's bedroom and slammed on the light, bathing the walls in retina-gouging pain. What he saw made his heart flee his body.

Danny's bed was empty.

Patrick lunged forward, then exhaled sharply as he spotted him on the floor. Danny had obviously rolled out before falling asleep again. Carefully, he picked his son up and replaced him in the bedsheets. There was a discernable chill in the air and Patrick made sure he was tucked in tight. Danny's breathing was shallow and miraculous.

Assured of his son's safety, his heart still racing, Patrick re-entered the hallway then burst into the front room, makeshift weapon raised. Ana turned round in shock, one arm in her coat sleeve. He cornered the umbrella behind the door, flicked the light switch.

'I'm off to the hotel,' she told him.

'You should have woken me.' He peered into every corner of the front room.

'What's the matter?'

'I thought I heard someone.'

'You heard *me*. Why are you so panicky?'

He flashed her an apologetic smile but it couldn't have been convincing; he'd been living alone for too long and the

85

roleplay required for twenty-four-hour human interaction was rusty from disuse.

'Give me a call tomorrow,' she said. 'I need to sleep in a proper bed. My neck hurts.'

'Have mine. I'll take the sofa.'

She looked at him, as though weighing up the offer. Would sleeping in his recently-vacated bed be too personal an act? The light was scalding. Her look too.

He crossed to the window. The street was, as it always was, empty. He was shaking.

'Can you look after Danny for a few days?' she asked.

'Of course. Why?'

'I've made plans.'

'Plans? You've only been back five seconds.' He knew his suspicion, his jealousy, was unattractive, but hiding it was like camouflaging a facial blemish – or cleft lip – there was only so much concealer you could cake on the affliction. It was who he was; he was a jealous man. 'Are you... seeing someone?'

'No. Are you?'

He shook his head. When were the two of them going to acknowledge the elephant in the room? When would the word *Divorce* get its first mention? 'Take my bed. I honestly don't mind. You don't really want to leave in this cold, do you?'

'Not really, no.'

But she left anyway. And in doing so, painted a clear picture of where their relationship, or lack of one, was at. Patrick stood by the window and watched her go, then remained there for the rest of the night, a sentry peering out into the glass-cold dark.

The next day, the day after, the day after that, Patrick took Danny far away from the regular world: to museums, play centres, toyshops, McDonalds. His son was delighted, constantly, and his energy was infectious and boundless. It was a far cry from the night-time world, in which Patrick lay in a fragile dark listening for tell-tale signs of teenage intruders as the calendar mocked him, drew him back to school.

Over New Year, they visited Patrick's mother, who seemed to ask, 'And how's your work, Patrick?' every five minutes, as everyone always did, defining him through what he did for a living instead of his politics, his ambitions, his personal library. Danny, of course, got the lion's share of the attention, but that was to be expected, while Patrick was told to 'be careful on the sauce' with each glass of wine. His response to his mother's Methodist asceticism was to sulk, obviously, and though he hated himself for falling into the teenage sarcasm trap, no one had told him to watch what he drank since his wife left. Ana was, of course, asked after. Patrick could only answer, truthfully, that he had no idea where she'd gone.

His mother's entire body tightened at moments like this. The split had been a major incursion upon her sensibilities; no one in their family had got divorced before and she dreaded the rumours which would fly around her book club if the Big D happened. While Patrick seemed to spend the whole time talking through his teeth, she dabbed her thin mouth with a red and green serviette, as though holding back the real questions she wanted to ask. Being a failed novelist, she wasn't predisposed to outward emotion. They didn't mention Dad once.

Patrick and Danny sat on the top deck of the bus on the way back, at the very front. Danny loved it, and seemed to believe he was genuinely flying over the streets of London. Patrick, as usual, was nervous about bumping into kids he taught. The smell of petrol and vomit and chips offended him, despite how used he now was to their aroma.

'Danny,' he began. 'Mummy's taking you back to Argentina soon. Have you enjoyed yourself?'

The boy shrugged, then said simply, 'Yeah.'

Patrick knew not to take it to heart. A child's mood changed from second to second.

'Would you like to stay here, with me?'

'Your flat's too small,' the boy stated.

'It's big enough.'

'In Argentina I have a *massive* room.' He spread his arms in demonstration. 'And a balcony. And it's hot. And I eat *jamon* every day.'

'What's *jamon*?'

'Ham.'

'Right.' Educated by his three-year-old. Nice. He paused, looked around him again. The streets clanked past, taillights beginning to glow as the evening scrolled over the horizon. 'You know I love you, don't you?'

'Yes.' Again, so matter-of-fact it hurt. For a long time, Patrick had assumed his son was autistic, but he'd eventually realised that all children, up to a certain age, spoke like this. 'I know you do. And so does Mummy. Maybe a bit more.'

'What do you mean?' To disguise his hurt, Patrick stared out the window at the Turkish restaurateurs as they scraped greasy slices of donner kebab into stale pitta clams.

'She laughs more.'

'She... laughs more?'

'And she doesn't look around her all the time.'

'Do I look around me all the time, Danny?'

'You've been doing it all day today and yesterday and the day before yesterday.'

Patrick pulled his son closer to him. It was all true. His mother offered him a larger, warmer, friendlier, and all round safer environment.

The two of them stared out of the curved windscreen at a mushrooming storm cloud, its ominous grey mass singed on the right-hand side by sunset. Patrick held his son still tighter, and wept silently into his sweet-smelling hair. When Ana came back, he decided, he wouldn't fight with her over what was going to happen to Danny. Danny would go where

Danny felt the most comfortable, and the boy, with cutthroat receptivity, had already convinced him it would be more sensible if he flew back with her.

After all, it would soon be time to return to Highfields. And Denis would be waiting for him.

THREE

Passing through the playground's crematoria-style entrance gates, Patrick's eyes flitted round the darker recesses as he headed for the front doors.

A few teachers said hello as he flew down the corridor, their greetings falsely chirpy. That part-timer in Humanities, a knock-kneed knob-end from Wood Green who looked as though his haircut had been bought over the internet, even had the audacity to ask him how his holiday had gone. A nameless teaching assistant whose wonky face was saved by inappropriate décolletage probably tried to smile at him, but it looked for all the world as though she was about to start crying so he hurried embarrassedly on.

The final flight of stairs was always trickier than the three previous, usually more on account of the accumulating chewing gum on his soles than Patrick's deteriorating levels of fitness. Through the rear windows, he saw Charlotte's effete, little car and was momentarily dumbstruck. It was in exactly the same position as they'd left it two weeks ago. The snow must have prevented it from being fixed before she flew off to Barbados or Bilbao or Bilauktaung. But seeing the car brought the events back home. Even the snow now seemed like it was returning properly after its own holiday, fluttering back onto the grassy verges, the basketball court, and those weeks off suddenly seemed inconsequential and forgotten.

He decided against turning the light on in the Art office. There was no need to advertise the fact he was there to anyone.

Patrick stared into the slowly dawning sky to find himself wondering whether his son thought about him much, or whether he thought more about Spiderman, or the Gruffalo, or *jamon*. 'Danny's Tune' was still very much a work in progress, but it had gained verses in his mind, and a middle eight. The problem was, it was now replete with his son's fresh absence and had morphed from rousing stadium anthem to the lonely plink-plonk of a nursery-room pullstring.

Danny was probably on the plane, right now. Patrick searched the pregnant snowclouds for his boy. He'd heard of refugees falling to their deaths from the wheel housings of aircraft, frozen and asphyxiated, in a desperate attempt to flee their war- or economy-ravaged countries. He believed he had some idea of that kind of desperation, and right now would gladly have taken the risk of falling to his death from Danny's plane.

Patrick slouched to the far side of the office and tugged his electric guitar out of the mire of other formerly loved bric-a-brac. He had more of a history, more of a relationship, with that instrument than the flesh and blood who shared the office with him. He knew its sounds and feels and emotions and, once upon a time, it had responded in kind to his. Though scratched and dusty, an object drawn by hundreds of children unaware of its pedigree, its weight against him felt good and he fastened the strap across his shoulder.

Adam had always been fiercely jealous of this guitar, coveted it the way Patrick had coveted Ana. Now both acquisitions were covered in dust, the poetic thing to have done, rather than let it rot in a London secondary school, would have been to send it to his former bandmate. But Patrick doubted Adam wanted anything from him these days and as he hugged the guitar close, breath coming in thin gasps, he hovered his right hand over the strings and cautiously strummed a slow E chord.

The note sagged derisorily out of tune.

'Morning.'

Patrick jumped a foot in the air as Harriet entered the office, accompanied by a drawn-out sigh which didn't herald from the door's stiff hinge. She wore a long turquoise skirt with a turquoise jumper, both the exact same shade as one another, and further betrayed her age by accompanying the combination with a gold floral brooch.

'Hi Harriet,' Patrick tendered, trying to sound normal. He replaced the guitar. 'Good Christmas?'

'I didn't sleep well last night. I never do before the first day back. Too nervous. You?'

'Not a wink.'

He had the Elevens period four.

Deny everything, right down to the bruises on Denis' face. Nothing happened. Just deny it, utterly. And make sure you're in a public place at all times.

'The kids will be bonkers,' Harriet mused, looking out the window at the kids beginning to limp into the playground. 'It's snowing again. Is the heating on?'

'Not that I can feel.'

'There'll be complaints about that.' She said this with genuine concern, grimacing so hard Patrick worried about being sucked into the corrugated fissures around her eyes. 'It's like Mr H is desperate to alert Ofsted again.'

The inspectors were overdue as it was and Highfields hadn't performed well previously. The climate around the school had been one of unparalleled anxiety since the September kick-off, a death row atmosphere hardly conducive to the teaching of children, and even Harriet, who'd seen off several such inspections in her time, wasn't immune to the panic. In fact, she suffered it worse than most.

'Charlotte's paperwork's all over the place and her GCSE grades are fucked up,' she confided quietly. Patrick had long ago become used to hearing someone his mother's age swearing so readily. 'She hasn't a clue how to control the youngsters. You remember what happened last time she was observed?'

Of course he did. His only regret was that he hadn't been there to see Charlotte's lesson first-hand. 'The odds of another heron flying through the window are highly unlikely, Harriet.'

'How were my kids in my absence?' Harriet checked her timetable above the kettle.

'Awful. Charlene was stealing other pupils' school bags and filling them with water at the sinks.'

She nodded. This kind of behaviour was hardly news.

It was good to have Harriet clocking in again. Her demeanour was no fresher but her pained-yet-defiant air was somehow reassuring. Patrick noticed, not for the first time, just how truly knackered Harriet looked. Her top lip sported a thicker wisping of hair than usual and she'd been scratching at her cheek, leaving it with the thin traces of sadistic fingernails.

'You... alright?'

'I'm counting the days.'

'Afraid there are still six weeks before half term.' If she looked this awful on the first day back there was no chance she'd last till then.

'I'm thinking beyond that, Patrick. I'm looking forward to *retirement*.'

'You're not going anytime soon, are you?' he asked with what he hoped she'd take as a flattering dismay. Charlotte hadn't mentioned anything about interviewing for a vacant post.

'Less than two years.'

'Doesn't sound long.'

'Not compared to the thirty I've already done, no. There *have* been good moments, don't get me wrong, but it's never been easy. In fact, it's got harder. The moment I feel on top of my job the curriculum changes or the government introduces something to pull the rug from under my feet. Twenty years ago, I considered leaving but thought I'd be unable to retrain. The irony is you have to retrain every five years or so to

93

remain in this job, or you get left behind. I was scared the money would be less if I went somewhere else, that I'd lose a secure career, that the holidays would be impossible to do without... I'm in the twilight of my career now. You're comparatively fresh. Trust me, Patrick, if you're not one hundred percent happy, *get out*.'

Patrick stared across the grey playground. There was little he felt he could say to a colleague who'd just admitted to being trapped in her job for a working lifetime. The Monday morning blues. They both had it.

But she hadn't punched a pupil.

Don't go anywhere near him. Don't look at him. Don't even say his name in the register.

Harriet was still looking at him, in that odd way. He tried to sound breezy, normal, but knew he sounded like the drunkard who attempts to overcompensate by adopting an unconvincing impression of sobriety. 'Why did you stay at this school?' he asked.

'They're all the same,' she whistled through three decades of throat polyps. 'I've got a Year Team meeting this week. It'll be full of keen newly-qualifieds with plans to be more positive with the youngsters. Letters of praise sent home when they fail to hit each other, that sort of thing... I just feel like I'm out of my depth sometimes, Patrick. Do you know what I mean?' She seemed to be prying for something. Perhaps she'd sensed his discomfort, his fear.

Three storeys beneath them, he saw Denis.

He parted the legions of huddled lower years as he swaggered through his jungle, bobbing like a rap star, a newly rethroned king. Patrick couldn't make out his usual expression of lofty enmity, or even if his face was bruised or not, but saw only the muscles in his neck, the firm lines of a prematurely broad back.

'I'm beginning to,' he replied.

Charlotte entered as the morning bell went.

94

'Good morning,' Harriet and Patrick both chimed.

'No it isn't,' she spat.

Patrick opened up the pouch linings in an old body warmer with a rusting scalpel and carefully inserted ceramic tiles from the bottom shelf of the kiln into the slits. They wouldn't stop a bullet but he doubted a knife could pass through, unless Denis was supremely lucky. In case the boy was after a kill, Patrick double-tiled the area in front of his hammering heart. He tried it on, beneath his jacket. It looked ridiculous, and was insanely heavy, but he would take no chances.

His teaching plumbed new depths. Fortunately, the kids were equally depressed to be back and were just about manageable. Some asked about the body warmer under his jacket but the lack of heating forgave him. Sometimes the tiles clanked together and, each time, to cover himself, he stamped down on the flooring as though it might be coming loose. He was vaguely aware that the kids were looking at him more strangely than usual.

When the time came, the Elevens began lining up. Sophia now had Miley Cyrus hair. Carlo's chin looked like he'd glued individual hairs onto it. Jenna's skirt had lost another two inches.

And there he was, near the back, alone.

He looked straight ahead, unreadable, untouchable. He seemed to have grown again, out as well as up.

'Come in,' Patrick squealed, standing at the door until the last few were due in and then slipping inside, so the majority of the class formed a human shield alongside him as Denis entered. His jacket clanked.

Denis found his seat, shrugged his bag off onto the floor.

'Today, um… Well, today… Let's see… Happy New Year…'

Denis sat inspecting his large, powerful hands.

Patrick tried to explain to the group that they were to begin their mock exam preparation today, showed them the paper, some past examples. He was pleased the pupils were listening, though it began to dawn on him that they were simply shocked by his appearance. As the clock ticked round, he waited for the insults, the threats, someone to throw a chair.

Nothing. Not yet.

Unusually quiet, the class began their brainstorms. Matthew Keane's empty seat was a reminder of Denis' unproved sociopathic tendencies, as the assailant in question sat there chewing the end of his pen, his eyes leaden with... Anger? Apathy? Hurt? It was like trying to decipher the soul of a statue. Nothing lurked within, and no clues gave anything away on the outside.

Sophia put up her hand.

'Sir, can I make an appointment for Wednesday?'

Reluctantly, he slid the parents' evening form round the room as the pupils selected an appointment time and jotted it down in their planners.

He hated parents' evenings more than he hated marking. Or teaching. Or the getting out of bed.

Jenna looked at the paper, then at him.

'Is there any point me filling this in, sir?' she asked, her eyes round with sarcasm. 'I mean, since you and my mother are...?'

'Probably not, no.'

He passed the sheet on to Hamza.

Soon, all except Jenna and one other pupil had filled in their timeslot. It sat in front of Denis, unnoticed.

Patrick stepped forward to take it back as Denis snatched out for the form. Casting his apathetic gaze over the available times, the boy chose a slot before skimming it back across the table to the teacher without a word.

'Thanks,' Patrick said. The tiles in his body warmer ground together, then gave out a loud clink as one fell through into the pouch underneath. Jenna looked at him under heavy lids that seemed to confirm a mortal disgust.

'Denis, you have thing on your face?' Cosmo asked, in his delightfully mangled English.

The room, silent before, was an instant, fearful vacuum. Cosmo smiled dumbly at Denis.

'I used to have a harelip,' Denis stated, calm, composed.

'No. Your eye.' Cosmo pointed to his own, left eye.

Patrick saw now. The bruise had retreated over Christmas, but could still be seen around the socket in the form of a faintly blotched, rash-like contusion. Denis put his finger to it, then observed the sailing clouds out the window. Nothing was said.

Somehow, time passed.

When the class stood as one on the bell, Patrick jumped in shock. The pushing back of stools was the scrape of fingernails on chalkboards.

Patrick swam back to reality. It was lunchtime and he was sitting on the toilet.

He couldn't remember the previous, sleepwalked lesson. He could barely remember the last seven years, how they'd passed in a drowned heartbeat of time.

What was he supposed to have made of that last hour? On the surface, nothing had changed. Denis wasn't, for the time being, dragging Patrick's broken body through the alleyways of Union City. But it was a false victory. The white bone of reality had been revealed to Patrick. He was a dead man walking.

Had Denis even spoken? Had he looked his way at all? What the hell had happened? And how long had the inevitable retaliation been delayed for? And why?

Patrick almost wished Denis had attacked him.

He stared at the back of the toilet door and listened without listening to the footsteps, the locking doors, the unbucklings. He considered, in that most unsanitary of environments, the infinity of time which had passed before his birth and the infinity of time which would follow his death. He considered the notion that he was here, by the remotest probability, at this living, breathing moment, this tiny, tiny snatch of time, and he screamed out silence. He knew he should have been out in the world, making things happen. Living his life. So much time had passed already.

It had been so promising, once. The move to London. The formation of the band. Meeting Ana. Then, ashes. What had happened to those dreams?

But dreams, of course, aren't real. Civilisations aren't built on fantasies and dreams can so easily dry up and blow away.

The footsteps. The flushes. The expulsions. Some of the staff washed their hands, some didn't.

The snows came again, singing over the sharp lines of Union City, feathering the estate with the unfamiliar presence of nature.

Trudging home, Patrick rang Ana's mother.

The harsh, intermittent buzz of an international call sounded, before being answered by a Spanish voice.

'Ana?'

'No. Lo siento. Esta es su madre. ¿Quién llama?'

The stupid cow knew exactly who it was. 'It's Patrick, Adana. Can I speak to Ana please?' He didn't want to speak to Ana, he wanted to speak to Danny. It felt to him sometimes that it had never really been Ana he'd wanted to spend time with, not once Danny had learned to talk and fight and draw and dream. That was almost definitely why they weren't together any more.

'She no here.'

'Any idea when she'll be back?'

'She no say. She in England. They no here.'

'You're wrong. They flew back yesterday.'

It must be a translation issue, he told himself. Or maybe Ana was there in the room but just didn't want to speak to him.

He hung up when he began receiving another call. It was Sarah. He deliberated, then answered.

He might have imagined it, but he thought she sounded relieved. 'Hello. I thought you'd died.'

'I was away for Christmas. Sorry, didn't I tell you?'

She asked him how he'd been, enquired as to his holiday, and he asked her if she'd tried to call him often and she replied, 'Only a couple of times'. He knew this was a lie; he'd counted at least ten attempts in the aftermath of their hotel date.

'Jenna's at her father's tonight. Why don't you come over?'

He paused, looked along the pathway that led to the end section of the estate, the ground upon which he'd stood and thrown his fist at his least favourite Year Eleven pupil.

'What's the address?'

He walked out onto Albert Road and hailed a minicab.

The driver had such tired eyes, and the luggage underneath them was so circular, it was as though he wore spectacles of flesh. 'Where you going, fella?'

Patrick recited the address.

'Bateman block? You must be kidding.' He powered off, leaving Patrick by the roadside.

Assuming the journey was such a short one it wasn't worth the boorish taxi driver's time, Patrick tugged up the collar of his coat and headed into the estate on foot. He found a crude council map on the corner of Stetson block. Bateman seemed to be seven blocks on.

He'd never plunged so deep in-between the high-rise of Union City before and couldn't believe how identical every block, quadrangle, alleyway and balcony looked. The corner of the estate he knew from his walk home had infinitely replicated itself, every confused and criss-crossing walkway an example in déjà vu, with only the names of the blocks and the graffiti changing. He might have been back where he started for all the variety he was afforded in the snow, slanting and drifting across a bloating moon. As water crept into his shoes through high-street stitching, he creaked hesitantly across packing ice in the manner of an octogenarian.

Unbidden, 'Danny's Tune' sought Patrick out. He rolled it around his mind before humming it to life. It calmed him, and the woes of Highfields retreated like figures in the snowfall. He added another verse.

And though you're hardly
Here with me
My love for you flows
Constantly

He was about four blocks into the conglomeration of shoebox silhouettes, very near Sarah's flat, when he passed two hooded shadows.

He kept his gaze low and walked as fast as the snow would allow. Inevitably, dozens of snowballs, hardened into ice by hot mitts, pelted him until his song was lost.

Round the next corner, the rest of the gang lurked.

There were seven of them, liveried in tracksuits and attitude, and they waited like a checkpoint militia, silent, expectant. Most of them were tooled up: one held a golf club, another at the far end of the line had gone for the traditional baseball bat. They all wore bandanas across their faces, eyes showing in thin, ninja slits.

Patrick approached, keeping to what he assumed was the path. The tinny, rapid sound of hip-hop rang out from an iPhone as the snow gave out compacting squeaks beneath his shoes. Snowflakes were black ash against the white night sky.

The golf club kid, broad-shouldered and tall, stood up from his place on a low wall segregating refuse bins from the residential area, and walked slowly towards Patrick until he blocked his way. He wore a grey and white Palestinian-style scarf across his face and he bounced his club, once, twice, three times against his leg. The eyes were brown, cynical, familiar.

The taste of fear was bile in Patrick's throat.

Denis sidled right up to a paralysed Patrick and grabbed him by the elbow, as one might an elderly relative. He steered him through the quadrangle. It was civil but urgent and Patrick had no choice but to obey.

As he was led through the masked gang he noticed a couple were female. One of whom quivered in her too-short school skirt, beneath a fur coat and a girly-pink bandana. He hoped Jenna wouldn't recognise him in his own inadequate winter gear. Or maybe it wasn't Jenna. Wasn't she supposed to be at her father's?

To Patrick's surprise – and towering relief – the grip on his arm was suddenly lessened. The boy's footsteps dissipating behind him, he squinted into the blizzard. The estate had transformed its dimensions in the snowy dark, and Patrick was no longer sure about the direction he was supposed to go. Crunching on, he pondered his release; the ironclad atmosphere hinted at something about to happen, something big, uncivil, dangerous – was his adult presence a threat?

As he mused, the word 'Bateman', writ large beneath graffiti on a sign half-screwed into brickwork, loomed out of the murk. He counted the door numbers up to Sarah's flat and was about to mount the steps towards a fracturing balcony when the worry that Jenna was observing span him back to face the youths.

Dissolving in a filmic whiteout, the gang were already just formless spectres behind the soggy, bright night.

FOUR

'You look shaken. What's up?' Though her broad smile betrayed just how pleased she was to see him again, Sarah's eyebrows surged into a pincer of concern. 'Those hoodies at the end of the street again?' She brushed ice off his shoulders and slapped the front door closed. Her skirt was shorter than he'd ever seen her daughter's.

'There were a few kids, yeah. Nothing worth stressing about. I'm a pro.'

There was no embarrassment about where she lived; inside it was bigger than his own flat, tidier, cleaner, more contemporarily furnished. Only the view bordered on war-torn. She took his coat and hooked it behind the door alongside others. Her fake fur was absent – did mother and daughter share the same coat?

'Does Jenna ever hang around with that lot?' he asked, jerking his thumb back at the snowflakes twisting to earth outside.

Sarah fired him a sideways look. 'Of course not,' she almost snapped, indicating the way to the front room.

On the coffee table sat a few weeks-old newspapers, their supplements unthumbed. Patrick got the impression from her dusty CD pile that the genres – indie, sixties rock and roll, lots of greatest hits – represented old tastes. He couldn't locate his own debut album, which she'd claimed to love. The books dotted about might easily have been Jenna's GCSE texts – Austen, Brontë, Plath – and he spotted all seven *Harry*

*Potter*s and the *Fifty Shades* trilogy. The films were either rom-coms, foreign language or starred Audrey Hepburn. A man had never lived in this home.

Patrick noticed some pages of hand-scribbled notation on a table and, following his eyes towards them, Sarah hastily swept the sheets onto a nearby chair, albeit in considered, tidy fashion.

'Boring, job-related stuff…' she explained.

From the mantelpiece a young girl smiled down, the traditional school portrait of big teeth in front of a clouded surface. A pink-costumed Barbie beside the photo struck Patrick as an odd memento of Jenna's childhood, or at least a peculiar place to store it.

A noise from outside, like a violent folding of metal.

'What was that?'

Patrick drew back a curtain and peered through the whiteness to see the gang in the quadrangle below, uniformly dressed in grey-hooded nonchalance. There were eight – no, nine – of them now, doing nothing, waiting, braving the inclemency. Perhaps it was the sheer fact that they were out, an audacious safety in numbers, that transmitted hostility. One sat upon a bike, smoked a cigarette and kicked at litter from his saddle as though playing some urban game of polo while others sprayed tags on a bin. They still held their makeshift weapons, rapiers for the teenage rulers of the estate. How old were they? Fourteen? Fifteen? When Patrick was their age he was still impressed by kids who could 'round the world' their yo-yos. Where were their parents?

Jenna – or the girl who closely resembled her – was nowhere to be seen.

'Doesn't this annoy you? The noise?' One of the group was battering a litter bin with a cricket bat, as though sounding an alarm, or summons.

'I'm immune now,' she said. 'People complain but nothing ever comes of it. The police will only come if something

103

massive happens. I worry about Jenna, of course, but… She stays out of trouble. It's just how it is round here.'

He stared into the swirling snows. 'How long have you lived here?'

'Oh, forever…'

'It must be difficult…' he said, taking in the blackened carcasses of an unwanted mattress and sofa, the sulking sky above an asphalt playground that was once brightly painted. 'I know how draining, financially, emotionally, a separation can be, even when the parties concerned are determined to… Sorry. I didn't come round to discuss social anthropology, did I?'

But that last question, and its vaguely licentious edge, seemed inappropriate. He doubted Sarah was going to lead him straight to the bedroom, especially after their previous failed tryst, and yet the way she looked at him worried him slightly. There was hunger there. And something else…

'I mean, what did you want to talk to me about?' he rephrased.

'Oh. Nothing. Just wanted to see how you were.' She took a step into him and he dropped the curtain. 'I was thinking about you quite a bit over the last few days.'

'I thought about you too,' he confessed.

'Really? What did you think about me? Specifically?'

She'd pressed him against the window, her eyes wide, pleading orbs.

From outside came a terrifying roar, followed by the clash of steel, breaking glass, and he sprang round and tugged back the curtain.

About twenty young people were fighting in the quadrangle, crunching into one another with rugby tackles, bare-knuckled blows. It was an ugly and unprofessional brawl, with little sense of fairness. Here, four on one. There, five against two. Kids used planks, poles, kicked one another as they rolled in the snow, pulled clothes over heads to disorientate. He saw Denis, still with his golf club, swinging it wildly at a group of boys armed with kitchen knives. Patrick wasn't sure how one side even distinguished themselves from the other. The diplomacy of last summer, when boys played football in their school colours, was long gone.

Lights blinked on all over Bateman block and silhouettes appeared against yellow, floating squares, adults holding themselves back from the glass.

'Rival gangs sorting out their differences,' Sarah said, nowhere near as nonplussed as she would have liked to think she sounded.

The sky burst with an explosion. Fiction frequently mixes gunshots and the backfiring of cars but while Patrick hadn't heard much of either noise in his life he doubted there were many cars backfiring in the pedestrian-only walkway behind Sarah's flat. It scattered the swarm of youths in all directions, as it did the nesting gulls in the roofs. One boy clutched his shoulder and sank to his knees as the blast echoed throughout the estate. From three stories up, Patrick could make out red spots in the snow.

Too late, the ray-gun wail of sirens began to simmer in the distance and the remaining kids picked themselves up and trudged away. It was all over by the time the blue lights came, swirling the blizzard in all directions. Despite what had looked like significant brutality, no one hung around to get caught by the police, and no bodies remained for transportation into the belly of the ambulance which meandered unwanted into the quadrangle, leaving two snaking trails in its wake. Even the boy who'd collapsed after the gunshot had bled away into some dark alleyway.

In the kids' place, innocent snow was left rusted and scarred. It took an hour to dig the ambulance's rear wheels out.

The blue lights flickered one final time across the Monet print tethered to the lounge wall as Sarah served a packet curry. She lit two tall candles which had never had their wicks singed before.

Before it was even on his plate, she asked, 'You want to stay the night?' She crossed her legs and her thighs showed all the way to her underwear.

'We'll see,' he said, and what had sounded non-committal in his head simply came across as teasing. Her invitation, based as much on the brawl having freaked him out as on the snows rendering the estate impassable, *could* have been platonic.

Sarah shifted the conversation at whim and it was hard to get a foothold. She seemed more nervous than the last time they met and he wondered if it was because of his own obvious unease, or whether – heaven forbid – she'd developed feelings for him. It felt like he was being probed somehow, almost as though she was firing out questions scattergun in the hope that something stuck. The band. *No thanks.* University. *Not today.* His marriage. *Are you kidding me?* An exhaustion he'd rarely felt before fell over him almost as soon as she asked about school.

In the end, she fell back on the easiest subject of them all. If two people in a room both have children, that's what they end up discussing. Every time.

'What's his name?' she asked.

'Danny.'

'Lovely. Named after the boy in *The Shining*?'

He assumed that had been a joke, until her awaiting expression told him otherwise.

'No, it was my dad's name.'

'Was?'

He took a small photo of his father from his wallet, a suntanned image of him relaxing in Dubrovnik, and passed it across. It had been hard, at first, for Patrick to remember his father as he was in that holiday snap, to push into the background the yellow skin of renal failure, the desperate succession of 'final' rattles in his throat as the oxygen left his body, making it seem as though he watched him die a dozen times. Even once time had passed, the overriding emotion that established itself was guilt. Guilt that he hadn't spent enough time with him. Guilt that he hadn't spotted how frail he'd become until it was too late, when the only treatment for the untreatable was palliative care and cannulised limbs.

But there was also the guilt at the relief he felt that his father was no longer there to ignore him. Guilt at the bitterness that struck him when he recalled the efforts to gain his father's affection, only for it to fall on tone-deaf ears. Naming his son after the man hadn't been his idea – in fact, it had been everyone's idea *but* his, mooted because it felt 'right' at a time when the pregnancy was public knowledge and his father still clung to this accident we call life – but he'd gone along with it. Now that his father was smoke, he had to admit to himself that he'd allowed his son to be called Danny for one reason only: it was a final, desperate attempt to seek a scrap of attention from his old man.

'He died four weeks after our son was born. Cancer.'

She scrutinised the image. 'I'm sorry.'

They ate in silence for a bit.

'You got any photos of Danny?'

Patrick moved his chair closer to her, took out his phone and showed him image after image of his son's visit at Christmas.

'These are recent?' she asked, surprised.

He explained about Ana's visit. 'They're funny at that age, aren't they? Just about everything they do is brilliant. But you have to treat the things they say as gold dust, as the most important things in the world, because *to them* they are, and you don't want them to stop telling you that stuff. I mean, two is a nightmare. They're famously difficult at that age. But three… Three is… I just…' He didn't go on. He couldn't.

Patrick pushed his chair back round the other side and resumed his meal. He felt her watching him for a while but she didn't say anything, her fork stirring her rice in slow, irregular circles.

'Shall we go to the sofa?' she asked, once he'd finished. Something in her voice told him she was no longer nervous. Maybe she'd prised what she wanted from him already.

Though they sat with barely a foot gap between them, he got the impression she bottled further sexual invitations. She eventually pulled her bare legs up next to her, a large glass of wine cradled in her lap, and eyed him drowsily.

'You love your son very much.'

'Of course. I'm programmed that way.'

'Well, you say that, but I know of men – well, I use the term "men" – who felt nothing, soon as they saw their children, but the urge to run away.'

Patrick watched the chip of cork floating in his wine for a time. 'I do love him, but… In a way, that doesn't come close to describing it. I would literally put my life on the line if it meant protecting him from anything so much as a scratch. And yet, when the three of us were living together, there were times when I found his presence unbearable.' He fished the offending object from his drink. 'I mean, it's hard, isn't it? It's exhausting. And I, quite unreasonably, somehow blamed him for my life being ushered along a different path. Maybe the breakdown of our relationship put a strain on my love for my son. Or maybe the strain of my love for my son broke our marriage. I don't know. All I know is that I miss him so much… I never thought I would feel such a, a rift. My father – and this will sound awful – I miss far less, even though he was in my life much longer. I think it's the ownership thing. You invest in the things you create. But he'll fall from me, as I fell from my father. I wonder, too, about his age… My first memories stem from the days when I was the age he is now. Will he even remember living in England? Will his first memory be of his father leaving him? Because that's what it will seem like. I hope, one day, he'll realise that it wasn't my choice, that it was she who took him from me…'

It was with eyes itching with tears that he turned to see Sarah slackjawed and snoring beside him.

He finished off the wine, then helped himself to hers. There was a third left in the bottle and he had that too. He would make his way home soon, despite the snow and the violence outside. She'd probably be hurt in the morning, but he felt unashamedly wounded that she'd fallen asleep during that speech.

The journey back would be cold and slow-going but it didn't matter. Highfields would be closed again tomorrow, due to the risks involved with pupils travelling. It was depressing how happy this notion made him.

He lay back and closed his eyes, just for a moment.

He woke under a blanket in pretty much the same position. His left arm had gone to sleep, hanging off the sofa, and Sarah was gone.

Then he heard the voices.

Even if his senses hadn't been heightened by the bloodshed he'd witnessed earlier, he would still have discerned the murmuring from one of the bedrooms. He assumed it was Jenna, home again and on her phone, but then an urgent but quiet male voice could be heard in reply. He lay in the dark and strained to hear more.

The murmurs from the neighbouring room carried on for two minutes before Patrick eventually let his curiosity steal him into the hallway, where a thin strip of yellow glowed under a door.

The voices stopped again.

In a brief moment of awareness, he saw what he must have looked like, lurking in the dark outside what was, in all probability, the bedroom of one of his female students. But curiosity got the better of him, and, soundlessly, he crouched forward and placed his eye to the girl's keyhole.

She was on her knees, still wearing her mother's coat. There was no sign of anyone else in the room. Patrick watched as she wriggled herself back out from under the bed, empty-handed, and slunk towards the door.

He snatched his eye away and bolted to one side and, as Jenna's bulb was extinguished and his bearings became misplaced, he kicked open another door by accident, slamming it back against something solid.

A bedside light snapped on and Sarah shot up in bed.

'What the…?'

He stood in her doorway, fumbling for an excuse. 'I couldn't sleep. I was looking for the bathroom.'

She eyed him in sleepy terror.

'I wasn't spying on anyone. I was in the living room, watching the foxes from the window. Then I went looking for the toilet. That's all I was doing.'

'Patrick, why are you whispering? It's just us.' He caught the icy tone of distrust in her voice.

'Right. Sorry.'

'Don't let them kids get to you.' She tossed a rattling box towards him across the bed. 'Sleeping pills. They might help.'

Patrick inspected the packet of sedatives and saw they promised to stimulate more of a coma than sleep. Sarah blearily indicated the near side of the bed, patted it down to indicate he could join her, and he sat in heavy silence.

'They don't seem to have helped you,' he said.

'A rock star kicked my bedroom door down.'

After that, there was nothing else to do but kiss. It took several minutes this time before she pulled away and he recognised the same crestfallen, guilty look that he'd received at the hotel. He lay back on the pillow and stared at the ceiling and when he heard a soft snuffling from her side of the bed dismissed it as a ghosted echo of the last weeks of his marriage. It was too soon for tears.

But when she moved in closer to him, he found a face wet with them.

'Bollocks,' she hissed, softly. 'This is the last thing you want, isn't it?'

'What's the matter?'

110

She dragged herself up a little in the bed, smeared a hand across her face. 'I'm sorry. This is part of it, I'm afraid.'

He sat up too. 'Part of…?'

'Mike couldn't take it in the end. Few couples, statistically, survive the death of…'

She didn't finish, but Patrick worked it out, and as he did so knew the stiffening of his torso gave his astonishment away. She'd spoken as though he had foreknowledge of her bereavement. Maybe she assumed, as Jenna's teacher, he was already privy to this information.

After a few minutes, Sarah wormed free of his shoulder, snatched a handful of tissues from a box by the bed, and blew her nose. 'I need to know you're for real,' she said. 'I need to know… you're with me because you want to be. Am I making any sense?'

'I'm for real.' He tried to sound as reassuring as possible, despite the inner voice gnawing at him. *Was* he for real? What did that even mean? A nerve in his eye was twitching.

'I'm trying to deal with it but… My psychiatrist suggested I write down how I feel, so I don't bottle it all up.' Patrick recalled the pages of notes scattered across the table in the front room. 'I don't think it's working, do you?'

'What was her name?' he asked.

Sarah looked at him, her eyes vivid. She either laughed or sobbed as her hands wrung at the duvet, and she forced herself to take deep breaths which stuttered on their journey from her lungs. 'Millie.'

'Is that her photo on the lounge mantelpiece?'

She nodded.

The archaeology of her unhappiness revealed, Patrick scrabbled over clichéd words of apology. So inadequate were his attempts, she asked him to stop and the pair sat there for a long time, staring blindly into the converging vanishing points of the past and present. After the evening's rampage, it seemed unnaturally quiet outside. He could have punched himself in the head, there and then, for going on and on about Danny all evening.

'Your turn,' she said.

'My what?'

Sarah's grin appeared theatrical in its intensity as she pressed his shoulder. 'We've told each other so little about ourselves. You must have had your heart broken at some point. Everybody has.'

He sank down into the bed. Not only did a swapping of bereavements strike him as crude but his past had never felt so redundant. 'Seriously. I don't... Nothing worth telling.' He attempted a placatory smile. A humidifier hummed through a circle of corrugated plastic on the wall.

Sarah turned and snapped off the bedside lamp. 'Fair enough,' she said, bedding herself back into the sheets with her back to him.

Patrick, horribly aware of Sarah's wakefulness, could only chase the same questions around his head. Who was in Jenna's room earlier and where had he suddenly disappeared to? What had she been hiding under her bed? Why was she hanging out with Denis, the boy who'd molested her?

Since Sarah was no longer on speaking terms with her ex-husband, Jenna could claim to be waltzing off to her father's whenever the need arose. It was the perfect scenario if she felt the need to hang out with questionable friends.

Or gang members.

Patrick turned and, without thinking, draped his arm over Sarah's hip. Perhaps just as involuntarily, she reached down and threaded her fingers through his.

'Compared to your life story, mine's nowhere near as... dramatic.' The wrong word.

'Go on.'

She was clearly as intrigued, as intimidated, by his past life as he was by hers, yet he had but a small reservoir of hurt, compared to Sarah, from which to draw his confessional. His wife's suitcase in the hallway. Cold hands unfurling, dissolving his aloof father into death alongside his cancer. His little boy, waving obliviously from the back of a taxi bound for Heathrow. Only his most painful experiences would make the grade here, and he silently thanked her for the opportunity to exorcise a demon.

'The band had been my identity for a long time,' he said, pressed against her. Pale streetlight smudged the room. It was an unhealthy, yellow hue. 'My *entire* identity… When it broke up… I didn't take it well. But I still had Ana. Then she and I, in the time-honoured way, drifted apart… Or maybe I pushed her away…'

'I remember something about…'

'Ana had been Adam's girlfriend. Adam was our singer. I stole her off him, in short.'

'You cad.' Sarah was only trying to gee him on but had managed to decorate the story as a humorous one before he'd even begun.

'I broke up the band for the love of a woman. I continued to gig for a while, solo stuff, wrote a few songs for other people, then, when Ana and I got married and started talking about the possibility of a family, I started teaching, for security really, always thinking I could session here and there. When Ana left me, it felt like losing the band all over again. What had that sacrifice been for? I resented her for that, for doing to me what she'd once done to Adam.'

'He was so good-looking…' Sarah cooed in the dark. 'As were you,' she quickly added. 'As *are* you.'

'Everyone fancied Adam, which is why certain magazines were so shocked when she left him for me. The Forsaken may or may not have gone supersonic anyway, who knows? And I still have my memories of that period in my life…' But Patrick seldom bothered to remember the happier times. His pride in his achievements was usurped by the poisoning knowledge that his band mates – men who should, at the very least, have been drinking partners for life – blamed him for the smoking ruins of their music careers.

'All my ambition had been for nothing. To keep myself from the pain of it all, I embraced the change of direction; giving up music completely seemed strangely appealing, though I now consider that to have been nothing more than a form of sulking. Lately... I don't know. Failure doesn't feel good. I arrive home totally knackered. I can't write songs any more, or I've got no time to. I see these young, hip indie guys making music for a living and... it burns me. '

'I don't think you've failed.' The bedside light scalded his eyes and Sarah crossed to a silver, balloon-shaped CD player in the corner of the bedroom. 'I thought I'd failed as a mother but... Look, sometimes you think you're on the wrong track, but all regret does is speed you past stations you've never heard of.' This sounded like her psychotherapy talking. 'Sadly, you can't always get off and board another train.' She held up a CD case. An album cover showed four men, fresh-faced and long-haired. Two members of this quartet, including a face that barely resembled Patrick Owen's any longer, looked moodily to the left while the other two stared at the camera. They all wore black and the photo, as befitting the contemplative poses, was shot in monochrome. Behind them, the hopeful, arrogant vista of London, full of promise.

She wasn't embarrassed to admit she'd been listening to his work. She wanted him to see the album, just as she'd obviously wanted him to spot her therapy notes earlier. She wanted him to see her as she was, and he felt his heart dance a little closer towards something that could, perhaps, one day, be love.

He recalled the reviews of this, their first album. 'One of the better bands from the current crop,' a reporter in the know had begun. 'Undoubted talent,' heralded another. 'Cuts a swathe into the zeitgeist.' But no one bought their second album of doubtful, murky compositions, avant-garde melodies forged in the inferno of his and Ana's adultery.

'Please don't put it on,' he said.

She smiled. 'What would you say if they wanted to give it another go?'

Ana's betrayals fermenting anew within his mind, Patrick's reply was instant. 'I'd tell her to get lost.'

'I meant the band.'

'Oh.' Patrick slumped into the recess Sarah left in her pillow. He contemplated the brutal monotony of his teaching career, squaring it alongside the day The Forsaken played Glastonbury and Iggy Pop asked him for a cigarette backstage. 'I think I'd rejoin, yeah.'

Sarah smiled and slipped back into bed, then curled herself up, somewhat defensively.

'Night, Patrick.'

At that moment, he knew he'd wait until Sarah's snoring insulted his insomnia before scribbling out his note of apology and leaving it on her bedside. He knew the night busses wouldn't be running and a long, freezing trudge back home under a pale, cartridge paper sky awaited him. But, right then, despite his growing feelings for this woman, and the deepening mysteries surrounding her daughter, he wanted nothing more than to sleep fitfully in his son's unmade bed with the neighbour's violin playing a hymnal and the certainty of snow shutting Highfields.

He'd stick to the shadows on the way home, and pray Denis was sleeping too.

FIVE

There was a doll on his desk, a plastic newborn with flapping eyelids and a mouth puckered into the inverse of a feeding bottle's teat. Like some kind of perverse voodoo offering, a cigarette had been burnt into the crotch, its stub a crude, protruding sexual organ. Across the chest, the word PEEDO had been scrawled in lipstick.

He regarded it for a while, wondering whether or not to get PC Thomas in again, but eventually decided it wasn't obvious whether it was an insult directed at him or a sixth former's work of art. In any case, teachers have always had to endure pupils giving them insulting nicknames, but Patrick was aware that, in the twenty-first century, nothing hits harder than insinuations of paedophilia. He was hopeful this sinister rumour – if that's what it was – would fade into history alongside the gossip concerning Mr Jackson's toupee (true), Mrs Edgar's 'love of blacks' (a misinterpretation of a some-time proclivity) and Mr Malcolm's wooden penis (baseless falsehood), but he knew children had little sense of quietude; information was no good battened down. Like money, gossip was designed to be spent and, as all good capitalists in a recession are urged to do, he knew children spent recklessly given the chance. The notion that he was 'seeing' the mother of a pupil had perhaps snowballed into a grotesquery, maybe after Jenna herself had admitted it to one of her scandalised friends.

Patrick had long prided himself on keeping his private

life and work separate and, having no desire to see that change, didn't mention the doll to anyone. If these were yet more off-stage boos, an unquiet critiquing of his skills from the stalls, then so what? Reporting it would have meant hours of form-filling and emails.

He threw the doll in the bin then, from the window, sought answers in the ambling figures of children entering the playground and surmised the identity of several gang members. Karl Simpson sported a limp, a deep scratch on his cheek and an amateur repair to cut knuckles. Quincy Ofulu was contused, battered and beaming with adrenaline. Halil Mostafa walked with his head high, showing off the bruising to his neck which hung like a necklace of hickies. No one with an injury seemed to speak to anyone else with an injury, and they moved as scarred islands among the innocent flock. The watery snow had been scraped off the playground but a few kids had gathered ammunition from goodness knows where, and a tamer version of Monday night's brawl was taking place by the fence. Denis was playing basketball, seemingly unscathed, spinning the ball up into a basket with its netting torn. He had even developed an extra bob to his already boastful swagger and somehow there was a new purpose to him, a sense of the untouchable as he laughed and bickered with another pupil, revealing a camaraderie and playfulness Patrick seldom saw in his classroom.

The boy's vengeance was to be a slow one, was it? What would come next? Razor blades hidden inside his pigeon hole? A nail up through his chair? The thought of his parents' evening appointment later on was a dark twist in Patrick's heart.

Never far from Denis' side, a brunette in a skirt far too short for the season exposed an approximation of her mother's legs, clung and whinnied over his very presence.

Was this evidence of a personality trait Patrick needed to let Sarah know about? Might the loss of a father figure have forced Jenna to pine over boys who mistreated her? Did

Denis actually *like* Jenna, or was he, for reasons unknown, merely convincing her he did?

When the bell sounded, Denis stood, ran his hand through Jenna's hair and ambled away from the school building. Jenna looked without expression in the boy's wake before turning and glancing up at Patrick's window.

He wouldn't report the doll. In seeing Jenna's mother, he was already kicking the hornet's nest. He probably didn't need to stick his dick in there as well.

She appeared at his door later that day, refusing to look him in the eye. He couldn't blame her, and tried to imagine how he'd have felt if he'd believed his mother had been carrying on with one of his secondary school teachers. He'd probably have killed himself.

She wasn't the only one who had trouble looking at him either. Matthew was back, an external fixator on his arm, pins bolted deep into iodine-stained flesh.

'Good to have you back,' Patrick said. 'How's the arm?'

'It's better,' was the sheepish reply. No doubt the pride with which he'd been previously showing off his injury was acutely tempered whenever he faced someone who was actually there, who'd heard his screams. The boy was on a cocktail of anti-coagulants and painkillers; his eyes were two full stops in his face and his hair was an electric shock of toilet-brush. It seemed Matthew had sustained far more damage than simply popping his shoulder out of its socket. He'd snapped his radius just below the elbow.

'Surely you're not fit to be back yet?'

'Ride or die, sir.' Matthew was a different specimen to Denis. His rage might have been natural but his over-confidence wasn't. This was the kind of boy who laughed over teachers' altered entries on Wikipedia using his mobile phone then allowed that exact same phone to be confiscated.

Matthew had recently been added to the unofficial SEN register, due to 'behavioural issues', but that seemed to

Patrick no more than a cover for his real problem: he no longer gave a shit. Academically, Matthew Keane had lapsed into one of those marginal students, a D grader, borderline C, who could potentially scupper an entire year's exam results. Come GCSE time, it was kids like Matthew who received more attention than they deserved, like swing states in American elections. Without help, Matthew, and others akin to him, would be listlessly plodding from room to room, truanting the odd class and generally underachieving to their hearts' content.

'So how *exactly* did you do that then?' Patrick asked, as flippantly as he felt he could get away with.

Matthew shrugged, followed it with a vague wince of remembrance. 'Careless, wasn't I?' He began to walk to his seat, as fast as his analgesics permitted.

'No. Really. How did it happen?'

Matthew, realising escape was impossible, stopped and turned. 'I told this story, like, five hundred fucking times already. I might've got a knock. There were too many people pushing.'

'You sure?'

The boy looked at his teacher as though he were the biggest dunce in the school. He held up his forearm and the metal sparkled. 'Yes sir. I *think* so.'

He took his seat.

Patrick outlined the day's task. Each student was to create a half-decent replica of their own head from clay and he took the class through the basics, then patrolled the room, waiting for the carnage. Denis hadn't entered the room with the rest of them, and he kept looking towards the door, waiting for the latecomer to gatecrash with an explosive act of violence. His tile-armoured body warmer was giving him terrible neck ache.

It was Jenna who fashioned the first grenade, tamely lobbing it over to Marie, a pretty, gothic-looking girl whose dark hair was betrayed by ginger eyebrows. She caught the clay easily and asked Jenna something Patrick couldn't quite discern, though he heard Denis' name mentioned. Jenna dismissed the enquiry in a guilty, complicit manner, betraying the fact she had information to hide. Indeed, her friend sang back a childish 'Oooh' at which Jenna visibly blushed.

Were Jenna and Denis, unthinkably, friends? More than friends? He'd seen her in the group just before the brawl but didn't really believe she would be so stupid as to become mixed up romantically with the boy. And yet, here she was, coyly skirting the issue with a teenage lack of dexterity at odds with her appearance (it was impossible to ignore the similarities between her and her mother: the same small, precise features; the eyes a comparable multiplicity of colours; the same slightly nervous mannerisms hidden by the brash voice of the metropolis). Jenna even managed to draw in an angry, juvenile way these days, which didn't do her already scratchy and disjointed style any favours whatsoever. She chewed gum, masticating exaggeratedly, and when he told her to spit it out she plucked it from her mouth and contemptuously fastened it beneath her table. Almost overnight, he'd created a delinquent.

Miraculously, the carnage of clay never interfered with the lesson's usual undercurrent of disruptive childishness, and it wasn't until the hour's end that Denis appeared.

Patrick sensed him, even before he knew he was there. His presence was heralded by a poltergeist-flicker of lights, which seemed to suddenly deposit the boy in the blink of an eye at his classroom door. Matthew was certainly spooked out, and didn't leave his stool with the others, visibly shrinking from his former friend. But Denis, hands in his pockets, eyes unseeing, seemed to be waiting only for Jenna.

'Tonight,' Denis growled at her, and then was gone.

Patrick saw Christophe glance over, then unsubtly swivel his eyes towards an uneven stack of papers on his desk before rechecking the spelling of DuPont on his name card with dark and knitted brows.

The Arts and Humanities subjects, a loose umbrella title which also incorporated Modern Foreign Languages and PE (the dads would be all over Miss Bates, Patrick knew, who wore a pair of yoga trousers which left no mystery whatsoever as to her figure's exact geometry), were gathered in the hall, while Science, Maths and English – the important, 'Core' subjects – hid in the gym. Charlotte sat filing her nails to Patrick's left, a bored Harriet to his right.

Patrick normally objected to this way of meeting the parents, and knew of nearby schools where teachers remained in their teaching rooms while the pupils' progenitors toured the lost corridors, but was grateful that, tonight, a degree of impersonal protection was assumed as a result of the all-in-one arrangement.

At first everyone had been able to hear Mr Pfister refer to Cindy Granger as 'keen and disciplined' and stress how, if he'd been her father, he would have sent her to an entirely different school but, as more parents began streaming in, the hall bloomed with noise and only the conversations from the immediate other side of the desks could be heard. Patrick sat alone for some time. 6:15 stood out on his appointment sheet as though inked in blood, but he didn't unduly concern himself with the fact. Neither Denis nor his mother had been particularly frequent attendees of parents' evenings over the last four years.

Patrick rang Ana's mother.

'*¿Quién llama?*'

'Can I speak to Ana? I tried Skype yesterday. Is everything okay? Did they make it back alright?'

'I tell you she no here.'

'They flew back days ago.'

'No here. She and Danny in England.'

'You're mistaken.'

'No, you mistaken. Ring hotel.'

'Listen, there is no way my son would be in London without me knowing. They were due to catch a flight Monday. Just ask her to call me, will you?'

Derek Pertwee's mother bowled over and Patrick hung up.

Just as the teaching of drawing is all about *re*drawing, modifying and refining mistakes, so Patrick knew he also had to mould his parents' evening performance around the personalities and expectations of his carousel of visitors, some of whom would be supportive, others hostile. At one point, when faced with a huge bouncer of a parent he suspected would pounce upon any criticism of his lackadaisical daughter with very real violence, he even affected a South London accent. The truth of the matter was that parents' evenings at Highfields were just as frightening as being in the classroom.

Sarah and Jenna breezed into the hall.

The pupils were required to wear uniform at these events and it was interesting to note that Jenna had rolled her skirt back down at the back to repair its length. In contrast, Sarah had dressed as though attending a gala premiere, dressed in a tiny black number which courted considerable attention. She waved at Patrick across the hall and he waved back, then looked around to see who'd noticed. Nobody except Christophe had.

Jenna hadn't made an appointment of course, and to have done so would have been suicidal, but that didn't stop Sarah from tottering over while her daughter spoke to Mary in 11C.

She stood in front of him, hand on hip, chest thrust forward. 'I got your Dear John,' she said before bending forward at the waist and putting her mouth to his ear. 'Just imagine,' she breathed. 'Me. You. This desk. All these people watching.' And then she was gone.

Charlotte's face remained blank, and he had to respect that. Harriet began a coughing fit. It wouldn't be long before she took another week off.

Parents and pupils came and went as Patrick's eyes calloused themselves harder with tiredness. He could tell more-or-less off the bat how the encounters were going to go. Praise worked best of course, even if it wasn't deserved, and generally sent both parent and pupil off happily nonplussed. Occasionally, the room erupted with laughter and everyone looked with suspicion, more often than not, towards the dads at Miss Bates' table.

At about six, it seemed to get darker, the oxygen retreated and something approaching quiet fell over the hall like a fire blanket. Denis Roberts and his mother had arrived.

Patrick watched them amble near Mr Stewart and hunker on the chairs aligned around the perimeter of the hall. Mrs Roberts was a large woman, especially weighty around the neck, wrists and ankles, as though out of some hideous deference to gravity, and her complexion was as rugged and blotched as someone who'd spent years working on a farm while eating nothing but chips. Despite all this, there was a trace of something once-beautiful in the shape of the face and the sideways olivedrops of her eyes, but anger and Western sedentism had set in and ruined her.

Mr Stewart was finishing his conversation with Amy Stoppard's mum and smiled over at the Roberts duo to let them know they were next. Mrs Roberts looked back at him with a cold, unmoved gaze then heaved herself from her chair.

While Denis moved very little, his mother occasionally looked towards her boy but it was hard to tell their emotions, not least because Miriam Dylan's father sat before Patrick trying to ascertain, in irate fashion, exactly why his daughter had earned an E and not an A* on her latest report.

Patrick clichéd his way through the rest of the meeting with Miriam's father and the moment he left, muttering something about modern professionalism, Denis and his mother edged forward to take their places. Instinctively,

Patrick's eyes flicked round the hall for nearby fire exits. Sarah and Jenna still worked their way round the room.

'Hello, Denis,' Patrick offered, his voice a convincing falsetto for the first time in his life.

'Alright,' the boy replied, slumping almost horizontally in a chair opposite.

Denis looked defeated already and Patrick wondered what monstrous bribe had been dangled to drag Denis here. His mother's face was fierce with the expectation of criticism. She neither offered recognition nor her hand.

Patrick turned matters over, straight away, to Denis. 'So, Denis. Tell me. How do you think it's going?'

Denis looked up. There was more than a trace of confusion in the shaved eyebrows.

'Alright,' he shrugged again.

Patrick attempted to turn on the charm, looked to the mother and half-rolled his eyes. 'They all say that,' he demurred. 'I would say that Denis is a very capable student. Very talented.'

'Is he applying himself?' she asked, clearly suspecting the answer.

'No.'

There was a silence amid the din of the hall. Mother and son both sighed in dismal acceptance and Patrick wondered, if this was what they'd been expecting, why they'd bothered turning up.

'What does he need to do?' she enquired.

'He needs to produce a year and a half's worth of artwork in the next four months.'

She turned to face her son. 'Am I going to get this from everybody tonight?'

'Probably,' Denis replied.

'What do you expect to be? You need to get some qualifications, Denis. You want to end up like your father?'

Denis flashed a look that said she'd crossed a line. 'Shut up,' he spat.

Mrs Roberts looked at Patrick as though she'd been slapped. 'Is this how he speaks to you, Mr Owers?' she asked.

Denis looked at the teacher, his eyes dulled by disrespect and boredom.

'No. He's very polite actually. Never had any problems like that, have we Denis?'

The boy turned away, fixed his eyes on Jenna. 'No, sir.'

A brief moment of pride, or defeat, recomposed his mother's face before she pulled her chair in slightly closer. By degrees she might have been warming to Patrick.

'So, why doesn't he work? What's stopping him?'

'Shall we ask him?' Patrick turned to Denis.

'You think you can make something of yourself without school, is that right?' his mum accused.

'What's the point?' he asked. 'What's the point of working hard for a shitty job selling burgers? Or so I can sit in front of a computer all day? Or what? Become a *teacher*?'

His mother indicated Patrick. 'Mr Owers has got a decent job. He worked hard for this.'

Denis laughed, his point made.

Mrs Roberts inspected her chubby hands. 'I don't know what to do, Denis, I really don't. You don't help yourself.'

Had Patrick been expecting Denis' mother to be a demonic version of her son, a genetic blueprint for his latent wrath? Or a simpering, weak-willed subservient, unable to control her raging child? She was neither. She was exasperated and powerless, jilted by her own son. A normal parent. When he'd first caught a glimpse of her fierce face opposite, he'd almost, unimaginably, expected to come away feeling sorry for Denis, but she was no more overbearing than any parent of a child like Denis might be. She wasn't the explanation for his character. It wasn't her fault.

'So,' he asked, 'Mr Roberts couldn't make it this evening, I guess?' He sensed he was in dodgy territory.

'Not tonight, or any other night,' she said. 'And in a way I'm glad.'

Denis rounded on her. 'What are you…?'

'If he could see you… He'd be turning in his grave if he was still alive…'

Denis stood. 'Bitch.'

They both watched him walk purposefully towards the hall doors. His mother's lip wobbled.

'Take a moment,' Patrick suggested. 'I'm sorry. I had no idea. I shouldn't have…'

'No, no. It's fine. You didn't know.' She dabbed at her eyes, disregarding the looks of nearby parents. 'Denis and his father… It was complicated.'

Perhaps Denis might have turned out differently had the events of his thirteenth birthday not occurred. Maybe they made no difference in the long run. Maybe they changed him completely. Patrick could never know. He'd known him before and he'd known him afterwards, and he appeared, on the surface, to be the same.

Denis' father had died when Denis was five years old and Denis had always been led to believe that a traffic accident had taken him. For some reason, his mother decided that he would be told the truth when he turned thirteen and so the whole sorry lie came out. He was deemed old enough to know the facts; his father had been murdered. Happy birthday.

His father had been part of a crew in the estate, had sold drugs, handguns, anything. He'd hung out with known fascists and violent criminals. Nice people. On the afternoon of his death he'd been due in court over the armed robbery of a corner shop, but instead had decided to go for a drink at a pub only four streets from the courthouse. There, he become involved in an altercation with a couple of men over some cocaine he'd sold them some time ago, which resulted in Roberts Senior throwing off his coat and challenging both men to a fight outside. They duly obliged and, one single punch later, Denis' dad was dead of a brain aneurysm.

'His dad was a hero to him,' his mother snuffled, a queue of parents now building up behind her. 'I mean, I guess a kid eventually forgets the beatings and the drunkenness... But once Denis found out how he died, he lost that respect. He told me. I mean, it was something he talked about only once, but I got the sense that it hurt him. Like, right after his thirteenth birthday, he had a growth spurt, became bigger, taller, and closed himself up. But, one day, he came home looking like he'd been crying – of course he would never have admitted this – and I noticed he had a bruise on his face – fresh-looking, y'know – and I asked him about it. He told me he'd been jumped in the playground by a boy, that it was a long-standing argument between the two. He told me that this particular boy had learned about his dad in some old newspaper cuttings and was giving him grief about it. I think most of his fights are about his dad. We talked a bit about it. The way he looked at me and said, 'One punch...?' told me the way his dad died hurt Denis more than him not being around did.'

Patrick nodded. He could imagine that the conflict between defending his father's honour and the shame caused by others knowing the truth about his murder would tear at the boy. He was struck by memories of his own father's death, his conflicted feelings regarding his demise, and it occurred to Patrick that he had something in common with Denis after all.

'Of course, thirteen-year-olds don't like their parents anyway,' she continued, 'but this didn't add, you know, gold or whatever to the myth of his dad and I wouldn't be surprised to learn that he hates me too, after my attempt to tell him some truths about his old man backfired. But he's a good boy, deep down. He wouldn't do you no harm.' She looked at her appointment sheet. The entire queue behind her had given up and moved on. 'I'm late for Maths.'

She stood, and left.

Patrick waited a while, looked around him, then stood and took his coat from the back of his chair. He was done.

And Christophe, still watching him between the heads of pupils and parents, revealed nothing but disappointment in those tired Gaelic greys.

Patrick was on his way to the bus stop when he saw him.

The bus sailed past and the shelter display mocked him by announcing an eleven-minute wait for the next. He was following Denis before he knew what he was doing.

Denis was ambling at a narcotically lobotomised pace, with little or no sense of time's scarcity, his expression set in its usual irate mask. He stopped at a privately owned garage a couple of streets south before turning back on himself. Patrick froze, unsure whether to dive for cover.

But Denis was too busy checking out the garage forecourt to have seen him. The boy stopped again, took another walk past, then loped calmly into what looked like an unoccupied service area to the left. He was gone about ten seconds before reappearing with his jacket bulkier than before. The robbery had been unambitious and obvious but no one except Patrick seemed to have observed it.

The boy doubled back, head down, faster.

Patrick quarried him from the other side of the street, past torched bins set like improbable jellies on the kerbside, boarded shop windows. From the doorway of an arcade the tinny squeal of simulation racing games and one-armed bandits hollered for attention over the sugary aroma of junk food. A snooker hall sign, shiny reds and greens now faded to pink and lime.

Denis stuck to the main road before ducking up an alleyway into the estate.

Patrick peered after him into a corridor of sweet wrappers. There was no sign of the boy.

He took short, hesitant steps across jagged droplets of glass. At the end of the passageway, several walkways bloomed above his head and a concrete maze of straight lines – the tangible outcome of a nineteen-fifties' vision of the future, now exposed as impossibly ill-conceived and dystopian – presented him with four potential directions. Finally coming to his senses, he began walking back the way he'd come.

Swung into the wall, a guttural thud was torn from his lungs.

'You following me?' the boy demanded, his voice storm-raged, demonic. There was madness in Denis' eyes. The smell of gasoline was strong.

The teacher tried for indignity and affront but couldn't muster either properly and instead squealed, 'I was on my way home.'

Denis had a forearm across Patrick's chest. 'I saw you following.'

Something sloshed under the boy's jacket as his right arm was removed and flashed a thin slice of gunmetal sky.

Denis teased the blade across Patrick's neck. It was cold, watery, the itch of a needle before the injection. The wall behind Patrick was unyielding and damp.

Whatever passed for a grin on Denis' face didn't convince Patrick there was anything rational sparking in the muddied neurotransmitters inside the boy's head. His cleft lip scar was livid and scarlet. His teeth were bared. 'I want you to beg,' Denis hissed.

'What?'

'Say "Please don't stab me".'

Patrick had one, proud thought: so far, he'd failed to soil himself. 'Please don't stab me.'

'Say it like you mean it, pussy.'

'I *do* mean it, Denis.'

'Say it in a girl's voice.'

Patrick remained silent. A very small part of him was still this boy's teacher. He would have to look at him the following day through chalk dust spinning in beams of morning sunlight. Denis' mother was still at Highfields, suffering the parents' evening from which they'd both recently escaped. 'This is…'

Denis edged the knife a little further into Patrick's neck. As the weapon pricked skin and he felt the warm liquid run, he saw a kind of stalemate had been reached. Something had flickered briefly in Denis' chasming pupils. Something like fear.

Patrick turned to follow Denis' eyes, saw a shadow behind them at the end of the alley.

'Swear down. I got plans for you,' Denis sneered. 'I'm keeping you a little longer.'

He stashed the knife back in a pocket and, as Denis released him, Patrick caught another potent whiff of petrol.

'We ain't even yet, sir,' the boy called before he rounded the corner and, wasted, wild-eyed, was gone.

Patrick shrank, gasping, to the ground. The shadow reached him.

'You okay?' a bearded man in his late fifties asked. He smelt awful, his hair matted into natural, grey dreadlocks.

'You just saved my life.'

'Did you get a good look at him?' It was asked without excitement or disbelief, just a dull disaffection that suggested the homeless bum saw such violence on a daily basis. Patrick wondered why he didn't take his cardboard boxes and sleeping bag five miles down the road. Surely he was freer than some of Union City's residents.

'Never seen him before,' Patrick shrugged, touching his fingertips to his stinging neck and bringing them away sodden with blood.

SIX

He was led to a seat at the kitchen table, where the wound was tended with biting antiseptic. The blood was slow to cease and Sarah replaced the first bandage almost immediately, the used dressing sporting a dark red smear at its centre.

Patrick tried to keep his voice temperate. 'I slipped on the way out the school gate.' He knew he wasn't pulling off a capable performance and to avert discovery of his trembling hands he palmed them together and thrust them between his thighs. 'A patch of ice,' he added.

'And there wasn't anyone at the school who could have helped?'

'The school nurse leaves at four. As I say, I was in the area.'

She wasn't convinced, pushed a mug containing a bobbing teabag towards him. He reached for it with tremulous, dirty hands, his fingernails containing half-moons of Art teacher grime. Sarah's hands closed around his.

'What's the matter?'

He stilled himself with short, shallow breaths. His back was a mess of knots and pain tore up his spine. This superlative stress and exhaustion, last experienced in the nuclear fallout of his marriage, had returned for another bout. He'd never been threatened with a knife before. The look in Denis' eyes had been supernatural, psychopathic.

Jenna swanned past the kitchen wearing more make-up than Ronald McDonald.

'Hold on, young lady,' Sarah shouted, but her daughter's feet were already a drum roll on the steps outside. Sarah flung an apology Patrick's way then hurried out after Jenna.

Realising his opportunity, Patrick darted to Jenna's bedroom.

It was messy, cold and smelt of cheap perfume. The mirror on her dresser featured blu-tacked photos of familiar classmates: Marie Rallings from 11B; Rochelle McNamara from 11F. The room contained a TV and DVD player, some maths books and – in a touching display of childhood fighting valiantly against adolescence – a small collection of teddies. An unknown rapper was crucified to her wall, topless and bejewelled with thick, gold chains and sovereign-encrusted digits.

He lifted the mattress to find a plethora of magazines and clothes in bin liners. The smell was musky, damp.

Upon spotting the shoebox, he slid the bedframe from the wall and, flipping the lid, found nothing but papers and notebooks, a black, spiral bound diary.

He flicked through it, disappointed that was all she'd been hiding. The majority of it was unreadable, like her sketchbook annotations over the last eighteen months. Patrick wondered if there was much about him in the journal, the way he'd muscled in on her mother and moved from her classroom to her home in no time at all.

The papers the diary had been sitting on weren't lying completely true and Patrick lifted them as the sound of feet echoed from the steps outside.

The moment he saw what lurked underneath he dropped the bed and slammed it back against the wall. On his flight from the room he noticed the window was open about two centimetres, an unaccountably risky lapse considering what he'd just seen beneath her bed. He was back in the kitchen just as Sarah and Jenna emerged from outside.

'Did you forget our curfew, young lady?' he heard Sarah yell. 'And *where* did you think you were off to dressed like that? Haven't you got homework to do?'

'Yeah. Your *boyfriend's*.' The teenager crashed herself into the house. Anger, like ambition, was a quick-fire, youthful emotion, Patrick reflected. Injustice required longer and longer run ups as he zeroed in on middle age. He couldn't remember the last time he'd slammed a door.

'I told you. Nothing's going on.'

'Oh, right. So you just fucked him. That's disgusting.'

'Actually we haven't even…'

'Why not? He got a small dick or something?'

'You do know I'm standing here, right?' Patrick interjected.

There was a moment's silence, then mother and daughter went out into the living room and whispered in urgent, angry voices. He finished his tea as Sarah re-entered.

'Everything okay?' he asked.

'It's a bit delicate. I'm very attracted to you, Patrick, but my daughter comes first. It's an important year and I don't want her distracted.' It was a rebuttal that informed Patrick she still protected Jenna, that he was, naturally, in second place.

'What are you saying?'

'I'm saying I like you…'

'*But*?'

'…I just think we need to tone things down a bit.'

'Tone things *down*?'

The hands snaked back. 'Look… I *do* like you. It feels right. It's just that I don't know that Jenna seeing us together is such a good idea. I told her…' She tailed off.

'That there was nothing going on? That you dumped me? That I was a mistake? What?'

'More or less all the above.' Her index finger hooked his left thumb. 'The bottom line is: if – *if* – we decide we do want to see each other again, and she finds out about us, it's over.'

'And do you want to see me again?'

She waited until he was looking at her. 'Yes. Do you?'

'Yes.' The word surprised him. But he'd meant it.

'In which case, you should go.'

Patrick walked silently to the front door as appalling music blasted from Jenna's bedroom. On the welcome mat, he turned.

'You remember that business with Jenna and Denis,' he mumbled. 'Has she mentioned it since?'

'No. Why?'

Patrick and Sarah had never mentioned 'that business' either. She clearly assumed the matter was over with, that he'd dealt with it through the proper channels. 'It's just that… I've seen them hanging around a bit.' Sarah's mouth fell open. 'I mean, it might not be anything to get worried about. It may just be something that blows over…'

'I… I can't believe she's hanging out with someone like… like *him*. After he…' She collected herself. 'I'll have a word with the little madam right away.'

'Please don't. Not yet,' he whispered. 'It must be weird enough that a teacher's in her home. I don't want her thinking I'm sticking my beak in any further than I should be. I'm just letting you know. I really wouldn't mention it. Please.'

She wasn't happy, but had to concede his point was valid. He shouldn't be abusing his position.

'She's all I have left,' she said, defeat in her throat. 'Keep an eye on her for me, Patrick.'

He already had been. But how could he tell Sarah about the goods under Jenna's bed without admitting he'd been rummaging?

'Sarah. I don't know how to say this…'

He watched her brace herself. The hardening of the nostrils, the sudden deadness behind the eyes, publicised her expectation of another betrayal.

'…I have reason to believe Jenna's hiding cannabis in her room.'

She narrowed her eyes. 'How do you…?'

'I can smell it. When she opens the door.'

134

Sarah bounded to her daughter's room, rapped upon the wood and sniffed the air. Without waiting for a reply she pushed her way in, then yelled out Patrick's name.

He raced to join her and found her desperately rifling through her daughter's dirty laundry. He turned off Jenna's CD player.

'Where's she gone?' Sarah asked.

The window was closed now, but unlocked.

He watched as Sarah pulled out the contents of a chest of drawers, deposited it in a heap on the carpet.

'Perhaps under the bed?' Patrick suggested.

Sarah sunk to her knees and began extracting random folders and boxes. Patrick was bracing himself for the finding as she screamed.

She'd unearthed not the shoebox full of papers, diary and grass, but something far more odious and adult.

Patrick didn't know the first thing about makes of guns. It was a dirty-grey colour, with an odd metal loop at the rear and a snub-nosed end giving it a squat, unbalanced appearance. The trigger was large compared to the hexagonal barrel, and the handle was chunky with gangland runes scratched on one side. Something tugged at Patrick's memory; it was unmistakably the pistol from the video he'd watched with Christophe.

Sarah cast the gun to the carpet as though it burned her fingers.

Slowly, Patrick lifted the bed and pulled out the two bags of grass, dumped them down beside the weapon. Sarah wept.

'I'm calling the police,' she said, before jabbing the phone back and slumping on the armchair beside it. 'I don't know what to do… Will there be repercussions if she loses someone's stash? Will she be accused of… snitching?'

'I think snaking is the term nowadays.'

Patrick sunk into the sofa and willed the clock to move at a normal speed. In the company of Sarah's hysteria the present was everlasting, a Dali-like stretching of the clockface. Patrick had been as good as dismissed from the home already but didn't feel he could leave while she paced, kicked furniture, stared with rabid eyes at Millie's photograph on the mantel.

Sometime later, there came the sound of breaking glass and shouting. Being nothing unusual, Sarah ignored it, but curiosity led Patrick to draw back a curtain. Across the road, a second-floor flat rippled ablaze.

'Sarah... Look at this.'

She came to join him, angry flames reflected across her face. 'Do you think there's anyone in there?' she gasped.

By way of reply, the burning flat's front door exploded in a burst of copper sparks. Two figures flew from the flat and hit the balcony walkway coughing. No locals ran to drag them free, which Patrick thought bizarre. Instead, many seemed to shrink from the spectacle. The pair, a half-naked man of large build and a slightly older woman of mixed race, spluttered their lungs of noxious fumes.

The man, now raging at the fire which cast long, inconstant shadows across the quadrangle, looked familiar. In fact, he looked a lot like an older version of Matthew. Was it Sean Keane's apartment in flames?

Music started again. Sarah ran to Jenna's bedroom and smashed her way in.

'What are you doing?' her daughter shouted. 'Have you gone *completely* mad? Look at the state of my room!'

Patrick followed to find the drugs and gun gone, and Sarah on her knees sweeping her arm under the bed. The window was open and cold air set the curtain in a sail. Patrick strode over, looked down. Using an overflow pipe, three window ledges and rudimentary mountaineering skills, the route up from the alley could be traversed. The blue lights of a fire engine sprayed the brickwork, its accompanying siren yowl dying as the unseen vehicle handbraked to a halt. What truly frightened Patrick was the knowledge that those sirens, those livid flames, were neither the culmination of a series of events nor the start of something bigger. It was life. It was 'just how it is round here'.

'Where are they?' Sarah demanded from her daughter.

'Where are *what*?'

Sarah turned. 'What do I do, Patrick?'

He looked blankly at the space the illegalities used to occupy on the floor.

'We should tell the police.' The determination in Sarah's voice was probably intended to scare Jenna, rather than allude to her own resolve.

'Are you crazy?' Jenna exploded, indignation creasing her face. 'There's nothing here.'

'Jenna, we both saw it.' Patrick hated himself for wading in.

'We're having all the locks and windows changed. As of tomorrow,' Sarah said. 'This ends. That... *stuff* never comes back, okay? Ever.'

Jenna persisted in her defence. 'I don't know what you're talking about.'

'You could go to prison for this, Jenna. Oh God. Do I report my own daughter? What do I *do*, Patrick?' She continued to use 'I' and not 'we'. His involvement was officially acknowledged as that of a bystander. 'Whose was it, Jenna?' she pleaded, shaking her daughter. 'Whose was it?' She slapped a stinger across Jenna's cheek.

Jenna held her mother's gaze with defiance, condescension. 'I have no idea what you're *talking about*.'

With so much anger and disappointment in the home, a stoic daughter remaining tight-lipped in the face of a mother's rage, it would have been impossible for him to stay. When the debris settled, questions answered or not, Sarah might well have wanted a man about the place, for support, for protection, but they'd coped for a long time without him.

He took a few paces backwards as they quarrelled, then turned and left.

Outside, the fire-fighters had managed to douse the flames and most onlookers had returned to their homes. There was little now to see; only faint curlicues of smoke dimpling the night on their way to obscure the stars.

When Sarah's landline number flashed on his phone at two in the morning he pounced, but the voice on the other end was unfamiliar and otherworldly. 'Please come over,' it begged, in-between gulping silences, the catarrhy lacunae of distress. 'It's an emergency.'

'Jenna? What's happened?'

'Please. Straight away.' She hung up.

Panicked, he tore that day's clothes back over his body. His mind was blank as he hurried to the main road in search of a taxi. Convinced something terrible had happened to Sarah, fear and adrenaline synthesised into primal shutdown, an urge merely to arrive at the side of his summoner in as little time as possible.

It didn't take him long to locate a taxi, the twenty-four-hour ubiquity of minicabs being one of London's only certainties, and persuade the driver to slalom his way to Union City. He was dropped off a couple of blocks short of Bateman, for reasons now clear to Patrick, and once the money had changed hands the cab skidded off without pause.

Lightning in the distance, sweeping closer. And 'Danny's Tune' repeating, repeating. A majestic melody from G to A, from A to D, from D to…

It was so familiar to him now, this tune. He'd been gestating it for what seemed his entire life. The most transcendent melodies always seemed as though they'd always been 'out there', demanding plagiarism royalties on behalf of the universe.

…E minor, from E minor to G, from G to A, from…

'Bollocks.'

It came to him, finally. 'Danny's Tune' wasn't his. It was Adam's 'Find the Ocean', 'the worst kind of mainstream, sub-Beatles singalong crap' Patrick had allegedly ever heard in his life, the song they'd famously argued about in the dying days of their tense studio time together. He'd never uttered the quote attributed to him on their Wikipedia page but, still, of all the tunes on Earth, how had that one managed to invade him so commandingly?

Patrick hurried past a weaving circus of 50CC bikes, child riders yelling at each other with broken voices. The smell of burning fuel, caustic and metallic, like spent matches. A car alarm squealing. An estate map being pissed against.

Bateman block, by contrast, was silent. As was the block opposite. Hours earlier, the fire had set ablaze the community, but not one fire-fighter now remained and the building across from Sarah's had been reduced to little more than a blackened husk, a charred, glassless stacking of bricks and beams.

A black shape was sitting on the west staircase, three steps shy of the third floor. Jenna had her arms curled protectively around her knees and looked up, dog-eyed, as he approached.

'What's…?'

He was immediately shushed. 'Follow me,' she said, her words brittle.

Jenna had never been like the other kids, had always seemed to carry baggage, and even in Year Eight had possessed nothing like the nonchalance of other twelve-year-olds. But this was different. Something was very wrong. The girl was as beset and brow-beaten as any adult could ever be.

She led him into the flat. 'Keep quiet. Mum's asleep.'

Patrick was taken aback. 'Asleep?'

Even before the door closed, she collapsed into shivers. 'I didn't know who else to call… I found your number on Mum's phone.' A long line of grey mascara had etched itself from her left eye to midway down her cheek and at its tip hung a tiny tear. He watched it roll, picking up speed on its way to the chin. The soft pink buds of her lips drew back, revealing a gnawing of white teeth. The light bulb bathed her in ugliness.

Patrick, in dread anticipation, felt water pooling on his breastbone. No teacher training had prepared him for this.

Surrealism poured from Jenna's mouth. '…He was here… They'll know it… oh God oh God oh God…'

Uselessly, he tried to comfort her with an aged and inappropriate arm on the shoulder. She walked to her bedroom, indicating he ought to follow, and then pushed the door almost closed behind them.

The hairs on Patrick's neck stalked. Standing with Jenna in her bedroom, as her mother slept through the wall, felt nothing short of treacherous. He wondered whether Sarah had taken one of her sleeping pills, if she'd be passed out for hours.

'What's happened?'

'I…' She steadied herself against the end of her bed, all traces of youth pulled from her face.

'Tell me.'

'He was at my window. He kept knocking. I was worried Mum might hear, so I opened up…'

'Who? Who was at your window?'

'…Denis.' She could barely say the name.

'Was it his gun you were keeping?'

She looked at him askance. 'What do you think, Patrick?'

Her use of 'Patrick' startled him. In that moment, there was something like understanding between them. He wasn't the teacher and she had stopped being the pupil. And then she collapsed in tears on the bed and the understanding dissipated. But it had been enough. Enough time for her to suspect Patrick knew more than he was letting on. Enough time for him to realise he didn't know the half of it.

Why had she contacted *him*? Why not a friend? Why not her father?

'He was…' she sobbed into the pillow, drawing the duvet around her.

In an attempt to coax the story from her, he crouched by the bed, offered a tissue. 'Why did you call me? What is it you think your mother can't help you with?'

For a long while they remained in their places. A gentle rain auditioned at the window.

'I killed Denis,' she said.

SEVEN

Jenna ran a glistening nostril along her sleeve and attempted to garland her pronouncement with some detail. 'He'd climbed up to my window. It's how we... I... come and go. When I don't want Mum to know.'

'I guessed that much.' Patrick waited as patiently as he could while the story unfolded in staccato, tearful fashion, fingernails cutting into his palms, ashamed of his own fascination. 'And he... tried to...?'

'He wanted his gun. Said he needed protection.'

'But... where was the gun when your mum confronted you in here? And the cannabis?'

She indicated the small of her back, implying she'd stashed at least the gun under her clothes.

'Did your mum call the police in the end? I'm guessing not.'

With obvious difficulty, she swallowed. 'I felt like if I gave him the gun I was going to regret it. I tried to shout for Mum but he put his hand over my mouth and... made him tell me where it was. He stank of petrol. I heard him laughing as he followed me out the window...' Jenna spoke like a girl possessed; perhaps the action of recounting helped foster the pretence that these were already memories, events she could outlive. 'I ran round the estate, in a kind of circle, and when I thought I'd lost him I hid by the recycling bins at the end here. Then, like all of a sudden, he had the gun at my head.'

Patrick awaited the grim climax as Jenna mined inside herself for the confidence to finish. She muttered, in a quieter voice, 'He's under the stairwell at the end of the block, between the bins.' She lashed out and grabbed Patrick's arm at the wrist. The level of her distress went some strides to convincing him she spoke the truth.

But information was missing. 'Jenna... *How* did you kill him?'

'I was trying to push the gun away.'

'And you shot him?'

'The gun... My prints are on it for sure. I thought about going back and... cleaning up. No one will find him until the morning. You probably walked past him just now and didn't even realise...'

Patrick saw the reason he'd been summoned. He was no shoulder to cry on.

Of course, it wasn't really as simple as collecting the gun from the corpse; there would doubtless be more proof of her presence at the scene. Footprints, lint, skin cells under the boy's nails.

'There are many things to consider here, Jenna. If it was self-defence, you might...'

'Get away with it?' She sat, wiped her face on the pillow. 'I killed someone. I *killed* someone.'

'Are you sure he's...?'

Jenna appeared to genuinely consider this; her unblinking eyes swivelled top left, her shoulders minutely contracting. 'Maybe... you should go down there, just to check things out? And get the gun?'

It would kill her mother, if Jenna were to be sent away for this. And hadn't he promised Sarah earlier that day he'd look out for her daughter? He stared up at Jenna's face, her skin smooth and clear, features soft despite the tears and re-pieced with hope into innocence. Denis' scarred face flashed into his mind, the boy's strong hands creeping up Jenna's skirt. Despite her attempts to use him, Patrick felt deeply sorry for her.

'Jenna. I'm not going down there. I'm sorry. This is a police matter. You have to explain to them what happened. Wake your mum and let her know everything immediately.'

'No one will see you.' In her hysteria, she hadn't heard him. 'You'll be careful, won't you? In fact, why don't you change your clothes?' She grabbed a black bin liner from under her bed, and he caught again the scent of damp. 'This was stuff Denis left here. It might be useful.'

She tipped the bag's contents out onto the bed. Grey tracksuit trousers, a dark hoodie. Almost funereal, Patrick thought. At the bottom of the bag were several empty wallets and a couple of de-SIMed mobile phones. A Morrison's shopping bag hid a pair of sweat-smelling gold trainers and a white cap. It was the same apparel pulled from the victim in the video he and Christophe watched; Denis clearly liked to safeguard his gang's ill-gotten gains here. 'You could take the window?' Jenna suggested.

'You must be joking.'

She slumped back on the bed, her face contorted in desperation. 'You have to get that gun. *Please.*'

'There's no way I'm wearing those clothes and there's no way I'm going to forage in the dark and collect your murder weapon. Even by telling me about this I'm complicit. If you don't inform the police, I will.' He spoke louder, in the hope of waking Sarah. Was she so terrified about retribution from Denis' gang that she'd chosen to confide in him rather than someone her own age? 'The police can give you protection, Jenna.'

She actually *laughed.* 'You *must* collect that gun for me.'

'No.' He backed from her, angry now, his stomach knotting in autonomic fight or flight response. 'If you wanted to cover this up, you should've collected it yourself. I can't believe you're even involving me. Now I've no choice but to let the police know.'

'Please, Patrick.'

'Stop. I won't do it. I know what's happened is… truly horrible, but I can't get that gun. Surely you can see that?'

Jenna's nostrils flared. 'Patrick…' There was a new steel in the girl's voice, a mature hiss which belied her youth, and he was struck by how much she resembled her mother. 'You're going to get that gun for me. I know you are.' She crossed to a drawer, pulled out a black, slimline torch, and held it out to him.

Patrick set his eyes on the door handle. 'There's nothing you can say which will convince me to do this.'

'Nothing?'

He paused, but not without confidence. '*Absolutely nothing.*'

He descended the stairs and entered the rain, taking pains to avoid the cold gaze of slowly swinging CCTV the way a neurotic avoids cracks in the pavement. He took another left, then another, electing to find Denis via a circuitous route in case he'd been seen leaving Sarah's flat. Less than half the streetlights were working but it wouldn't have been hard for onlookers to spot his hunted gait as he searched the night for his courage.

When he saw the shadow approach he ducked into an old, unloved phone box which smelt of urine and featured *Tremor10* and *GalDiamondz* inked across pimpled steel behind a shattered phone. The ominous outline of Bateman block reared tall outside as he waited for the shadow – now identifiably a man, walking with the agonising slowness of a drunkard – to pass. The figure splashed by without even looking, legs carrying their sleepwalking owner home via the routes of memory.

Patrick left the box and walked up a flight of unlit stairs. There were no cameras there, and no occasion to be seen from neighbouring flats, but he was no longer following a conscious resolution to hide; he was putting off his task. On the balcony he stopped and gathered what remained of his thoughts. His hands were translucent with shaking. He was soaked to the skin and it wasn't due to the downpour.

When he emerged from the darkness, he was faking the teenage walk he so hated, figuring that if he'd been forced to wear such ridiculous garb he might as well go the extra mile and conduct his journey with an arrogant, swinging limp. It was slow going, walking like an idiot and wearing a pair of large gold trainers filled around the toes with toilet paper.

He moved at the periphery of the barely lit gloom, where the orange rain met the purple shadow of no man's land, and peered up to Sarah's flat. The lights were off.

Voices alerted him, and he pressed himself into a small recess in the brickwork as several kids, peddling so languidly they were practically hanging off the backs of their bikes, moved as ghosts towards him through drenched moonlight. They talked as loudly as they would during the day, if not louder, while one saddled youngster kicked a discarded beer can and sent it skittering in the direction of Patrick's hiding place. It came to rest nearby with a hollow, aluminium rattle. Patrick couldn't comprehend what made them pedal so slowly, in such bleak weather. Had they anywhere to go?

Once they'd weaved to the other side of the little square, Patrick faded himself back into the dark and limped towards the far steps.

If Jenna was right, and Denis' corpse was under there, then he'd already come too far not to pervert the course of justice. Patrick was the boy's teacher, not his deity, and Sarah and her estate weren't his responsibility, no matter how convincing Jenna's smiling blackmail. But though every sinew in his body screamed at him to walk away, now he was here he needed to see for himself the proof of Denis' union with the cold and loveless night. No longer would he find desks doused with paint, arms broken on stairwells. It was over. Denis was gone.

A flash of lightning startled him as he stalked through the gunning raindrops. He fingered the torch Jenna had given him, felt the length of its rubber grip for the switch.

Patrick ducked and stepped beneath the stairs.

On top of the rank stench of two weeks' refuse was something altogether fouler. The potent retch of flesh, the appalling mineral musk of innards never intended to meet air. Copper, sewage and red meat. One side of the boy's head was missing and his right fist was clenched, frozen in one final unaccomplished act of violence. Denis' remaining eye stared up in incredulity, no light behind it, as a stray tabby ceased licking at the casserole of brains beside the boy and shot through Patrick's quaking legs to freedom. It didn't take a ballistics doctorate to surmise his head injuries were consistent with a bullet fired at point-blank range.

Patrick tasted vomit, turned his body towards the dark, dispassionate estate. Despite a gunshot having ricocheted through the block not so long ago, no one had investigated. Thank goodness, Patrick thought, for the apathy of a place in which bullets in the night weren't uncommon. *Watch the wall, my darling, while the Gentlemen go by.* The whole estate was insanely afraid of its new masters, the teenage Mafioso.

He took a lung-swelling breath, adrenaline fooling him into courage, and jabbed the torch back in the body's direction, swilled it around the blackness, but the light couldn't penetrate the dark fully, defied him by showing only the corpse. No matter how far he widened his search, he saw blood.

It was at this point that Patrick's brain, perhaps understandably, began to play tricks. Accrediting the heavy breathing filling the shadows to someone other than himself, he stabbed the torchlight back across the corpse and let out a sharp cry, taking a step backwards, as the boy's eye appeared to focus upon him. Underneath his foot was something raised and unyielding. He lifted his leg and dazzled the gun with light, then fumbled out a pair of gloves from the large pocket at the front of his borrowed hoodie. After spending what felt like half an hour struggling to pull them over his trembling fingers, Patrick stooped to pick up the weapon before stuffing it inside the same pocket. Muddy scuff marks on the ground evidenced a struggle, but there was nothing he could do about those; the important thing was not to add anything else to the scene. At least his footwear was of a false size, and concrete, he assumed, permitted no trace of prints. Water was dripping from the stairs above and a swelling puddle had almost reached the blood. The police could never hope to uncover any evidence after this deluge.

He clicked off the torch and fled the scene.

Sticking to the shadows, he sprinted faster than he'd ever managed before, in case the man who used to be Patrick Owen caught up and questioned the oncoming eternity of covering his tracks. The walkways whistled in the wet wind. The gun felt heavy, powerful. He thought a viscous liquid was bleeding through the gloves and he wiped at the tracksuit trousers. As he reached the balcony leading to Sarah's flat, the rain lashed with renewed vigour and, dizzy with fear, he approached the unlatched door and stepped inside.

He headed straight to the bathroom and fumbled for the light switch, then the basin. Blood seemed to adorn everything he'd touched, red on enamel white, and he retched again.

He'd spent endless nights on the cancer ward, in the uncomfortable chair beside his father's bed, had seen the horrors of chemotherapy first-hand, the way it rips open grown men, but nothing had prepared him for the sight of that body under the stairwell, the butchery a sixteen-year-old girl had inflicted upon another human being.

A voice slurred, 'Patrick,' and he attempted to hide the reddened gloves behind his back, heart crashing in his temples.

It was Jenna.

Patrick set about cleaning the blood and Jenna assisted him in silence. The front door handle. The bathroom basin. The taps. He checked the bottom of his shoes to determine whether an incriminating trail of haemoglobin was trod through the flat. His wet clothes were hauled off and shoved back into the bin liner alongside the gloves, then he tossed the blood-splattered gun in too. He knew exactly what he'd do with all that in the morning. Patrick washed his hands five times.

Slipping quietly to Sarah's bedroom, he pushed the door open a matter of centimetres. She was in a drugged sleep, part-foetal, her arms thrust out into the plains of her bed, as though cradling a small ghost. Her eyelids flickered and her mouth twitched in neither smile nor grimace. A strap of her nightgown had fallen away to expose one perfect shoulder.

Watching her, he was struck anew by the purity inherent in a sleeping person, their innate infancy and helplessness. His burgeoning affection for her had not been diluted by recent actions and he felt an overwhelming urge to join her under the duvet, to take refuge in those empty arms, to melt his nightmare into her seemingly temperate dreams.

He closed the door and returned to Jenna's room. With nothing to say to her, he stood at the opposing end of a flokati rug and waited while she smiled nervously, as one would out of a sense of duty to an unsolicited houseguest. But he was anything but a cold caller; he was now and forever her co-conspirator.

'Patrick...' Again, the use of his forename shocked him. The casting off of 'Mr Owen' spoke of mock familiarity, as though, even after all he'd just done for her, she talked down to him. 'Was he...?'

'Very.'

She was determined to shock him with her casual tone, youth trying to get the better of its elder, but she couldn't muster the necessary hardness, and the equanimity didn't suit her either.

She said, 'No one knew the gun was here, except you and Mum.'

Patrick could barely bring himself to look at her. 'Between us, we'll need to keep her quiet about that. But I don't know how likely that's going to be. Once word of the murd... accident gets out...'

This slip of the tongue retriggered a hushed sobbing from Jenna.

'Damn you,' he said. 'I'll think of something.'

'And what about this?' She produced the two bags of cannabis from the bottom of her chest of drawers.

He snatched the bags and thrust them into the black bin liner alongside the other incriminating artefacts. 'Anything else?' he asked with acerbity, knowing their eyes could never meet again in living or class room, kitchen or canteen.

'Jenna, did he sexually assault you?'

She shook her head, but he couldn't be sure it was the truth. Jenna still wanted to remain a peripheral character in the drama, and he could hardly blame her. Her eyes were dead. She didn't seem to have a clue what was going on any more.

'This is done now,' he warned. 'You can't go to a doctor, or a...'

'He didn't. Not this time.'

Every hair on Patrick's body stood on end. 'Anything else to link you to this? Think hard.'

'No. Nothing.'

'Look at me, Jenna.' He threw the bag over his shoulder. 'I haven't been here. Whatever happens, this *never* happened. You slept all night. Denis didn't come over. I didn't come over. And we *never* talk about this. Okay?'

She walked him stiffly into the hallway. 'Whatever happens,' she echoed.

PART
THREE

PART
THREE

BREAKING NEWS: MURDER PROBE AFTER BODY FOUND IN UNION CITY

A murder inquiry has begun after a body was found in the western section of Union City in South West London on Thursday morning.

Det Ch Insp Meadows, of the Metropolitan Police, said the identity and age of the body was not yet known and officers were asking locals to come forward 'as a matter of urgency' if they know of any missing persons.

The force has confirmed the body was that of a male.

Cold cases reviewed

A refuse collector made the discovery at Union City in the early hours of the morning. The area has been cordoned off.

"We are at the very early stages of the investigation and it could be a complex inquiry," said DCI Meadows.

"The body hasn't been in situ for a long time but I can't comment any further on that. The circumstances suggest this is a murder case and we are looking at missing persons reports and cold cases, both locally and nationwide."

Forensic tests

Forensic science experts are carrying out a detailed search of the area - about two hundred yards from the troubled Highfields Secondary School.

DCI Meadows said it was not yet clear if the man was killed at the scene or taken there after his death.

The body is expected to be recovered later and taken to the King James Hospital, where post-mortem tests will take place.

Highfields School would not comment on the discovery, saying it was a "matter for the police".

Related Stories

School fails Ofsted inspection 28 JANUARY 2016, LONDON

'Last chance' for failing headteacher 01 FEBRUARY 2016, LONDON

Gang crime 'ignored' say Union City residents 07 APRIL 2016, LONDON

ONE

The school was a cemetery of silence as Patrick led the tall, grey-suited, grey-haired Detective Chief Inspector Meadows past peeling displays to his classroom. Half an hour beforehand, he'd witnessed the man barter an assembly of a thousand pupils into electric silence with his sullen, businesslike comportment before giving the exclusive: the death of Denis Roberts.

They arrived at his classroom and Patrick toed open the door.

The ill-proportioned portraits of twelve-year-olds on the far wall greeted them. The chalk faces had been tacked there for three years but it'd seldom occurred to Patrick that one of the smudged, tone-free images had been made by Denis when he was in Year Eight. In many ways, the anonymity of the portrait was reassuring: if it'd been anything near an exact likeness there was no way he could have accepted it glowering across at him day after day.

The Inspector muttered something that sounded like 'Large room,' before sitting on a front table. Patrick perched himself on the edge of his desk, facing Meadows. Dry streaks of white emulsion still besmirched its surface.

Through the wall, the kiln droned.

'Sorry about the smell,' Patrick said. 'Harriet missed the end of term pottery bake and decided to stuff the kiln with clay this morning.'

The kiln had almost reached its top temperature, its door

automatically locked by pyrometric controls until the firing process was complete. By that time, Patrick hoped most of the evidence, thrown inside first thing that morning, would be ash.

The Inspector looked at him sideways, frowned a generous pair of white eyebrows.

'A rough place, Union City,' Patrick said. 'Very bad.' The presence of an authority higher than himself in his own classroom inspired a courteous honesty, and he saw the need to repaint a portrait of an area deep-fried in teenage unrest.

'What do you mean?' There was little emotion in the voice; its ambiguity was Meadows' bread and butter. This stripping away of sentiment left Patrick feeling autistic, unable to read what the man wanted. 'What's wrong with it?'

'There was practically a small war Monday night.'

'Indeed. Bateman block. A few youths making a fuss, I gather.' He spoke with the non-committal amiability only a policeman of many years' standing can manage.

'And a fire opposite, last night. There's a charred space where there used to be a flat.'

'"Opposite"? Perhaps you could explain where you live.'

'Where…?'

The ringing in Patrick's ears had shifted into a higher pitch since the morning. The latest symptom of a life out of control.

'Where you *live*, Mr Owen.'

'Oh, I live to the west of the borough but last night I spent a small part of the evening – the *early* part of the evening – with Sarah Ellis. *She* lives in the estate.'

'I see.' Inspector Meadows jotted something on a pad.

'She's the mother of a pupil here, actually.'

Meadows nodded, giving nothing away. 'Is this pupil "Jenna"? Someone suggested she might be Denis' girlfriend.'

Paranoid, Patrick fell firmly towards the defensive. 'Don't know. Kind of.'

'"Kind of" is her daughter or "kind of" was Denis' girlfriend?'

'She *is* her daughter and *might've* been his girlfriend. To complicate matters, I teach – taught – both of them. Jenna *and* Denis.' His eyes flicked towards Denis' dreadful portrait at the back of the classroom.

'Well, that's why I'm here, Mr Owen. What did you make of Denis?'

Patrick's pause was noticed. The Inspector hastened to cajole his memory of the boy. 'Good kid? Bad kid?'

Patrick opted for diplomacy. 'He wasn't the easiest kid to teach.' He stopped short of saying the things one expects to hear about those who've died prematurely – that they were a credit to society, a straight A student, well-liked – but Patrick trumpeted Denis, and made him sound more well-rounded and personable than he had been, merely by concealing his general loathing of the boy. 'Though certainly intelligent, he liked to throw his weight around, if you know what I mean. In Art, he showed... aptitude... and that helped. You've got to praise kids to get the best out of them.'

'Adults too,' the Inspector mused, chewing a pencil. 'You don't need to pull any punches, Mr Owen. I'm not a journalist. The kid wasn't much liked by the staff here at Highfields was he?'

'He... wasn't liked by everyone, no. But he had a few acolytes amongst the students. Kids like that always do. Do you think he got mixed up in drugs?'

The look the Inspector shot Patrick had suspicion written throughout. 'We're keeping an open mind, Mr Owen. Do *you* think he was involved in drugs?'

'I've no idea...'

Meadows broke his pencil nib and thrust a hand into his jacket to retrieve a biro. 'I'm aware this is shocking for you. It must be terrible knowing a child you teach has died, more so when you're personally involved.'

'Sorry, I woke up with this damned soprano singing in my head... When I'm personally...?'

'Are you dating Jenna's mother, Mr Owen?'

'I don't know.'

'Let me rephrase. Are you sleeping with her?'

The crudeness of the question flushed Patrick's cheeks, and Meadows clearly inferred a positive answer from this. Patrick didn't correct him.

His first lie.

'Then you're personally involved. Don't think you've heard the last of this.' The manner was polite, but his smile nonexistent. Maybe it was just his technique; his policeman's poker face. 'How did you find out about the death?'

'Like everybody else, I guess. The rumours had started by breaktime. I overheard some boys in the sixth form talking about it.'

The biro hovered over the notebook. 'Is there anything more you can tell me about Denis? Was he involved in a gang that you know of? What was your impression of the way he spent his spare time?'

'I saw him from Sarah's window, in the fight. To the outsider it looked like there were two gangs.'

'And would you recognise any other members of these gangs, Mr Owen?'

'I could direct you to a few. Many of them attend this school.'

Meadows flipped over his pad. 'We've got some names already. Fire away; maybe you can fill in the gaps.'

Once Patrick had reeled off the list of pupils he'd seen with black eyes and assorted injuries, Meadows replaced his notebook and wandered to the window. 'Ugly place, isn't?' he said, surveying the flat greyness of Union City. 'Solid concrete for three miles. Where were you last night, by the way?' He kept his back to the teacher. 'Overnight. Between the hours of, say, midnight and five?'

'I was asleep, at home.'

Meadows nodded almost imperceptibly, then turned to face Patrick. 'You live with anyone?'

'My wife and I are separated.'

Meadows furnished Patrick with the Homicide Command phone number then walked towards the classroom door. He stopped and turned one-hundred-and-eighty.

'If there's anything else you think you ought to tell me, please don't hesitate, Mr Owen. Anything at all.' He slipped through the door.

Alone, Patrick's heartbeat began to stabilise. Perhaps, he allowed himself to fantasise, that would be the last he'd see of Detective Chief Inspector Meadows.

It was over to Jenna now.

He rang the bell. Trepidation had rusted his throat and breathing was no longer the easy activity it used to be.

Patrick took a step back when a man answered. The same diminutive features as Jenna. A small, not quite retroussé nose and identical, cynical eyes, black-ringed by long lashes.

'I'm from Jenna's school…' Patrick introduced.

The stranger looked him up and down. 'And …?'

Patrick couldn't quell his dislike of the man. He was more attractive than Patrick, certainly, and his stubble, though it had barely been allowed to grow, was dark and expansive. Everything about him made Patrick feel inadequate. The bulge in the trousers seemed substantial. The muscular forearms were swept with a pelt of primordial hair.

'She's fine,' Jenna's father said, and it rang with the crashing timbre of a conversation closer.

'Right,' Patrick said, taking a further step back. 'Good.'

When Sarah appeared, Jenna's father looked him over one last time before retreating back inside the flat.

'Sarah? Everything alri…?'

She joined him on the balcony walkway, briefly folded herself into his embrace. Her voice, when she spoke, was quietly hysterical. 'I got back from work about an hour ago.

I'd heard, on the news, about the shooting but when I found out who it was… Jenna was nowhere to be seen until just recently. When she came in, she wouldn't tell me where she'd been.'

'Don't take it personally. Maybe she's upset.'

'About that… *boy*?' The venom was directed, in a sweeping hand movement, at the ground below, as though the street itself were shorthand for Denis Roberts. 'I'm her mother. Why isn't she talking to me about this?'

'Has anyone spoken to you about it? The police?'

'Why would they?'

'The connection between your daughter and Denis is substantial enough to warrant police interest. They've spoken to me.'

She visibly paled.

Patrick, though he knew Meadows had already discovered the link between Jenna and Denis, couldn't help but feel he'd led the inquiry to Sarah's door himself. 'Look, I wonder, if they do want to speak to you, whether you should mention… You know how we found…' In the fierce cold, sweat dripped off him.

'That's what I keep thinking about. We can't keep quiet about that now a boy's died, can we? Could it have been the gun that killed him? Perhaps Jenna knows something.'

'She'd have mentioned it already, wouldn't she? To the police?'

'Would she? It's not cool to snitch – *snake* – is it? If there's a connection… I *have* to tell the police, Patrick.'

'I really don't think you should. Why drag her into this? It might be dangerous.'

'It's already dangerous. I mean…' She lowered her voice. 'I read that his brains had been completely *blown out*.'

Patrick drew his collar up against the needles of ice in the exhaust fume wind and attempted a look of sympathy. The irony of the situation wasn't lost on him; it was he who'd led her to the gun in the first place, trying to build up honesty points by showing her the cannabis. When he looked down he saw he was holding both of her tight, cold hands in his. Shame wept through his veins.

'Sarah, have you seen those posters for Operation Trident? You can go down for keeping someone else's piece. And anyway it was just the once, she said so. The stuff's gone now.'

'How can you be so sure?'

Patrick hesitated. 'She promised you, didn't she?'

The phone rang inside. A male voice answered then called for Sarah.

'What's he doing here anyway?' Patrick nodded his head towards the unseen ex.

Sarah pecked a kiss in Patrick's direction and disconnected her hands from his before disappearing back into her flat. As she did so, it was as though an electrical source turned itself off.

Patrick smashed his watch into the wall. It was a pointless act and he regretted it instantly. Worse, he drew the attention of the token pair of policemen now patrolling the estate, clicking through the fast-forming frost.

It had dropped ten degrees in an hour.

Inside the police cordon, he could make out forensic experts hunting in crackling boiler suits as the squat white tent concealed the murder scene from the last of the day's sunlight.

He cursed Jenna's name, the perfect blackmail she'd laid down. If he'd helped to exonerate her, it wasn't because he'd been moved by her tears; philanthropy didn't justify a life on the hoof from the law and inner peace. Nor were his deeds a selfless fulfilment of a promise to Sarah – 'Keep an eye on her for me,' she'd said. 'She's all I have.' No, he was saving his own skin, at the behest of a teenager's cunning.

Patrick knew that Jenna, even if the police failed to extract the full facts from her, even if they never found out about her concealment of Denis' gun, could still wake up one morning and turn herself in. In any case, as Patrick had flicked the torch over the dead body he'd felt the image sear into his brain, bedding itself down forever. Jenna's mindset wasn't his only concern: one day, he knew, that image would give him away. It was a matter of who would crack first.

Life was supposed to crawl onwards now, in a rebuttal of the unlikely, macabre events of his day, but he breathed culpability, reeked of it, and knew his appearance at Sarah's flat had only been to promote the pretence of innocence while revisiting, just once, the scene of his crime.

Tired and light-headed, his spine torn with pain, he stepped with flat feet to avoid the reeling floor, the shrieking in his ears seemingly exacerbated by Union City's silence. Normally there were bikers, or workers returning, but tonight the residents stayed away; like villagers during the time of the plague, they saw the reaper in the alleyways.

As he passed the end of Moore block, his eyes were drawn to an art form he'd never much cared for. At least one other had been out tonight; the graffiti was still wet.

He stared in horror at the image on the wall as his phone buzzed a foreign number.

'Ana. Thank God. I've been…'

'Is Adana. She still no here Patrick. Have you heard of her? I very worried. Is not like her.'

Ana's mother didn't, as a rule, *do* flustered. This was serious.

He didn't, couldn't, take his eyes off the graffiti. 'Slow down. When was the last time you spoke to her?'

'She call me Monday and tell me they no come home. Like I tell you. She still in England.'

'Adana, it's great that we're on the same page finally. I mean, now we're both worried. What did Ana say she was doing over here? Why did she stay on? Why didn't she tell me?'

'I not know. Did you telephone her hotel like I suggest?'

'What hotel?' Even before he asked, he knew which one.

Union City's very bricks mocked him. Before him, in amateur but passable fashion, was the stencil of a face with the bannered surtitle: 'D-Man. RIP Union Soulja.'

Patrick studied the image. There were the eyes he'd hated, crudely daubed. The slack jaw. The proud lips and their tiny scar.

The boy, conceited, violent and lacking basic manners, was already a martyr.

'Patrick, you still there? Patrick?'

Patrick, aware no secondary school Art teacher could ever be the subject of such a tribute, moved on without a backward glance into the night. The piece got full marks for impact but scored poorly for execution.

The Lionswater Hotel wouldn't give out the name of anyone staying within its walls, so Patrick headed over on foot. Thawing out with a questionable whisky, he propped up the bar until the receptionist left her chair at the desk, then bolted with no attempt at subtlety up the thickly carpeted, eggshell stairs.

Room four was halfway down the hall, sentried by two potted rubber plants which had been dusted so hard he thought he could still hear them squeaking. A 'Do not disturb' message hung from the door handle.

He knocked.

There was the sound of rustling, then light, padding footsteps. 'Who is it?' a female voice called back. Through the wood of the door, it could have been anyone.

'It's me. Patrick.'

The door opened a crack to reveal a bronzed complexion. She wore a towel, her hair in dripping ringlets. 'Who?'

Patrick took a step back, immediately realising not only the mistake but his larger, very genuine lapse from reality. 'I'm sorry,' he mumbled. 'I think I've got the wrong room.'

'I should think you have,' the stranger growled with undisguised irritation, snapping the door closed in his face.

TWO

On his way to work Friday morning, Patrick picked up a popular but unchallenging tabloid. 'Another Young Victim of Broken Britain,' the headline screamed.

The traditional picture of the victim stared out of the front page. His Year Nine photo, all teeth and choppily waxed hair; he could have been anyone's son. Even Patrick, who'd had cause to dislike the boy more than most, thought he looked sensible and confident – Denis' smug arrogance didn't translate through the dot matrix of the printing presses.

Inside the paper, Patrick read how 'feral groups of angry young people roam Union City' and, in place of 'parental role models', a 'tribal loyalty is firmly established and a gang culture based on violence and drugs is a way of life'. The paper was sympathetic towards the victim but scathing about London's population for its inability to prevent the killing. Indeed, the incident seemed to be sold as a microcosm of the country's problems. 'How did we let this happen to one of our children?' The witch-hunt of society continued apace on the editorial page. 'Another innocent lies in a mortuary tonight as we look the other way.'

The last line on the matter read: 'Police are investigating a possible link between the murder and a flat fire in the area, in which a large quantity of cannabis was destroyed.'

Patrick wheeled the page over, then jabbed off his iPod in disbelief. A photo of him lumbering out of the school the evening before, face cuffed red by the cold, complemented the story's headline – 'School Mourns Gun Crime Star Pupil'. A second photo was of the crime scene, police-taped and low-lit, a few shifty coppers squeaking black gloves together in the cold.

Patrick hadn't been aware of any photographers outside the school the day before, but then he'd hardly been aware of a great deal lately. Probably they'd telephotoed several teachers leaving Highfields in the aftermath of the murder's revelation and Mr Owen's visage was deemed the most tragic, the most burdened by the death. Funny that.

He was still flicking through the paper as he passed through the school gates into the playground. Inspector Meadows was in a long brown coat, speaking with Mr Llendl, one of the more officious idiots from the Maths department. Patrick, off-guard, rang out a hello in breezier terms than tradition dictated.

'Oh, morning,' Mr Llendl offered, his words as gaunt and discourteous as his general disposition.

'Thank you for your time,' Meadows closed, now turning his attention to Patrick, as though he'd been waiting for him all along.

Mr Llendl limped away as the inspector approached Patrick with his head raised, affecting a height and authority he'd no need to, such was the innate gravitas honed over his years of intruding into other people's homes and histories. He nodded at the paper in Patrick's hands. 'Have you noticed how innocent the dead become? All this "we have failed him" and "society's shame". Apparently we're *all* culpable for the sins of our killers.'

Patrick wiggled a finger in his ear. 'Kids need guidance. In many ways, adults are the worst kind of role models.'

'You agree with what you've been reading, Mr Owen?'

'I never believe what I read in the papers.'

Quick, confident feet resounded across the playground, the gait of senior management, and a ponytailed policewoman of comparable age to Patrick arrived by Meadows' side, the skin around her eyes heavily pouched, as though replete with tears. A strand of dark hair tumbled from beneath her hat and a smooth blueberry of a mole sat, ostentatious and supermodelesque, above her mouth. Meadows refused to introduce the policewoman, which Patrick interpreted as an act of pulling rank.

'So what's all this about Matthew's brother then?' Patrick asked, waving the newspaper.

Meadows jacketed his notebook and took the paper off him, his eyes slitting. 'I don't follow.' He pulled out a pair of reading glasses.

'The house that burnt down... The drugs...'

The Inspector cast heavy, distrustful eyes over Patrick before finally acknowledging his partner. 'This is Mary Haynes from the Murder Investigation Team. She's assisting me on the case.'

'Actually, officially, you're assisting *me* on the case,' she said.

Meadows didn't return her smile. 'Let's not split hairs.'

The radio at her collarbone crackled. 'Have you told Mr Owen about...?'

'There's going to be a press conference this weekend,' he snapped, 'calling upon the public for information regarding the killing. Can you make it?'

Patrick looked between the two of them. 'Well... yeah, I guess.'

Mary gave Meadows a sidelong glance. Her attractiveness must have made her job difficult at times and maybe it was this that the older man objected to, the aesthetic impediment to professionalism. Conversely, a latent misogyny might have been stoked by the fact that it didn't seem to affect her professionalism one bit.

'You're a familiar face, Patrick,' the Inspector explained. 'In more ways than one.' He shook the paper. 'I hear you used to be in the public eye...'

'I was in a band, a long time ago.'

'We need someone to say a few words about Denis. You're local and... I think it could really help.'

'You want me to speak at this press conference?'

'If possible. How's the hearing?'

'Um... Better. Thanks.'

'My brother used to be a banker,' Meadows confided. 'He had a stressful job – like you, I guess – and at one point he developed a hearing problem. It was caused by anxiety, though he was embarrassed to admit as much.' He left a knowing silence hang between them. 'A bit like the sore back you keep massaging.' Patrick expected the Inspector to go on: the red holes that used to be his eyes; the dry tracings of eczema around the brows. 'If you don't want to help, if you think it would be too much for you, that's fine. I understand. But Denis' killer is still walking around and any assistance you can give might aid us in putting this nasty matter to bed...' It was all sung to the tune of emotional blackmail.

'When do you need an answer?' Patrick asked, looking from Meadows to Mary and finding no comfort in either pair of tired eyes.

Meadows' tone relaxed, secure of his gambit. 'Anytime. Anytime between now and the end of this conversation.'

Patrick's Elevens were noiseless as they waited outside his classroom, stunned back to their scared-shitless, Year Seven selves by the violent realism of a world previously only glimpsed on illegal downloads. After thirty minutes of first period had elapsed, Edward – far from the shiniest soldier in the toy box – announced, 'I saw you in the paper, sir,' cajoling one or two to join in with their own testimonies. Another duly produced the paper.

The newspaper was stuffed back into a bag when Jenna entered with all the appearance of a sacrificial victim. Short steps. Head bowed. She'd developed strange hand mannerisms, a fragile chewing of one fist into another, a repeated washing of imperceptible bloodstains. It was her first public appearance after killing Denis and she too wanted to keep up a normal facade. She wasn't managing it.

Patrick thought it doubtful she'd speak to him, or indeed anyone, and no one else engaged in conversation either. He'd never known such silence in a classroom.

The group were still sculpting their clay heads. None of them had mastered an exact reproduction but most had obtained vaguely accurate facial proportions and only three pupils had included spliffs poking from their mouths. Jenna seemed absorbed in her work until Patrick closed a window and summoned from the snapping latch the approximate sound of a gunshot. He could do nothing but smile weakly at her as the girl fled the room, drawing a sigh of relief and a torrent of 'fucking hells' from her classmates.

Christophe's email, flagged high priority, pinged up on his laptop.

Seven o'clock. O'Sullivan's Snooker Club.

He stared at it for a while, then concealed his phone beneath the desk, switched it on and counted seven pings, the sound of messages from varying news agencies and well-meaning old friends racking up like debtor's demands. Nothing from Ana. Nothing from Ana's mother. Nothing from Sarah.

Through the wall, he heard the kiln cease whirring. It had entered its cooling phase and would be safe to open within a matter of hours. Lost, he stood and wandered the room as the pupils worked steadily if not skilfully. He was attempting to aggressively rub a smear of green chalk dust from his groin when a man of mixed race with a three-day-old goatee, an ill-fitting suit and a black leather folder slid into the classroom.

Patrick sidled up to the stranger. 'Can I help?'

'My name's Jack,' the man replied, in accentless English. He offered his hand, which Patrick only looked at. 'This your classroom?'

It was the way the man looked around, his tiny dead eyes soaking up information like the shutters of a camera, which led Patrick to suspect Jack was a Hack.

'How did you get in here?' He could picture the news story follow-up: a school which bred thugs and gang members had security scanners anyone could walk past and an Art teacher who permitted GCSE students to throw erasers at visitors.

'Pick that up, Daniel,' Patrick snapped.

The journalist smiled. 'Mr Hutchinson said I could look around. Please, pretend I'm not here.' He indicated, with a theatrical casting of his hands, that he wished the teacher to perform for him.

'I'm going to have to ask you to leave. I'm sure I'd have heard if the head was allowing you lot in.'

At this, the journalist merely smiled and paced to the corner of the room. Having picked up on their teacher's fractious body language, the children, seldom fans of outsiders stalking them round their classroom, of which they naturally felt ownership, viewed the journalist with interest and suspicion. Patrick decided this wasn't the class he wanted the Fourth Estate watching.

He walked from the classroom, leaving his startled visitor to experience alone the timeless joy that is teaching, to play the underpaid security guard in the eternal battle between the Id and Superego. He swore his way through the Art office door and picked up the telephone.

'What the hell's going on?' he demanded from reception. 'Some journalist's swanned into my classroom. Which cretin let him up?'

'We didn't send anyone,' a defensive voice replied, with more contrition than sincerity.

'Look, just send PC Thomas up to get rid of him.' The journo had probably got in via the fire doors behind the kitchen, as the canteen staff routinely did. That was how Patrick smuggled the gun in on Thursday morning, after all.

Harriet whispered his name and he swung to face her. He hadn't even noticed her sitting there.

'You look terrible,' she said. 'You should take some time off.'

This, from Harriet. Things were bad.

Patrick returned to his classroom to find Jack the Hack looking uneasy in the doorway. Aidan Humphries and Joe Coe were standing, dark grey streaks across their faces and clothes, obviously savouring the aftermath of a mini clay fight. Patrick hoped the reporter wasn't wearing the kind of buttonhole video camera he'd seen on exposé documentaries.

The journalist advised, 'I don't think it's a good idea to leave the room, mate,' nodding his head towards the miscreants.

'Piss off,' Patrick snarled, barging him into the corridor and sending shorthand notation scattering across the floor.

Amid the delighted whoops of Patrick's class, the journalist aimed a few choice words at Mr Owen.

'Bang him up, sir!' someone shouted.

It was then that Patrick became aware of a black shape moving in an ungainly but rapid manner in their direction down the corridor.

'There you are,' Patrick said to PC Thomas. 'I need this guy...'

He didn't get any further. The resident policeman, flak-vested and wielding his truncheon, slid on a sheet from the journalist's folder and crashed legs-first with terrific force into the intruder, scissoring him to the ground. He then incapacitated him by use of a clumsy half-Nelson and cuffed a pair of flailing arms behind his back while the victim, through a profuse nosebleed, angrily conceived new combinations of Anglo-Saxon obscenities which Patrick's class would be quoting long into their remaining schooldays.

Patrick's classroom door opened at the end of the day and Charlotte, no doubt bored of sitting three feet from Harriet in the characterless Art office emailing silent memos back and forth, smiled with fake glee. 'Here he is! Mr Celebrity!' He'd made a tiny return to his glorious years of recognition, but underneath her fascination was palpable distrust: he was punching reporters and appearing in the papers. If that wasn't milking the dead boy story, what was?

'I need to use the kiln,' she said. 'It's an emergency.'

Patrick had his mobile in front of him on the desk and had been watching it for almost his entire fifth period. Still nothing from Ana. Nothing from Sarah.

Too late, it dawned on him what Charlotte was up to. Before he could conjure a reason for stopping her she'd stormed across his room, produced her mammoth set of keys and unlocked the annex at the rear.

He launched himself across the room and tore through the door after her. The annex was small and dusty, the large brick kiln stood in the middle, its green door still mercifully closed.

'Fucking hell, I can't get the bloody thing open,' she complained, tugging at the handle.

If the chamber remained in excess of seventy degrees the kiln door wouldn't have unlocked but Patrick knew it sometimes stuck a little anyway and he made a big deal of checking the clasps on the side, trying to prise them open. The pyrometric controls verified the oven was off. 'It's definitely jammed,' he said. 'The mechanism's broken.'

'How much will it cost to get fixed?'

'A small fortune probably. I'd suggest you get your kids to use air-drying clay.'

This, it seemed, was too much for Charlotte. She wrenched at the handle with a possessed fury, screamed 'Bullshit!' at the summit of her lungs and succeeded in tearing the kiln wide open, hitting Patrick with the familiar burning smell that had lurked at the back of his classroom since he'd accepted the job. She stared aghast into the kiln's innards.

'What's... this?'

At the front, obscuring whatever smouldering traces of the murder evidence remained, was a wall of half-finished Year Seven sculpture Patrick, in a rare moment of forward-thinking, had thrown in the morning before.

'Oh, that's my Key Stage Three stuff. It's kind of... abstract.'

'Right... While you clear this out, I'll go and get my pieces.'

As Patrick watched her flounce out, he wondered what his head of department's ambitions might once have been, whether she felt her dreams of being a famous watercolourist or curator slipping away with the passing of each holiday. Her response to the kiln door jamming, their profession's latest trivial crisis, had been as absurd as expected.

He removed, fast, his pottery from the kiln then worried his hand into a small pile of black ash at the bottom, feeling around for anything which had proved incombustible. There it was, the only piece of evidence the thirteen hundred degrees couldn't have incinerated.

A hexagonal, snub-nosed barrel. Chunky handle. Small loop above the rear sight. The gun's polymer frame had bubbled in the extreme heat and reset in a stuccoed manner, stippled like the grip on the handle. It was hard to tell what had happened to the steel intestines of the pistol but he assumed the extent of its warping would have prevented the weapon from ever firing again. He stood there with the warm gun for a moment in contemplation, turning it over in his hands, weighing the heaviness of it. The clothes and trainers had been comprehensively barbequed.

A thin voice shot behind him. 'Here we are...'

He turned to see her staring at the gun in his hand when the lights failed.

Patrick swore, stabbed the gun into his pocket. He took out his phone and held it in exactly the same position as he'd been holding the gun. The haunted lights flickered back on again.

172

'You scared the life out of me!' he gasped, clutching with genuine panic at his flailing heart.

She hovered at the doorway to the annex, confusion adorning her handsome features, her arms laden with an assortment of sculptures: a doughnut; a cake slice; a half-peeled banana. They weren't bad representations, for a Year Seven, but he suspected they'd been fashioned by one of her sixth formers. He made a big deal of putting his phone back in his pocket then took her sculptures and placed them, piece by piece, above the cindered remnants of his immoral collusion.

'I thought…' she began.

'What?'

'Nothing… That poor boy… What do you think happened?'

The smell came again, as it had, on and off, for the last two days. A sweet, coppery scent mixed with defecation, burnt hair, natural gas. Raw meat. Death.

'What do you mean?' He removed the last slice of clay pizza from her hands, a giant cupcake, an oversized apple with a cartoon worm crawling from a bite.

'Do you think it was inevitable? You know, that he'd end up this way?'

'Not inevitable, no. He got mixed up in some dangerous business, that's all.'

He swung the kiln door closed, fastened it, then turned to face his head of department.

'I wonder where Denis is now,' Charlotte considered, a faraway look glazing her eyes. 'Maybe he's looking down on us this very moment.'

'I don't believe in an afterlife.' What was more, Patrick thought it unlikely the boy could have developed a soul all of a sudden.

'I thought you were a Christian, Patrick.'

'God, no,' he said, aware of the ironic invocation in this very denial. He pressed some digits on the kiln's temperature

173

gauge. 'All that magic apple, talking snake and missing rib nonsense. I'm not four years old.' Patrick's father hadn't bothered with religion, even when under the heel of chemotherapy, had never turned to Jesus or Mohammad or Krishna. He never talked about death in those final days. He just got on with the business, the art, of dying.

'I wonder if he knew who killed him.' Charlotte tried another tack. 'What would make someone do that? Take someone else's life? It's disgusting. You may not believe in heaven but I hope there's a *hell*. And I'm praying Denis' killer goes there.'

The silence which followed this comment was broken by a student walking past, blaring hip hop through a mobile phone.

'I better go,' Charlotte muttered. 'Thanks for that, Patrick. It's not often we get to talk, is it? Not so *deeply* anyway.'

Once she'd hurried to her classroom, and he'd mentally rewound their one-sided exchange and hunted in vain for anything that might constitute 'deep', he swept his arm across a table of art materials, screamed, and smashed it all sideways, sending charcoal, pencils and canvases spinning to the floor. The mess this created was nowhere near satisfying enough so he grabbed two bottles of poster paint and squeezed a few Pollockian arcs of blue and yellow atop the debris.

His head whining, Patrick slid over to the window to watch Highfields' kids streaming into the estate. No child seemed to be managing an even line; these were not the straight migratory patterns of wild creatures seeking warmer waters, but the random bearings of domestic pets, pampered creatures on their way to Xboxes and YouTube videos. Patrick straddled their world for a while, all-seeing, as the sun skimmed down behind the jagged skyline. Jenna's accomplice had survived another day.

He considered resigning, but knew it would look suspicious. His blood pressure might benefit, but there was more at stake than his reputation as a teacher, which he admittedly considered a hilarious oxymoron: he had his innocence to prove. Jenna and he shared a terrible secret, it was true, and yet he needed to keep her on a long string, let her exist in her own, separate purgatory while remaining on speaking terms, at the very least, with her mother. His line of work was a legitimate point of contact with the Moris/ Ellis household.

A light cough signified a presence behind him and Patrick checked the reflection in the window to see, framed in his doorway against the dirty orange streaks of sunset, a shadow in a padded police vest. The kiln-chewed gun in Patrick's pocket trebled in size, burned, and made a profound thud as he span round and its barrel struck the front table.

'Hello… Mary, was it?' he asked, breezily. 'Caught the bugger yet?'

'What's this on your door?' the beauty-spotted Murder Investigation Officer asked.

Patrick walked over to take a look.

'PEEDO' was sprayed a metre high in blood red letters.

'But… that's impossible…'

He stared in disbelief at the vandalism. Denis was dead. He was *dead*. Who was doing this? The CCTV camera in the corridor had brewer's droop.

Officer Haynes peered into the classroom, then wandered in to inspect the strewn drawing materials, the sweeps of paint on the floor.

'Someone really hates you.' She poked at the chaos with a toecap. 'I'll come straight to the point, Mr Owen. We're both busy professionals. I was wondering why you never mentioned the gun or cannabis Jenna had been storing under her bed.'

'The gun… and…?' It took all of Patrick's strength to remain upright.

'Yes?'

'I guess… I've been protecting them.'

'Who?'

175

'Sarah. And Jenna. I thought it implicated her and...
You know.'

'I'm afraid I don't, Mr Owen.'

He croaked the words. 'Sarah and I... We didn't know
whether to tell you or not. She was keen to safeguard her
daughter and I was keen to... safeguard Sarah, I suppose.'

There was a hint of a smile on the officer's face. Suddenly,
Patrick missed DCI Meadows. 'Well that's very noble of
you. Fortunately, Sarah came to her senses before you did.
The child's at the station now, incidentally, clarifying any
little matters her "safeguarding" adults were too nervous to
disclose. Anything else I'm going to discover through another
source that you might as well just come straight out and tell
me about? Think carefully now.'

THREE

Patrick closed one eye, sighted his target. He took a deep breath and, keeping his guiding left hand still, applied the merest touch with his right.

His cue poked the white ball a quarter of the table's length, but pushed the targeted red over its intended pocket. Christophe laughed unconvincingly and bent for the same red, sank it. He then potted a nifty pink with side before powering home a straight red along the cushion. 'Can't normally get those,' he admitted.

Friday night had arrived, and with it mediocre snooker and tolerable ale. Sliding his colleague's points along the scoreboard, Patrick wondered how much time he had left.

It was the not knowing that ate at him. There was no way he could escape his limbo by contacting Jenna and asking whether she'd stuck to their 'deny everything' agreement. His paranoia worried whether it was wise to even contact Sarah, in case her phone had been tapped or his every move was being monitored.

'Alright?' Christophe asked.

'Sorry. I was miles away.'

'Like your shots.' He tapped the table with his cue. 'Your turn.' There were six balls fewer.

With little to go for, Patrick attempted a safety off a red on the bottom cushion. He messed it up but was lucky with the result, spinning the cue ball up behind the spotted green.

'Jammy bastard.'

'I'm not at my best today. Tired, I guess.'

'Seen your bit-on-the-side recently?' Perhaps Christophe considered himself astute enough to blame a man's poor sporting prowess on a woman, or perhaps this was finally the start of an inquisition which would unveil the real reasons for his 'high priority' summons.

'Yesterday, briefly.' He could already feel the first, high-risk flushes of drunkenness.

Christophe lined up his escape from the snooker. 'I reckon they're close to catching the killer.'

'Really?' Patrick failed to keep his voice stable. 'What makes you say that?'

'I spoke to Meadows earlier at the school. He wouldn't say what he looked like but apparently a figure was caught on CCTV the night Denis was killed. Did you see him?'

'I didn't see anything,' he replied in an instant. Then, realising his mistake, added, 'I mean, Mary from the Murder team popped by, but nothing about CCTV was mentioned.'

'The police are calling for any witnesses who might've seen someone in the estate at the time of the murder. The net's closing on him, that's for sure.'

Patrick didn't like the searching look Christophe threw him.

'Have they announced what this person looks like?'

'I don't think so. Maybe they're waiting to see if descriptions match up.'

'Mary Murder didn't tell me any of this.' Patrick kept his expression cool, stared at the mess of balls on the table. 'If they're not releasing a description, how can they expect identification?'

'I'm sure there's a reason. But they need to find him soon. What if Denis was just his first victim? What if he's one of those serial killers?'

'What makes you think it's a he?'

'Are you joking? Ninety-three point three percent of murders are committed by men.'

'You scare me.' Patrick struck the white too hard. The red went down but he messed up position on the blue and, though he potted it, missed the next red. With six points, he'd made his highest break of the evening.

'The popular bet's Sean Keane,' Christophe continued. 'You know he hasn't been seen since his flat was set alight?'

'You're putting two and two together and coming up with *cinque*, Chris.'

'Perhaps but, be honest, there's a connection, isn't there? I mean, there just *is*.'

Patrick watched him clear up the balk colours, until a lazy foul on the brown, but the point of no return had long been reached and Patrick was happy to concede.

'Shall I get the drinks in?' the Frenchman asked.

'Loser's privilege, surely.' Patrick headed to the bar and let his colleague rack up the balls for the next frame. On a whim, he ordered a double whisky and smashed it back without Christophe noticing. It was essential he kept his mouth shut and his head clear, but he needed to unknot himself; what Jenna said, or was saying, at the police station was out of his control. He couldn't stop looking at his shattered watch.

Christophe was refining his aim at the table when Patrick returned. 'Those guys are looking over,' the French teacher said, nodding to the far end of the snooker hall. Patrick's paranoia went into overdrive and he span round to face the cops. But they weren't cops. Just two kids, barely older than school age. Patrick was getting recognised in public again.

He bent forwards to take the break-off shot, fired the cue ball into the triangle of packed reds, sending them fizzing out across the table. One plopped in.

'Nice pot.'

'Yeah, watch your back.' Over-confident, Patrick missed an easy black off its spot. 'This game's impossible. I'm losing to a guy with arthritis.'

'I don't need to do much with my hands. They stay in more-or-less the same position.'

'I'm sorry, Chris.' The drink was already talking. 'Seriously. It must be painful.'

'They're not causing me too much of a problem at the moment,' was said knowingly enough to set off incendiary devices in Patrick's mind. If Christophe was getting his grass from Sean Keane, or via sources connected to him, the flat fire meant his supply would soon be drying up, if it hadn't already.

'Why's that then?' Patrick aimed for blithe but managed just shy of panic-stricken.

Christophe wasn't looking at him, and it was then that Patrick realised, all evening, in the run up to this moment, they'd been as nervous as each other. 'Oh. Well. I found two bags of skunk in my summer house. It's shitty stuff but it does the trick.'

Patrick swore.

The security light. The neighbour's barking dog. A twitched curtain.

Patrick had hurled the bags into the back of the summer house and bolted. For all Christophe's security features, he left his side gate unlocked. Patrick had no experience in evidence concealment, so could perhaps be forgiven for not thinking straight that night, and figured it was better to gift the evidence to a user, on the other side of London, and let them puff the stuff out of existence. He hadn't expected Christophe to find the stash so rapidly. What the hell had the man been doing in his summer house in the middle of winter?

Patrick said the words before he could veto them: 'Don't tell anyone, will you?' His voice was higher than usual as he leaned over the baize, lanced the cue ball onto the carpet. His hysteria was having pejorative influences upon his volume too. 'I mean, *God knows* where it came from,' he shouted.

Anxiety etched itself into Christophe's face. 'But what if someone wants it back?'

Patrick stooped to pluck up the white and placed it behind the balk-line, watched his friend tap it into the D with a careful stroke of his cue tip. He knew he should have just thrown the grass away, or burnt it in the kiln with the rest of the proof of Jenna's crime, stoning the whole third floor in the process. Now he'd handed the evidence to a man whom Meadows was informing firsthand about suspects.

'They won't. It's on your property. It's yours now.'

Christophe placed a steadying hand upon his colleague's shoulder. Patrick's flinch was almost controlled.

'But property is theft, Patrick. Remember? Let's stop the act now. I thought it was a very... kind gesture. If a little stupid.' The Frenchman stalked the table like a hunter, nervous smile illuminated archly by canopy lighting. He fired in a red, then the pink. 'Whose was it?' he asked, squatting golfer-like to eye up his next shot.

'Denis's,' Patrick replied, replacing the pink ball.

Christophe didn't even blink.

'Seven,' Patrick declared.

'Forgive my curiosity, but last week you made a startling announcement. Might that have some bearing on my recent gift?'

'Eight. Nice shot. Sadly, there is a connection, yes.'

The blue disappeared.

'Thirteen.'

Christophe paused to allow Patrick time to replace the ball. 'And by donating me my... pain relief... Are you asking me to keep quiet about what I know?'

'You don't know the half of it.'

'I've always been of the opinion that ignorance is bliss, Patrick, but in this case I think there's one piece of information I ought to be privy to.'

'I didn't kill him.'

Christophe straightened and looked Patrick in the eye. Relief shined an inner light. 'My friend, that's all I needed to know.'

The door buzzer propelled him into a world of pain.

Patrick slouched from his bed, smeared his hands across the dark hollows of his eyes. Hangovers now possessed a septic brutality they'd never attained in his twenties and the world lurched violently. What had happened after he'd left the snooker club? Why did the taste of kebab meat soil his mouth?

The buzzer went again and Patrick swore.

It was the police. It had to be.

Patrick shivered to recall the coward's words as she'd sat, so secure of her gambit, upon her bed that night:

'Denis told me you hit him.'

Jenna had a knowledge which put him at the vanguard of suspects and had made it clear she'd use such knowledge against him if he declined to help her.

She'd been desperate, but that alone didn't forgive her, nor him his collusion; he could have stood by his assertion to walk to the police station there and then. No, the real clincher was her threat of gang involvement. If he'd refused to help, she knew a plethora of barely pubic but dangerous people who could and would persuade him. It had seemed so much more civilised to keep his secret between them.

But Patrick hadn't been thinking properly that night. It wasn't their secret alone.

Denis had been with five of his gang the evening he'd hit him. Five mouths which, loyal to Denis in death, could have said anything to anyone by now.

Between his classroom encounter with Mary Haynes and the snooker hall confessions with Christophe, Patrick had found time to hastily replant the murder weapon in his Art room. It was safe for a few more days but if Meadows and his team had a warrant…

If only he could get the gun to Christophe's too. The Frenchman, though far from onside, was surely the one person he could trust at the moment.

The buzzer went again. And again.

It hurt his face to frown. Surely even the police wouldn't have been so persistent?

He walked slowly into the hallway, peered into the video monitor.

His son's monochrome face hovered inside the little television. 'Are you going to let us stand out here all morning?' Ana's voice sang off-screen.

He buzzed them up.

'DaddyDaddyDaddy!' his son was the first to arrive, tackling his legs and clinging like a vine.

'You look as shit as you do in the newspaper,' Ana said, arriving at his door. She slipped past him, taking a rapid look around his flat and making the kind of sigh only the perennially unsurprised can muster. The flat, messy and chaotic, was the physical manifestation of how Patrick currently felt.

Danny ran round in circles, interspersing his gymnastics with little jumps. 'DaddyDaddyDaddy!'

Ana was already clearing his coffee table of mugs. 'There's mould on this one. I wouldn't say no to a cup of tea. That's if you've got any cups left.' Gingerly fishing a teabag out of a mug, she dangled its dry carcass in front of him. She was dressed for battle: a black body warmer was her flak jacket; her tied-back hair shone like Kevlar.

'Sit down. I'll see what I can find us.' He hobbled into the kitchen, leaving his wife to pick her way to the sofa, peeling back jumpers and takeaway cartons.

'Hangover?' she called.

'Stop shouting. And where the hell have you been? You told me you were going back to Argentina. Your mother even called me.'

It was unknown territory, this. They were still married, but she didn't owe him an explanation. But his concern, for her, and especially for their son, was genuine and they both knew that. It wasn't an opportunity to score points.

'I was thinking.'

'You were *thinking*?' He walked back into the lounge.

Danny jumped from the sofa, to the armchair, to the sofa.

'Danny!' Ana shouted.

'It's okay.'

'See,' Danny chided. 'Daddy says it's okay! Daddy says it's okay!'

'You'll hurt yourself.'

Patrick scooped him up, held him close. The strong, warm limbs wrapped themselves around him again.

'What were you thinking about?' he asked.

'Us. Amongst other things.'

'I didn't think there was an Us.'

'I've got a job.'

'Where? Here? In London?'

She nodded.

'What job? Who have you been staying with? I've been calling all your friends.'

'I know you have.'

'Why didn't you call your mum? She was worried.'

'No. *You* worried her. I'm sorry. I just... needed some time.' She inspected her hair in the mirror above the sofa, expressed disappointment with something about it, then ran a hand through its front as if to unknot it.

'You could have left Danny with me.'

'Really?' She made a show of looking around the flat, its galleries of unkempt bachelorhood. 'You can't even look after yourself at the moment. Have you seen what you look like?'

Danny grabbed his father's cheeks and pulled them, laughing. 'You look silly, Daddy. You look like a poobum.'

'Seriously,' she asked. 'Are you okay?'

Though he longed to speak to a person removed from the darkness in Union City, this was never going to represent a normalcy of adult communication with his son tugging at his face. In any case, Ana couldn't be expected to provide her husband sanctuary any longer. Motherhood was, these days, her true subtext. Murder his alone.

Ana paused for a long time. He hadn't forgotten what the tonality of her silences meant; she wasn't going to let it go.

'Patrick... What's happened?'

'You read the paper. You know. One of my pupils died.'

'And that's all?'

He was taken aback by what, at first, seemed the almost uncaring nature of her question, but became quickly aware that the hiatus this engendered lent his reply the impression of being considered: 'Yes.'

'Would you like us to stay?' she asked.

Danny climbed down. 'Look at this,' their son demanded, performing a frankly laughable handstand. 'And I've got Spiderman pants.'

'I'd love you to stay,' Patrick admitted. 'But there's no room.'

'The other day, you said…'

'Look, I'm not being rude. But I don't want you mixed up in this.'

'Mixed up in what?'

'There's a press conference tomorrow which I've agreed to take part in. I'm going to be busy.'

'All the more reason for me to be around, to give you help.'

He looked at her, unable to hide his affection. But the affection fought too many other emotions now. Patrick was on the brink of caving in, but knew it would be so much worse for Danny if he was arrested while they stayed under his roof.

'I'm sorry. It's just not possible.'

'Patrick. Tell me. What is it?'

He couldn't bear her eyes upon him. His vocation was a second choice one, their marriage was in cinders, his body a wreck. He was an accomplice to murder.

'Danny,' she said, 'go and play in your room.'

'What's wrong with Daddy's eyes?'

'Just go.'

When she came for him, hugged him, he wanted to bawl like a baby but all he could do was shiver. She stirred fear, rather than self-remorse.

'What is it, Patrick? What is it?'

Danny was watching him through the crack in the door, as though this was all a brilliant excuse for a game of hide and seek. Caught in her arms, her familiar scent, Patrick knew this moment was probably about as good as things were going to get for a while.

The buzzer went again.

When he arrived at the hallway monitor, Sarah's face was pressed into the screen. He tiptoed back and closed the lounge door, then pushed the intercom.

'What are you doing here?'

'You invited me, remember? Last night?'

'I don't remember anything. I'm sorry but you can't come in. My... mother's here. How's Jenna?'

'She thinks I'm at the shops,' didn't answer his question. Both mother and daughter were sneaking out of home whenever the other's guard was down. 'Come on. Let me in. I came all this way. We *need* to talk.'

'What's happened?'

Sarah's expression darkened and she lowered her voice still further. Patrick had to lean in to hear her. 'I mentioned... the gun and stuff... to the police. I had to tell them, Patrick. They were at the flat with dogs. You know, sniffing the area, places he'd been. Jenna went to the station to explain everything. It's for the best. It was... It was *his* stuff. It was Denis's... I had to describe the gun. They seem to think it's the one that killed Denis. Jenna's room was searched and there's this dirty black powder left where they hunted for fingerprints... Come on. Let me in. It's freezing.'

Patrick struggled to recall whether he'd touched anything that night without his gloves, but he didn't think so. He also doubted it was possible to get a precise date from a fingerprint and, in any case, he'd been in Jenna's room with Sarah that evening; any prints were legit. Remaining blood traces were a bigger concern, in the hallway, the bathroom, despite how thoroughly teacher and student had cleaned everything. He knew next to nothing about forensics except that, in television drama, microscopic evidence was enough to catch the killer every episode.

What had Jenna coughed up? How much more did the police know? 'So, are we in the clear about...?'

Danny burst out of his room and ran to him.

'Found you! Found you! Hahahahahaha!'

'Patrick, what is going on? Why invite me over and...?'

'So... we're all clear. The gun and that...? They released her without charge?'

'They told me I'd done the right thing.' On the screen, she turned her head in profile and stared across the street, perhaps to drink in a middle-class view bereft of burning flats, patrolling gangs. The hushed austerity in her voice told him she was trying to convince herself. 'I did the right thing.'

Without another word, she left.

Patrick hoisted his son back up into his arms and walked into the front room.

Ana was standing at the window, watching Sarah stalk across the road. In her eyes he read rivalry, suspicion, relief, hurt. His wife, after all those years, was easy to translate, yet as closed as anyone had ever felt to him. She didn't say a word for a while as he waited for the façade to break, for a hint of how she felt to be transmitted to him. In the end, it all came with a sigh and a reminder for that promised cup of tea.

'It's complicated,' he explained.

'It always is, Patrick. It always is.'

FOUR

Patrick leaned against the stage stairs and attempted to look relaxed in the suit he'd been wearing for a whole term. This particular jacket had a retch of blue acrylic on the left sleeve and no matter how often he'd polished his shoes they'd steadfastly refused to shine.

Twenty or so journalists were already hunkered in Highfields' hall, before a plain white lectern sporting several microphones and the Metropolitan Police emblem on its front. A compact black television camera was set up in the aisle, standing high on fragile stilts, and there was a framed picture to the left of the stage, the same photo of Denis every paper was printing, blown up to A3.

Mr Hutchinson clearly loved the idea of Highfields hosting the press conference, seeing it as the perfect way to make up for the humiliating incident with the reporter whilst raking together some publicity for a school 'fighting from the front line', so was able to rush the idea past the governors. Guests were hooked out of the local pool of concerned parents and, such was the draw of Denis's murder, a full house was anticipated.

DCI Meadows went over, one last time, what was required of Patrick and Denis's mother as they watched the dignitaries arrive.

Denis's mother was almost unrecognisable. Her skin was blotchy beneath excessive make-up and her hair was a dark, mid-length nest of angry curls, specially dressed and dyed, he guessed, for this terrible occasion. If he'd been led to believe she might have been vaguely eye-catching once, before the sleepless midnights and chronic rosacea, she now looked several decades of heartache past her prime. The newly purchased black dress didn't disguise her obesity.

'Thank you for this.' She broke the silence once Meadows disappeared briefly to speak to his team. 'It's very, you know, *proper* of you.'

Another silence fell.

'What went wrong?' she sniffed

'What indeed?'

Patrick's question was as hypothetical as hers had been, but she appeared to genuinely think it over. When she replied she did so through a hardened jaw. 'You know something? When his dad died – five years old, he was – he stood on the sofa and volunteered to be his own daddy.'

The teacher rubbed his shoes together. He felt obliged to say something, but nothing came to him.

'Denis didn't get much of a chance,' she continued. It was a clichéd going-off-the-rails story, but her analysis, no doubt the condensed highlights from two days of fevered guilt, was a theory designed to absolve rather than lionise. Denis's father was abusive when drunk, weak when sober, and Denis, in line with his ten-year-old Oedipal suggestion, eschewed parental role models and took to the street, where he did become, to all intents and purposes, 'the daddy'. 'They searched my place all over, Mr Owers. I know there was rumours he was selling drugs but they found *nothin'*.' Was the pride in her voice because her son was sensible enough to hide his merchandise in someone else's bedroom, or because her confidence in him as a law-abider remained unchallenged?

He found himself saying, 'I'm happy to help, if I can. Whatever you need.' Teachers having no call for business cards, Patrick scribbled his number on a Sainsbury's receipt and passed it over. 'I mean it. Anything, just give me a call.'

Patrick caught Meadows' eye.

'I'll let you know when the funeral is, Mr Owers.'

Behind the Inspector, Sarah and Jenna shuffled towards empty seats. They both wore similar blue dresses, which Patrick doubted was deliberate – it was more likely an unfortunate symptom of the event's short notice. His heart sagged somewhat when he spotted Jenna's father with them. Jenna, as expected, couldn't look Patrick's way.

Sarah claimed the chair with her coat then made her way towards him.

'Hello,' he said, as Denis's mother peeled away. 'You're looking nice.'

Sarah smiled a non-committal smile. 'Is this okay? Talking to you?'

'It's fine by me. Sorry about yesterday. I'm *technically* still married and my mother's very... you know...' He nodded towards Sarah's ex, who sat checking for messages on his phone. 'I didn't know you'd *all* be here.'

'He was around, so...'

'He's been a good source of... support?' Patrick asked. He tried to lace the question with a degree of casualness, but jealousy dripped through.

'For Jenna, yes. I think so.'

'Diplomatic.'

'What does that mean?'

'Nothing. I don't know. You really do look very beautiful.'

Looking past him and scowling seemed to be her way of forcing herself not to blush. It didn't work.

'I mean it, you...'

'Alright. You told me.' The redder she blushed, the angrier she seemed to become. 'I better...' She indicated her seat.

'Okay. Thank you for coming. See you later?'

'Good luck tonight.'

Sarah strolled back up the aisle to sit next to Jenna, the adolescent shock absorber between parents. Patrick looked worriedly round the hall, knowing full well what cynicisms the recent paedophile taunts carried as their by-line.

Who had written that on his door on Friday? Had they been responsible for the vandalism and those accusations all along?

Two reporters shuffled past, nodded at Patrick's name badge.

By now the venue was almost full and many journos, presumably those who'd been seated since the advertised five thirty start (it was now quarter to six), showed signs of professional boredom on top of their glazed, overworked fatigue. The one injured by PC Thomas was sitting at the front, bandage like a miniature swing under his swollen snout, two seats to the left of a stony-faced Mr Hutchinson.

Finally, Ana slipped in, with Danny asleep in a pushchair. She braked his throne and perched herself in the back row. Suddenly, this felt very, very, real.

Meadows approached the lectern, lights casting dramatic shadows across his solemn face. Uniformed policemen lined the walls, watched his preliminary shuffling of blank papers.

'Good afternoon. Thank you all for coming...,' he began, and his audience bowed heads in note-taking contrition.

He gave out Denis's details, the location of the found body, dates, timelines, last sightings, and spoke with an easy beam, a surety, only once referring to his notes. He declared, 'possible witnesses are being interviewed.'

Patrick's speech fluttered in his hand.

Denis's mother was politely invited to the front and cameras fired off flashes as a monastic hush fell over the hall.

Meadows flanked her as she eulogised her offspring. It was the usual stuff: a caring boy, a loving son, taken too early. Most of her speech centred on finding the 'criminal', a word she pronounced as though it were a more vulgar term, and despite using the word 'justice', as opposed to revenge, everyone knew what she meant. The police investigation – which Meadows' team, at least at this point, didn't know how to advance; otherwise, Patrick rationalised, none of this would be necessary – was a sidebar to her disgust of humanity itself. Seeing her there, drenched in hellfire, there was a lot of Denis about her.

Towards the end, she deviated from the script and flapped a heavy arm towards 'Mr Owers' and thanked him for his 'dedication' before stuttering to the finish line, whereby she broke down in a fanfare of snot and animal noises and was gently steered off-stage by Mary Haynes of Murder Investigation, who'd rushed in like a boxer's trainer at the bell.

Meadows introduced Patrick.

Tomblike silence. The Art teacher walked into exploding flashbulbs, flattened a speech written by some budding Met bard out on the lectern and tried to focus on its nonsensical hieroglyphs. His heart punched in his throat and his ears whined. In the fourth row, Sarah's encouraging but nervous smile. In the last, his wife stared with mute suspicion at the back of Sarah's head.

'It's estimated there are one hundred and seventy gangs with five thousand members in London alone,' he read, 'children who assemble in expensive trainers, low-slung jeans and hoodies as dusk falls. They've replaced the names their parents gave them in favour of new identities, forging an alternative family. Their lifestyle breeds contempt for anyone not involved in the gang world: politicians, parents, teachers. Some join out of boredom and many have no qualifications so have to make money their own way. An honour code binds these young people to crime, to violence...' He paused for dramatic effect. '...And even to murder.'

As Meadows had explained to him, his presence was designed purely to capitalise on the media interest surrounding the case, not call upon the public at large to throw away their weapons. Yet the speech he'd been prepared was nothing short of tub-thumping. As he read, his teacher training kicked him into the moment and it sounded, even to his wounded ears, an inflected, impassioned plea.

'But not all our children are potential loaded guns. World-weariness doesn't lead inevitably to moral corruption. This is a senseless waste of a young life and we call upon anyone, if they should know anything, to come forward. All information will be treated in strictest confidence. We need to bring *union* to Union City. Thank you.'

As he prepared to walk off, a reporter threw a question.

'Mr Owen? A certain newspaper has suggested sending any teenager found carrying a weapon straight into the army. What are your opinions on this?'

'I really don't…' He looked to the back row for help but his wife could only offer an anxious smile.

The broken-nosed journalist seized his chance. 'And what about teachers, Mr Owen? Aren't they in some way accountable for failing to instil a moral code in young people?'

Patrick wasn't supposed to be taking part in any Q and A; that was Meadows' responsibility. But the Inspector still stood to one side, whispering with his colleagues.

Patrick coughed into the microphone and a squeal of feedback rang throughout the hall.

The broken-nosed journalist persevered. 'Three-quarters of all young, violent crime suspects are freed on bail while awaiting Crown Court trials, sending out the message that they can get away with anything. Youth crime was up a third last year. The government has failed. I repeat, what are schools doing to instil morals in our young?'

Mr Hutchinson flashed a concerned look at his Art teacher, dabbed a handkerchief to his soaking forehead.

'Look… I hardly think it's the fault of the schools,' Patrick explained. 'You quote a good statistic, but if anyone's to blame it's you lot. A kid gets stabbed on the street and it's front page news the next day. Instant glorification. '

There was murmuring from the audience. Whether it was of an approving or disapproving nature he couldn't tell.

'Most of the time you bang on about "our responsibilities", how "we" oughtn't fail low-achieving children but…' He

193

didn't know where he was going with this. Half the audience were looking at him with wide-eyed approval, as though he could steer them towards the cures to society's ills, and the other half, the half with Teeline shorthand in their blood, sharpened pencils. 'I mean...' How had Meadows put it? 'Have you noticed how innocent the dead become...?'

In the grim silence which followed, the hall's main doors opened.

It took Patrick very little time before he recognised the boy from the footage on Matthew's phone. He was dressed exactly the same. Gold trainers. Grey tracksuit trousers. Black top. White cap. Patrick felt his blood curdle in his veins: when he'd retrieved the gun from the murder site, *this* was what he'd been dressed like. The boy's presence, the way he looked idly for support over the heads of the audience, as though his very appearance were against his will, freaked Patrick out. Why had this unknown youth bought himself an identical set of clothes to the ones he'd been stripped of in the video? The clothes Patrick had burned in the kiln upstairs. What the hell was he doing in Highfields' school hall?

As one, the audience turned to look at the intruder. Except for Meadows, who glared with violating intensity straight at Patrick.

The boy was approached by a teacher and, after a brief conversation, walked his gold trainers out the way they'd come. Meadows stared Patrick's way a little longer, then walked up to the lectern.

The Art teacher tried to concentrate on what the Inspector was saying, but felt himself pulled into a bottomless underworld of fear.

Meadows knew. He *knew*.

'Ladies and Gentlemen, thank you for coming...'

A creak, stage left. A rattle of quick feet.

There came a whistling noise, the waspish sound of rope whipping through a pulley, followed by a loud crack as the ceiling fell and flapped about a metre behind Patrick and

Meadows. The gasps from the audience couldn't mask the drumroll of running feet behind the stage, nor the creaking of the projection screen swaying backwards and forwards after its violent deployment.

Meadows turned, whistled at the large image affixed to the screen.

The image of Patrick, stony-faced and official against the school photographer's off-white background, must've been taken from the school website. Someone had crudely photoshopped his eyes red and pasted two hands at the bottom of the picture, dripping with blood. Another vampiric trickle emanated from the corner of his mouth. Scrawled in scarlet across the top of the screen was one word.

Molester.

Mr Hutchinson was out of his chair, nervous laughter resounding through the hall, as fast hands attempted to tear the picture down and hoist the screen back into the rafters. But not before half the room stood to take a photo on their cameras and, as if in some awful re-imagining of *Spartacus*, the other half rose to record the incident on mobile phones. A handful of teachers searched backstage to no avail and, in the fourth row, Sarah's family scurried from their seats.

Through the bodies, he saw Ana reach into the pushchair and pull out Danny, who'd been rudely woken by the commotion just in time to see the photo of his daddy with blood on his hands and lips be torn to shreds by baying strangers. Even over the sound of the congregated governors, parents and journalists, Patrick could make out the pitiful wail of his terrified, confused son.

Meadows assuaged the remaining crowd with talk of gremlins in the machine but in the presence of youth's mutiny the press conference was inconsequential and insincere.

Slapping a counterfeit smile across his face, Patrick bolted from the hall.

FIVE

He found mother and daughter arguing in the playground, Jenna's father between them, attempting to coo the women into acquiescence. Several parent clusters braved shrill winds to view the showdown, to gossip about the fact or fiction which had unfurled above the hall stage.

Jenna's friend Marie stood nearby, smug and cold in plastic trousers and ten centimetre rubber heels. She dragged Jenna away when she saw Patrick approach. 'That was epic,' she muttered, as the two girls scurried off.

Patrick stood a short distance from Sarah, the ex-husband rising himself by a fraction but holding his ground, a leashed Doberman awaiting its command.

It was Sarah who spoke first. 'So...' she whistled. 'That went well...'

Patrick squinted to make her out. All the classrooms had been doused and the playground itself had no form of illumination. 'What were you and Jenna arguing about?'

He was aware of whispering behind him, a sparking of cigarettes.

'Patrick, you were just publicly accused of...' She lowered her voice. 'Maybe it's not worth it. I think people might be confused by your motives...'

'Motives?'

'My daughter's certainly not happy you've done this.'

'She wouldn't be.' It occurred to him that, in the aftermath of the conference, he should perhaps be more careful about what his tongue gave away. 'I mean, Denis attacked her. I haven't forgotten that. I know he wasn't an angel but I didn't write what I just read out. I'm not some colossal attention-seeker; I was essentially blackmailed into doing this.'

'Well, maybe now… Stop.' She stood closer, her tone so serious it scared him. 'Patrick, people might not understand why you're martyring yourself. They realise you care about the children you teach but… The killer always cries in front of the camera, doesn't he?'

Patrick felt a nasty, coppery sensation in his mouth, as though he'd bitten into an ulcer. She was right. He was firmly in the line of fire now.

Jenna's father sensed his opportunity to interrupt.

'Alright,' he said, stepping up to Patrick too, staring him down. 'I think this conversation has gone on long enough. Go home.'

'Pardon?'

'My daughter's upset. Seriously, piss off now, pal.'

The gruff pitch of voice was clear; the meathead was actually picking a fight with the one person specifically chosen by the Metropolitan Police to sell the press conference.

Patrick felt sufficiently emboldened to say, 'Or what?'

He'd been in few fights in his life – three in fact; two drunken and one very messy incident with his former lead singer – but he knew the element of surprise was the only way he was ever likely to come out on top against a man of Mike's build, and that element of surprise had been efficiently removed by his aggressor's unashamed grandstanding. The only option, surprise-wise, left to Patrick appeared to be to punch him first, before all the boring, macho preamble could be curtailed by sensible, female intervention. As he swung his fist, the disconcerting realisation that he'd lost his three previous fights hit him in return.

There came a joyful gasp from the crowd as his knuckles clipped Mike's chin.

The next moment, Patrick was on the playground tarmac and pain scorched his brain to a ragtime beat of steel drums. A crowd was gathering above him, dark silhouettes against a waning moon.

He heard an altercation between Sarah and Mike, gazed groggily upwards to see her grab him by the jacket and swing him away into the night.

Sarah bent down, helped him into a sitting position. 'Amateur welterweight boxing champion two years running. He got you with the classic counter punch. Does it hurt?'

'Yep.'

He let himself be helped to his feet and the onlookers stepped back. With one thing and another, he'd surely provided them enough entertainment tonight, but still they hung about for more.

Sarah reached out and prodded his cheekbone. Patrick winced.

'Nothing broken. He wasn't trying to kill you.'

'Charming.'

Ana stepped forward out of the crowd. 'See,' she cooed to Danny, pointing at Patrick, 'Daddy's alright. There he is, *with a strange lady touching his face*.'

Danny jumped from her and shyly lolled over to his father, reached his arms up so he could be lifted off the playground.

'I didn't know your *mother* would be here,' Sarah said mock-politely, indicating Ana.

The two women eyeballed one another with a strangely pleasant curiosity.

'Aren't you going to introduce us, Patrick?' Ana asked.

A door exploded and Mr Hutchinson barrelled out of reception. 'Mr Owen,' he boomed. 'A word, if you *don't mind*.'

Union City had its own heartbeat, an anomalous quickstep of slammed doors and distant yodels. A resonance. The world heard through the stomach of an expectant mother.

Mr Hutchinson and PC Thomas had grilled Patrick, with predictable banality, about who might have a grudge against him for an interminable time and, Sarah and Ana gone their own ways, he was now so tired he could barely walk straight. His right eye was a shameful coin of purple bruise and, though this was a corner of the estate he'd traversed a hundred times, Patrick had never felt such an outsider before. Every flickering streetlight or drip of water was a merciless assault on his senses and, as the heartbeat around him quickened, he stopped to inspect his surroundings. Windows were steamed by cooking pots and poor ventilation, bricks inscribed with initials of lovers or victims. Grand boasts amid the sameness.

His phone buzzed a text message. It was from Ana.

I DON'T TRUST HER

A shifting shadow awaited him underneath a fire exit, jade light across young features.

'How you doing, Mr Owen?'

The amplified voice was older than its face would suggest, a surly bass which echoed off his mildewed alcove. The boy was affecting a degree of power and, with the estate on all sides, achieved it.

Matthew had good reason to be confident. The police would almost definitely have interviewed him, over his brother's whereabouts if for nothing else, but gang members were easily backed up by the alibis of peers and his anonymity as a suspect was guaranteed. He was too young and too alive to make the news.

Patrick uttered the boy's name as though it repulsed him.

Matthew stepped forward, raised his nose and circled shoulders in defiance. One hand held a spliff and the other was bandaged waist-height by its cage of dull metal. The mix of the boy and the adult made him a curiously sinister specimen.

'Run into some beef back there, did you sir?'

'You need to learn to mind your own business.' Patrick walked on past the boy.

He wasn't Denis, that much was clear. Patrick could see through his ganglord pretensions. He'd met hundreds of teenagers in his time and knew genuine trouble when it accosted him. Matthew had never carried himself the way Denis did. It wasn't as easy for him.

'Maybe you do too, sir.'

Patrick stopped, turned around.

'What does that mean?'

Matthew inspected Patrick carefully. 'We don't like you talking on behalf of D-Man. Interfering.'

'I don't believe this. I was *forced into that press conference...*'

'Back off, sir. Leave us alone.'

What did it matter to Matthew what Patrick had or hadn't said about Denis? Did the boy see himself as a new general, stepping into Denis's shiny Nikes? Perhaps the media's inevitable immortalisation of D-Man had made the gang-leader position, if that's what Denis had held, more lustrous. Or maybe Matthew was in a rival gang and was worried a state-paid educator lauding his enemy's 'innocence in death' would detract credibility from his own crew, tar it with his very adulthood. Either way, Denis was an overnight martyr, with or without approval from Art teachers, and Matthew, wherever he sat in whichever gang's hierarchy, was probably sore about that.

Patrick, averting his head from Matthew's hiss of cannabis smoke, became aware of ten, eleven, twelve hooded shadows hovering at the corner of the block and then automatically searched above for evidence of CCTV. Predictably, he found none.

'I wasn't aware I was getting in anyone's way. Who am I supposed to "leave alone" exactly?'

'Stay out of my way. Stay out of the Souljas' way. And stay out of Jenna's way.'

Mention of Sarah's daughter winded Patrick. She was above such petty rivalries, surely?

She was a killer.

Matthew flicked his joint to the floor and scraped it to ribbons underfoot. Under the green light of the fire exit, Patrick could make out spots of brown paint upon his shoes. Warning bells rang in Patrick's head.

If there was one thing Patrick was an expert on, it was colour mixing; what looked like brown paint under green light wasn't brown at all. It was red.

'*You…?*'

Matthew followed Patrick's gaze down, shrugged. 'You can't prove nothing.'

Patrick thought better of correcting him on his grammar. Matthew may have had a tough older brother and an attitude copied from Denis, but his use of paedophile slurs only underscored his immaturity.

'And the doll on my desk…? The writing on my door…? God, you're pathetic. What was the point of that sick picture just now?' Patrick was struggling to keep his anger in check.

'Don't know what you're talking about, innit.' Something behind the cruel pair of dark eyes told him Matthew wasn't really there. They weren't having this conversation. 'Stay out of our business, stop all this shit about standing up to gangs and drugs and whatever, yeah?'

'Or *what*?'

'We don't want another front page, do we?' the boy threatened. The gang on the corner stood their ground. London's wind carried Siberia's winter from the north, whistled it through the crumbling passageways and impenetrable shadows of the estate. 'I know things about you.'

Patrick's breath was a ripple of mist between them. 'You don't know *anything* about me.'

'I know… what Jenna knows.'

The teacher's blood ran cold.

'I don't have a clue what you're talking about.'

'We don't speak to the police, as a rule. We deal with things ourselves. But they've been sniffing round my family for days. Maybe they'll leave us alone once they hear about your own reasons for popping D-Man. What do you think? Won't look too good, will it?' Despite the street patois, his threats were clear.

'I'll think about it.' It was an adult's standard postponement of a child's request, but Matthew had proved himself, against Patrick's expectations, to be somewhat more calculating than most children. He possessed a hand that could indict his elder of murder.

'I mean it,' Matthew pressed. 'Leave us alone.'

'Again the "us"? Who exactly are you speaking on behalf of?'

Matthew smirked. 'I'm speaking on behalf of my boys.'

And with that, Matthew walked back towards them.

Thirty metres on, Patrick risked a look over his shoulder and was relieved to find, once again, that it was only his own feet which echoed through the darkness.

My boys, Matthew had said. But Patrick was in little doubt his gang included girls too.

The phone rang just as he was getting ready for bed.

'Very handsome,' Sarah breathed into his ear.

'What?'

'I just caught your press conference on TV. You see it?'

'Of course not. Did they include…'

'You bet they did.'

'Bloody hell.'

'Patrick, I'm worried about her. Is this the sort of thing that's likely to send a child off the rails?' The abrupt change of subject told him they'd already arrived at the meat of the conversation, and that her announcement that he'd been labelled a child molester on national television was merely an opener.

'Daughters aren't really my field of expertise, Sarah. What were you two arguing about in the playground, anyway?'

She emitted a dismissive grunt, but he couldn't decipher the depth of her subsequent silence; they hadn't known each other long enough for such clairvoyance. It was the second time she'd evaded that question.

'Perhaps it's best to give her some space,' he suggested, 'but let her know you're there for her if she needs you. Is... what's-his-name still there?'

'Mike?'

'Yeah. I guess she's finding him a reassuring figure...'

'He left. *I* didn't find him a particularly "reassuring figure".'

'Right. Good. I must admit I didn't entirely warm to him.'

'Maybe you should stop picking fights in playgrounds.'

Patrick laughed a cold laugh. 'Actually, would it be possible to... speak to Jenna?' He knew it was risky but he had to know what Matthew knew, whether Jenna had gone back on her word. What had Matthew said? *I know what Jenna knows.* 'I wanted to apologise to her.'

'She's at her father's. Why do you think I'm risking calling you?'

They were still running round behind Jenna's back. Her emotions were conflicted, he knew that, but she still contacted him, came to visit. Was it only out of fear? Were they bonded purely by their terrible situation, or was there something more?

'I had a nice chat with your wife earlier.'

'Oh shit.'

'No, seriously. She's nice.'

'She is?' He recalled Ana's text message. The respect wasn't mutual.

'And your son's adorable. You're very lucky. And...'

A scream almost forced Patrick to drop the phone in alarm.

'What? *What?*'

She whispered. 'Outside. I saw...'

'What is it? Sarah?'

'At the window. I thought... I'll be back. Hold on.'

Patrick pressed his ear to the phone, imagined he could hear her walk across the carpet, her hesitation before she opened the front door. The handle would be cold and damp to the touch, transferring the chill of the outdoors. Maybe she was picking out an improvised weapon from beneath the coat rack as she swung open the door, wielding the shaking umbrella like a sword. The first thing she'd see would be her own shadow on the cracked balcony walkway, accompanied by a slide of footwear on broken tile. Across the street, the ruin of Matthew's brother's home. A few insects fluttering around streetlights. And then...

'You still there?' Her voice was loud, unsure.

Patrick spluttered in relief. 'Did you see anything? What was it?'

'Can I come over?' she asked. 'Right away?'

He buzzed her into the apartment building and she arrived at his door looking cold and miserable. There was a hunted, startled look about her and several times, even once indoors, she cast a look over her shoulder.

'What's the matter?'

'I might've been followed.'

He turned off the light and strode to the curtains, though saw very little except the glow of houses opposite. There was a shadow moving near the end of his street, but it turned out to be the old guy with the dodgy leg from number eleven putting out his recycling.

'There's no one there.'

She threw her arms around him, and he could feel her heart beating through their clothes.

'You're shivering with cold. Didn't you bring a coat?'

'I'm fine.'

'I'm running you a bath.' He went to the bathroom and twisted the hot water tap. When he returned she was at the window, biting her nails. 'Anything?'

'No.'

He had another look up and down the street. Nothing.

'Thank you,' she said. 'This is very kind of you.'

'There are towels in the airing cupboard next to the bath. I'll fix you something to eat.'

Obediently, she started on her way to the bathroom. Then she stopped. 'Your wife...'

'What about her?'

'She's not staying with you?'

'We're separated. I told you.'

Sarah looked around her, as though confirming his assertions. 'But, earlier, she seemed to be suggesting that...'

'What?'

'I don't know. Like, maybe, you were back on.'

'Was she now?' Patrick tried hard to hide the emotion in his voice and hid it so well he had no idea what the emotion even was. It irritated him that his wife would dare to say such a thing, and yet... Those vows weren't uttered out of tradition only. It was, after all, his wife's job to frighten off other women.

'But...' she continued, 'I'm the one who's here, aren't I?' She splayed her hands to illustrate the fact. 'I want you in my life, Patrick, but I'm worried you'll find all this too much. I was determined never to see you again, after Jenna found out about us, but circumstances keep forcing us together, don't they?'

'How romantic, Ms Ellis.'

'It's all an accident, isn't it? Attraction? I mean, no one falls for someone on purpose.'

'I guess not.'

And with that she walked to the bathroom and he heard the gurgle of pipes as she turned off the hot tap and added cold. He imagined her slipping off clothes, checking the water's temperature with a toe, and poured himself a large tumbler of whisky while listening out for the sound of the bathroom lock.

It never came.

He placed his liquor to one side, walked slowly to the hall. Standing with his nose to the bathroom door, caressing the wood grain with light fingertips, he listened for further proof that she summoned him.

The slapping of water on skin. The drip drip drip of a combination tap.

Though shielded from one another they were perhaps six feet apart, and the erotic power of the moment was more than Patrick could bear. He was simultaneously aroused and ashamed by his adulterous thoughts and yet, underneath it all, continued to psychoanalyse: of all the people in her life, it was him she'd run to in an emergency, his bath she soaped herself in. That had to mean something. His silent concentration, a desperate repression of breathing as he listened out for every ripple of water or splash or sigh, tightened further his grip on the door handle.

With a deep, slow breath, he pushed open the door.

Re: hello

Adam Roper 8:46

To: Patrick Owen

Hi Patrick,

Since you don't appear to be on facebook (what is that? some kind of teacher anonymous thing?) i thought i'd see if i could smoke you out on this old email address. If i don't get a reply then you've either abandoned this account (a possibility, but it's too much of a pain in the arse to shift all those contacts away from hotmail surely?) or read this but decided not to reply anyway. After all, you're a media darling now. I dropped my phucking Guinness when i saw you on TV last night man!

Are you still in touch with any of the uni lot? Pete? Paula? I still see a few of the old crowd but less and less it seems. Steve was always a fuckwit wasn't he? Except with none of the wit. I saw Toni the other night and she asked if i'd heard from you and then, like ten minutes later, Kismet Kate came on the jukebox. Weird huh?
So me and Kris have been throwing a few ideas around

and we've got some good stuff going. I'm not saying we're thinking of reforming or anything but if you've got a loose end hows about my old axeman dropping this Northern twat a line? Maybe we could meet up for a drink in the big smoke.

Wish i had some news to impart but its same old same old. Jenny dumped me then Ishani dumped me then i dumped Ruby then Jasmine turned out to be a lesbian. I'm too lazy to make a proper decision about my career and still see work as something that funds the rest of my life. Know what i mean? Just can't get my head around that whole living to work as opposed to working to live thing. Basically i'm back selling beds in Land of phucking Furniture and shagging my way through the workforce. No one knows about Jasmine yet but when she comes out i'm going to be a laughing stock man.

Hope this email finds you well.

All the best,
Adam

p.s I'm not going to pretend there isn't an elephant in the room. There is. It's painted like phucking Elmer, yeah? So i might as well address that elephant, for what its worth. I can't hold grudges for this long. Its tiring. I genuinely hope you and Ana are doing well.

p.p.s What's up with our Wiki page at the moment man? Have you seen it? Apparently we are all, and I quote, 'assmunching Mr Owen's peedo bumboys'????!

SIX

Patrick read the email again, looking for a nuance, subtext or piss-take that might have escaped him the first time.

Three times he tried to fashion a reply and three times he failed to affect the suitably convincing nonchalance he desired. For years he'd rehearsed their re-acquaintance speech but had been knocked off-key by Adam's self-deprecations, plain admissions and the line 'I'm not saying we're thinking of reforming or anything.'

In the end, he wrote:

> Hi Adam. Nice to hear from you. Yeah, I DO think you're a northern twat. My number's 07700 900556 and my career's pretty shit too.
> Patrick

It was flippant, curt, insincere. A worthy retort to seven years of cold shoulder. He pressed send and stared out the window for a long time, watching the rain lash the world beyond into an aquarium. It was imperative he keep a low profile now.

He determined to never again speak publicly about Denis Roberts or the fight against youth violence. He wouldn't go to Denis's funeral. He would abandon the assuagement, the public masking, of his culpability and just sit it out. Media appearances were fanning his own shame into a fire and, without recourse to actual proof of innocence, it was, as

Sarah suggested, beginning to look suspicious. And it had rankled the Souljas.

'Hi, hon,' Sarah yawned, entering his front room. She was already dressed in her previous night's clothes.

Patrick slapped his laptop closed. 'How did you sleep?' He rose.

'Not brilliantly. What time have you got to go to work?'

'School starts in half an hour.' He had no intention of going.

'You should've woken me.'

'You looked so… tranquil. Stay here if you want. Or should you get back before Jenna pops home?'

'I should, but not in order to keep up the pretence.' She pressed against him, her breath hot. 'I want it all out in the open. She needs to be taught a few things about honesty.'

'I couldn't agree more.'

'I don't want any more deceptions, Patrick. She's not stupid. She'll know what's going on if I try sneaking around behind her back. And I don't want to be sneaking around anymore.' She turned, ruffled her hair into shape using her reflection on his gold disk.

Was this it? Was this the *relationship* that would finally overthrow his marriage for good? How would Sarah's unfolding affections compare to Ana's? Would she build up his self-esteem over the course of many years only to erode and eventually discard it into adulterous, tearful chaos? Or might he be the one who crushed her ego, supplanting the violent jolt of desire he once felt for her with a newer, less complicated model? Or, was this in fact the mythical, perfect partnership that would carry him with companionable tolerance and sock-darning dotage towards a twinned grave?

He didn't want to even think about it.

'I'll call you a taxi.'

Patrick took her downstairs, shooting a surreptitious look up and down the empty street from under his umbrella. There was no way of knowing how their relationship would end up, and that was probably what made it so exciting last night.

But there wasn't the remotest chance Jenna would welcome her mother's news, which was precisely the reason he'd rung the speaking clock and not the taxi company – to give Jenna those extra few minutes to make her way to school. Things were getting more complicated by the hour and if there was anything he could do to keep Sarah and Jenna's respective secrets from the other then he damn well would.

After waiting another ten minutes, Patrick phoned the cab company and remonstrated with the operative about the car being late. The gruff voice on the other end had no idea what Patrick was angry about but agreed to send a replacement.

When the car arrived, Sarah climbed in. 'Thanks for last night,' she said, blowing him a regal kiss. 'You always seem to be around when I need you.'

As the car drove away, Patrick mimed the kiss landing a little too forcefully and grabbed his heart as if shot by a sniper. It was an act which inspired laughter from Sarah but bestowed him looks of pity from the neighbours marching past.

His mobile trilled and Adam's name flashed on the screen. In all those years, he'd not deleted his bandmate's number.

Patrick let it ring a few times before answering.

'Patrick?'

'Yes?' He threw in a tactical but unconvincing, 'Who's this?'

'Adam. How are you?'

'I'm… That was quick. I only just emailed you.'

'Been in the news I see?' Adam's voice was as sarcastic and carefree as it always had been, though Patrick thought most northerners sounded that way.

'Yeah. Tiresome, isn't it?'

'Shitty about that boy. Did you know him well?'

Patrick was hardly surprised by this line of questioning. It was the easy way in for Adam after so long.

'I can't comment, I'm afraid. Sorry.'

'Sure, sure. I can't believe you're a teacher, man. What do your kids make of you being an old rocker?'

'Most don't have a clue. Even fewer could care.' He was

willing to bet Adam was still living off the glories of rock stardom, milking every tale for more than it was worth down the local.

'So yeah, like I say, we was listening back over some of our stuff and me and Kris have boshed up a few more tracks and it seemed, y'know, a good opportunity to hook up with the old gang.' It wasn't a question, but he let it hang like one.

Patrick found himself walking. Despite the umbrella, the slanting rain had turned his hair into a sticky melange of wax. 'Go on...'

'I guess I just got a bit nostalgic, y'know. Realised I was too old to die young. And then seeing you on the telly. Jesus... I never really found a calling after the band, I'll be honest. I've been in bands me whole life and I got older by accident. I mean... I moved on and all, but... *Our* band, it's still the big thing people talk about to me. You know what I mean?'

Was Adam under the impression The Forsaken had been massive in their time? Even Sarah, who'd claimed to have been a fan, could only name their sole top five hit upon prompting. If Adam was hoping Patrick's recent press would bolster interest in the band, he was well adrift of the truth.

The conversation entered its winding down stage. Adam revealed he was off the methadone. Patrick lied and said he was still writing music.

'You mentioned coming down to London...' Patrick said.

'That's a great idea. Are you free any evenings soon?'

He was standing outside the pub on the corner and, even though it was locked-up for the morning, Patrick imagined he could smell its wet woods and sodden carpet, a ghostly infusion of pre-ban fags. He looked to the sign above the pub door. 'The Old Ale Emporium?' he suggested. 'Tomorrow? About seven?'

A familiar figure awaited him outside The Heights. A mixed-race man with plasters across his nose.

'Did you once hit Denis Roberts, Mr Owen?'

Patrick heard his own voice, from outside his body. 'What are you talking about?'

The well-built journalist swallowed, raised himself an inch. He was dressed in a brown, knee-length coat and green scarf. 'The paper's going to run with the piece but needs the teacher's side for balance. It will be in this evening's edition.'

Even through his stupor of confusion, Patrick knew this was unjust: he'd kept a low profile since being threatened by Matthew, had done what was asked of him.

'Do you have anything to say about these claims?'

'Are you so keen to get back at me for your broken nose that you're willing to risk publishing lies?'

The smile was well controlled. 'It's not editorial policy.'

Patrick barged past him and trembled his door key in the direction of the keyhole.

'Mr Owen, did you hit Denis? Yes or no?'

He succeeded in getting in, slammed the door in the journalist's face.

'Can I have a quote please?' the journalist shouted through the door.

Patrick pressed his middle finger against the glass. 'Quote this.'

Five minutes later, he dared draw back his curtain the width of a castle's arrow-slit to see if Jack the Hack still lurked outside. Instead, he saw four men smoking cigarettes, their cameras flashing while grey clouds swam above.

Stubble snagged fabric as Patrick lurched through restless sleep. He woke to the hallucinatory moaning of what sounded like the school bell and rose unsteadily from the sofa to locate the source of the noise, eventually identifying it as the telephone. Patrick knew, upon hearing the officious panic in Mr Hutchinson's voice, the story had hit.

'You're staying at home indefinitely,' he confirmed. 'There's some unfortunate scaremongering in one of the afternoon papers.' From the acoustics, he assumed the call originated from the boardroom. He was aware of voices in the background, one of which undoubtedly belonged to the gung-ho PC Thomas.

'This is bullshit.'

'You're telling me. Ofsted rang this morning – they're on their way.'

'Don't they have any compassion? A boy died last week.'

'Child safety, Patrick. There'd be uproar if they weren't investigating.' He dropped his voice to a sinister level, betraying his past life as a drama teacher, then added, 'I don't believe what's being said about you, by the way, but… You're in our thoughts.'

Patrick headed straight out to discover the extent of the damage, prising his way through the phalanx of thermos-supping photographers. 'Turn this way, gov,' one of them cried. 'Look sadder, Patrick,' hollered another. There was no 'sir' for the commodity he'd become.

A couple of photographers gave chase on foot. Another pair dived into their cars. The rest, assuming by Patrick's bare feet he'd return sooner rather than later, remained coolly stationary.

Out of breath, Patrick smashed through the door of the newsagent's and staggered towards a paper featuring a front page photograph of him next to Denis's mother in the school hall.

The headline screamed, 'Anti-Violence Teacher Claim: I Didn't Hit Dead Boy'.

Union City teemed with the blue jumpers of Highfields' children as they filed home, school-run fumes clogged the alleyways and an oily tang of fried food filled the air. The slamming of car doors. Scratching pebbles lodged in children's scooters.

He waited in the same Bateman block recess in which he'd hidden from the cycling youths on Monday night. The police cordon was still in place on the other side.

Jenna appeared at twenty-past-four, her face over-made-up but looking no more troubled than any other teenager's. He snapped her name as loudly as he dared and she instantly twisted to the direction of the voice. She was on edge after all.

Jenna looked about her, hesitated, then crossed to join him in the alcove.

'This is dangerous, Patrick.' It was a voice that had called him Mr Owen for most of the time they'd known each other, that had wavered in strength and pitch in the last few months, through phases of apathy, distrust, avoidance and conspiracy. Impeccably pronounced when she was at home, lazy and slanged when she mixed with her peers. Her eyes met his. 'Patrick, where are your shoes?'

'You still haven't told me what happened. Over there.' He nodded towards the white tent.

Confusion puckered her forehead. 'I told you everything.'

'I beg to differ. It was less of an accident than you made out, wasn't it? Denis had assaulted you previously and... you'd had enough...'

The inconsistencies in her character were solved. As he'd lain in wait for her, scrutinising the messed-up events of the last few days, everything had seemed to fall into place; she hadn't been attracted to Denis at all, she'd been reeling him in, awaiting an opportunity to see her abuser off. 'I think I have a right to know whether I'm an accomplice to manslaughter or cold-blooded murder. Well, Jenna? I've been well and truly framed, haven't I? You and Matthew and the others can sit pretty while the evidence mounts against me.'

She tried to make a run for it. He grabbed her at the elbow. 'Tell me, Jenna.'

'Why are you being like this? I told you what happened.'

'What's to stop me going to the police and explaining everything? How you killed him. How I hid the gun for you. You can still go down for this, you and the rest of the "Souljas".'

215

'Please, Patrick. You promised.'

'You've played me just as you played Denis. How did you do it?'

'I pulled the trigger. That's how guns kill, Patrick.'

She tried again to force her way past him. He tightened his grip on her elbow.

'Was it even you who killed him? Or are you just a small part of the general plot against me?'

She shook herself loose but stood her ground. 'I killed him,' she hissed. 'Every minute of every day I think about it, even when I sleep. Which I can't.'

'Your remorse doesn't make it any less premeditated. Did you lure him there?'

'What are you saying? That I… That I *offered myself*? I didn't mean to kill him… I hated him but I didn't want that to happen…'

'So why, if you hated him so much, were you always by his side? I saw you hanging out with Denis all the time. In the estate, in the playground. You looked very cosy.'

She finally succeeded in wrenching her eyes towards his. 'He terrified me, Patrick. He *terrified me*. I didn't know how to escape him. I didn't know what to do. Maybe, when I found myself with the opportunity to kill him, something… unconscious… took over but I certainly never led him there, never planned how to cover it over… It just happened.'

Patrick slumped against the wall. Crying women normally inspired apologies from him, but not this time. He didn't believe her.

'I hated him,' she confessed. 'But he was so… convincing.' It seemed the wrong choice of word. Perhaps she meant controlling, or persuasive, or exciting. Her tousled, aggrieved expression, as though she struggled to recollect something of great importance, told him even she didn't know whether she'd intended to kill him or not. '*He* chased *me*. He was the one with the bad intentions. I was just protecting myself. *I told you*.'

'How widespread was the knowledge that I once hit Denis?'

She looked about her, wiped her eyes. 'It's not the sort of thing Denis would've talked about. It wouldn't have made him look very good, would it? I certainly didn't tell anyone.'

'Well Matthew knows, and he's made my life very difficult.'

Jenna waited for a group of kids to amble past. 'To be honest, I think he's trying to get at me.' Her voice was becoming harder, unrepentant. 'It's complicated. There's history, sort of, between me, Denis and Matthew. We've known each other a little while, you know. We're all Union City kids... He wants everything Denis wanted, let's just put it like that. He's immature. He doesn't know what he's doing.'

'His "immaturity" is going to put *me* in jail.' Patrick wanted it spelt out: his actions had been riskier than hers. 'You lied to me, to get me to help you. You weren't the only person Denis told about me hitting him, were you?'

For the first time, she looked truly contrite. 'I don't know.' And then, as though to justify her dishonesty, 'He said there were others there at the time, but that they wouldn't talk. They weren't from Highfields. They didn't know you. I certainly don't believe Matthew would've known about it. Denis couldn't stand him.'

'Weren't Matthew and Denis in the same gang?'

Jenna shivered. 'There are things you don't understand about gang life. Gangs are supposed to remain solid, like families, but in reality... people leave. Again, like families.' Her eyes betrayed inner hurt. 'Denis was a natural leader but Matthew was just the younger brother of some local dealer. I guess now Denis is dead, Matthew's carrying on their rivalry by trying to claim his position. Trust me, there's no love lost there. That fire at Matthew's brother's house? Denis did it. He thought there was a quid or two to be made in selling and was trying to take out the opposition. He'd begun to play dangerous games with people. I honestly think

217

if I hadn't killed Denis, someone else would've sooner or later…'

'And I bet that makes you feel a lot better.'

She ignored him. 'Union Souljas was getting too big. That war in the estate was basically two sides within the same gang fighting each other. Denis was trying to separate himself from the old gang.'

'And which gang are you in?'

'Neither. I'm not stupid, Patrick.'

Only now did Patrick unpick her previous mention of "history" between her, Denis and Matthew. 'Were you and Matthew…?'

'No. God, no. I mean, there was that time when we were drunk… But that was nothing. Everybody does, don't they?'

'So who the hell's been telling people I hit Denis if not Matthew?'

'I swear I haven't told anybody.'

'But Matthew *knew*. He threatened me yesterday. He told me…' Patrick struggled to recall exactly what had been said, screwed his eyes tight to engage his brain through the uncertainty, the fear. 'He told me I had "reasons for popping D-Man". He told me that he, you and I shared knowledge of some kind.'

Patrick slapped a sudden, hard hand against his forehead.

'You're scaring me,' she said.

'He's been spying on your flat. He startled Sarah last night, looking through the window, and he's obviously seen me going in and out at odd hours. That's what his campaign of hatred against me's been about; the paedophile accusations only started once I began seeing your mother. He thinks, in his confused, jealous, teenage way, that I've been meeting *you*. And it explains the rivalry with Denis, doesn't it? He's besotted with you.'

'Yuk.' Jenna chewed her bottom lip. 'I didn't even enjoy it…'

'You claimed to have thrown paint on my desk that time, but you were covering for Denis. I knew that. And now

218

Matthew's copying his tactics. I know he was impressed by Denis's vandalism because he'd been revelling in some online examples on his phone. My Wikipedia entry, for starters. He may have been Denis's rival, but he held him in high regard as a petty criminal. And he insulted Denis in the lesson that time, remember? That was just after Denis touched you inappropriately. Matthew's jealousy got him his arm broken...'

Jenna winced. '...I see.'

'So if Matthew wasn't threatening me over hitting Denis, who is? How did the press get wind of—'

He was cut off as Jenna gasped and pressed against him. Brittle, avian fingers wormed at his jacket.

'It's Mum.'

Patrick peered over her and saw Sarah. She was scudding away from them, dressed as though bound for the office, unsteady on high heels and a mid-length grey skirt.

'Did she spot us?' he asked, pushing her off his right foot.

'We should get out of here.'

There came a wail of sirens, as though confirming her appeal.

In his terrified panic, thin wisps of an idea coalesced in Patrick's mind. 'Jenna, I can't admit to hitting Denis. It makes me a huge suspect. Maybe if...' The terrible drama of the press conference jackhammered in his mind, the gasps and poison chatter of the crowd as Matthew's slander was unfurled. 'Maybe if we stick this on Matthew somehow... Perhaps we can make out he's been saying these lies about me to... to deflect the blame from himself. The fact that he and Denis hated each other might just help our cause... Quickly, I need to know what you said at the police station. Our stories *must* tie up.'

'I told them nothing. Remember? Deny everything.' She held onto the words as though they were still appropriate. 'You want to frame *Matthew*? Is that really what you're saying?'

'I'm going to go down for this, Jenna. This is serious.'

'You'll find a way out. I did you a favour killing Denis, you know I did. He told me he was just biding his time…'

He stared at her. She may have had a point. 'I hardly think your act of charity compares with mine.'

The sirens grew louder, their dissonant droning drawing residents to their windows, hoping to catch sight of the culprit. Jenna, her eyes wide, fearful, still stared after her mother; she looked ready to run.

'Wait,' he protested. Patrick didn't know if he could truly trust her, but there was no one else. No time. 'I fucked up. I couldn't just vanish the gun away. It's in my classroom. Go in and take your clay head. You can say you need to work on it at home. The gun's inside. Clean it up and stick it on Matthew somehow. Do for me what I couldn't quite do for you. Hide the evidence properly. It's our only chance.'

His conspirator nodded, horrified, and melted away into the concrete as sirens converged.

Patrick hurried back the way he came. Every hooded face carried a sneer, as though the whole of Union City knew who he was, what he'd done, and a young mother grabbed the hand of her daughter, pulling her closer as he swept past barefoot.

A door slammed and a voice called Patrick's name.

The woman turned towards the swooping police and he heard her sigh, 'This area goes from bad to worse. Wonder who they're after this time?'

Patrick was already running.

He didn't get far. Another silver and orange BMW sliced off his route with a squealing handbrake slide and Inspector Meadows stepped from the passenger side wearing a far less affable face than usual. He strode up to Patrick and pinched his skin with a pair of shiny cuffs.

'You have the right to remain silent, but it may harm your defence if you fail to mention when questioned something you later come to rely on in court…'

PART
FOUR

PART
FOUR

ONE

'So what happened that day?' Meadows asked.

Patrick sat in a grey room no larger than a single garage, at a small wooden table and on a straight-backed padded chair. To his right was a window made up of thick misted blocks like the kind found in budget bathroom showrooms, behind which uniformed shadows ghosted past. The traditional one-way mirror hovered to Patrick's left, showing him bruised and dejected. A dehumidifier sat in the corner.

'What day?'

'The day you hit him.'

'I categorically deny ever hitting Denis Roberts.'

Meadows scratched his shoulder blade, allowed himself a thin smile. 'You met him on the way home before Christmas. There were six of them. He was about to remove something from a pocket. You punched him and he stayed down. You fled. Sound familiar?'

The truth beat in Patrick's temples, his rage rose. Under the unblinking eye of the Inspector, he cursed.

'You still deny it?'

'Of course.'

'So it's a lie that the pacifist Art teacher, who was seen striking Sarah Ellis's ex-husband in the school playground yesterday, hit one of his pupils?'

'Yes.'

Meadows rifled through the printout in front of him,

clicked the tip of his pen. 'Why would someone make this story up?'

'You'd have to ask them that. Which trustworthy member of society is this "someone"?'

Time passed slowly. He heard the ticking of a clock from far away and thought in colours and sounds as though under psychotropic influence, never far from breaching the surface of a dream. When he looked up Meadows was still there, impassive against the ashtray grey walls, adopting the same pathetic look of sympathy as the solicitor who'd dropped the news about The Forsaken's break-up.

'Look, I don't know why this rumour is doing the rounds,' Patrick said, 'but the Union Souljas are responsible. There's a whole underworld you don't have a clue about, operating in Union City. Not a clue. I dare you to walk around there after dark. Do something about them, for fuck's sake. They should be the ones behind bars. Not me.'

'You're not behind bars, Mr Owen.'

Patrick stared through the misted blocks to his right, the policemen and women beyond like pixelated sprites. 'You saw that badly photoshopped image at the press conference. It's a disguise, a smokescreen. It must be.'

'For what, Mr Owen?' His interviewer spoke with irksome calm.

'Matthew Keane's spreading rumours about me. Can't you see why he's doing it? *He* must've killed Denis.'

In the silence which followed Patrick knew he sounded like a man scraping for excuses. Had Jenna had enough time to get the gun out of his classroom? 'I mean... why's he using me like this? Why's he passing the blame?'

'One could also suggest *you're* passing the blame. Or question why you're using *him* like this.'

'I'm not using him. I haven't sabotaged an event he was involved in, or written "paedophile" across his door, or left little voodoo dolls on his desk.'

'You just said, "He must've killed Denis". That sounds

like passing the blame to me.' Patrick hadn't noticed the eye of a CCTV camera in the corner of the questioning room before. 'Did you kill Denis Roberts, Mr Owen?'

'This is insane.' Patrick could hardly speak for fear.

'Is it? This is what I think happened: you found Denis's gun in Jenna's room and it terrified you. You thought Denis was after revenge, and maybe he was, and you engineered a way to kill him. Where's the gun now?'

'Ask Matthew.'

Meadows leant in towards Patrick, his eyes almost sparkling. 'We have a warrant, Mr Owen, but you might like to just *tell us* where the gun is.'

'You've got the wrong person.' Patrick tasted blood in his mouth. His hands rattled on the tabletop. Meadows had pushed him to the precipice of shame. Ana would have heard news of his arrest by now, would be sitting in shocked silence as Danny asked her repeatedly, repeatedly where his father was.

'And you believe the *right* person to be... Matthew Keane?'

'He's not clever but he's got support and immunity. The weak have to play tough in a place like Union City. That's what a gang does. Kids who don't have any identity by themselves find strength in numbers. He and Denis hated each other. I know Denis broke Matthew's arm one time.' It was essential he seeded the notion that Denis and Matthew were sworn enemies. 'This was after Matthew insulted Denis following some intimacy between Denis and Jenna in my classroom.'

'You've proof of this?'

'Not exactly. But that's not all. Think about it: Matthew's brother went missing after the killing. Maybe there are drugs involved in all this... Maybe... Maybe Matthew was involved in drugs *as well* as Denis...?'

The Inspector bored his eyes deep into Patrick. 'You have evidence that Denis was selling?'

'The cannabis under Jenna's bed. You know, rivals are taken out all the time for dealing on someone else's turf. There was that corner shop that was smashed up…'

Meadows issued a slow puncture of a sigh. 'Mr Owen, Sean Keane was found hiding at a friend's house in East London yesterday night. He left Union City soon after his flat went up in flames, knowing whatever remained of his burnt cannabis would be found and that he'd subsequently be arrested. He was charged with possession with intent to sell, but had a cast-iron alibi for the night Denis was shot: he was meeting his broker, attempting to explain where twenty-five kilos of marijuana had gone. We've got a whole bunch of them awaiting trial; Sean spilled the beans all over the place. And as for Matthew, let me make this clear once and for all…' Meadows pointed towards Patrick's legs. 'I interviewed him in that very chair. He looked close to tears the whole time. The only thing that kid could've killed was a joke. Now, Mr Owen, answer me this. Did *you* murder Denis Roberts?'

Exasperation pierced Patrick's heart. Any clumsy planting of contaminated evidence – a gun stippled in his classroom's kiln – would only make him look doubly guilty. He would have confessed had the words not stuck in his throat. A braver man would have been sent down there and then.

'Where were you the night Denis died?'

'I've told you.'

He smoothed his papers with his fist. 'You claim to have been at home. You can be sure of that?'

'Yes.'

'Did you stay home all night? You didn't get up and wander the estate at any point? You're prone to doing that, if this afternoon's anything to go by.'

'I was in the estate that evening,' he croaked, 'but I went home.'

'Yes, Sarah and Jenna confirmed that in their interviews. You left just after the fire. But let me tell you something interesting: two people were seen around the time of the murder. One of them fits your description.'

'Perhaps your source got the time wrong.' Patrick didn't have the energy to look at his inquisitor.

'Maybe. Did *you* see anyone in the estate? On your way home perhaps?'

There was the merest whiff of melodrama about Meadows' techniques.

'I *wasn't there.*'

'No one who looked suspicious? No one at all?' The lines around his hopeful green eyes folded upon themselves like ancient tapestry.

Meadows hadn't appeared so old when Patrick first met him – he'd been too imposing, too tall – but he was sixty if a day. Though he had good bone structure, there was no trace of a young man in his features anymore and his eyebrows were thick, old-mannish, with only a touch of black still to them. There were lines in places Patrick never realised a face could acquire lines. The chin. The wilting skin before the ears.

'The rumours that surround you are interesting to say the least,' Meadows said. 'Namely, the relationship with the mother of Denis's apparent girlfriend and the punch you once delivered the deceased. You've looked out of sorts to me ever since we first met, and I've seen the aftermath of gunshots fired in enclosed spaces before and more than once hearing problems have ensued…'

Just keep denying everything, Patrick told himself, as he'd once told Jenna. Did she have to sit through these mind games too? How did she cope?

'Look, Inspector…'

'Detective Chief Inspector.'

'Where's the hard evidence against me? Even if I did hit Denis, he can hardly press charges. And you're being remarkably cagey about where you've got your information, which tells me the person who told you this rumour is either hiding their identity or can't be trusted. There's nothing. And a "witness" who "saw me" on the night of the murder means even less…'

'I'll tell you what,' Meadows said. 'I'll give you five minutes.' He stood, picked up his papers, and walked out the room.

Patrick sat alone, with the feeling he'd just said something incredibly stupid. He tried to recall what had happened over the last ten, fifteen minutes. What he'd denied. What he'd confessed to.

He started humming, softly under his breath, songs his mother would sing him as a child. And then, out of nowhere, a tune he'd lost months ago flickered briefly. What had once wriggled and twisted from his thoughts, a tune he'd struggled to compose at his kitchen table and had considered calling 'Sixteen', returned. The music couldn't have chosen a more ludicrous time to unlock itself. Even as he determined to keep hold of it, this time, it had already gone.

And in its place: G to A. A to D. D to E minor. E minor to G.

That was certainly one persistent, overpowering melody. It may not have been 'Danny's Tune' any longer but he felt a strong sense of ownership. Yes, another musician got there first but Patrick Owen still owned the emotional rights. Not that he could have ever improved on Adam's original; he knew his limitations as an artist these days. In fact, as Patrick scanned his mind's eye over the emotive lyrics of 'Find the Ocean' he found them superior in every way to his own version. Though he'd never seen it before, its narrative so clearly concerned a man explaining the true nature of his quest for meaning amid multiple disappointments to someone else. As originally written, it was a farewell from Adam to Ana, an apology for not being Patrick, dressed in the poetry of the stream's journey to the river and, ultimately, to the death or freedom of the ocean. But, like the best songs, it meant different things to different people. Patrick hadn't appreciated it at the time, but now he'd rewritten its meaning to allow an absent father to apologise to his son for his departure.

It was still 'Danny's Tune'.

The door opened again. Meadows, clutching a blue document wallet, was accompanied by Mary Haynes.

'Hello Patrick,' Mary said in her clipped, authoritative voice. She was still baggy eyed, still pretty, still neatly uniformed.

Over the next ten minutes they went over the same ground as before, a recap designed to build back up to the big reveal, and while the newcomer asked her questions with the confident, elegant cadences that arrive with expertise and implacable professionalism, it was clear Meadows was the one leading. At times, it even seemed as though Meadows was showing off to the woman. Perhaps something still stirred in the old boy's loins.

'Right,' the Inspector announced. 'This is what's going to happen. In this file are five statements by witnesses, people living in the estate who saw something strange that night.' He stabbed the file on the desk with a long forefinger. 'They all tally. They all claim to have seen the same person. If you tell me who you think killed Denis Roberts – and if your description of them matches the descriptions in here – I'll take it seriously. Understand?'

Patrick straightened. Christophe had mentioned the police had a suspect, but that the description was being held back. That 'suspect' must have either fitted Jenna's description or...

'I wasn't there.'

'So you keep saying.'

The room constricted. He had an opportunity to give a description of someone wearing gold trainers, hoodie and cap, clothes which were now up in smoke, untraceable. He could pass the blame onto a stranger, a fiction.

'Come on, Patrick. Might you have seen someone suspicious on the estate that night? Think carefully...'

Meadows was leading him now, that much was clear, doggedly beating the same line of enquiry to death.

'I don't *know* anything. I feel dizzy.' Patrick heard his own voice, feeble and exhausted, a Year Seven accused of a sixth former's crime.

'Describe this person and you can go free. You'll have helped us solve the case *and* absolved yourself of these nasty rumours at the same time. Come on, Patrick. You have to tell us.' The voice was so soothing it was almost servile, even as Meadows' searching look bored into him…

That look. Where had he seen it before?

It occurred to him at once.

The boy who appeared through the hall doors at the press conference had been planted by Meadows to catch Patrick's reaction. The Inspector had watched the Art teacher like a hawk and translated murder in Patrick's mystification. He saw the same inquisitive gaze on Meadows' face now, and more than a degree of desperation.

This was a trap. If he described the boy it proved only one thing: that he *was* at the scene of the crime.

'I saw nothing. I have no idea who killed Denis Roberts.' Patrick stated this confidently and the woman's shoulders perceptibly sagged. Meadows wore his defeat well, relaxed back in his chair.

'Patrick. Let me tell you something about police work, as one professional to another. It's boring. Bits of paper… loose threads… You're always one step behind, always chasing your tail.'

'Sounds familiar.'

'But then… a chance comes to solve the senseless murder of a teenager and… You want to do the right thing, don't you Patrick? You've been so helpful so far. The press conference and everything. You gave Denis's mother your phone number I understand. I mean I *was* suspicious but… now's your chance to not only clear your name of all those ugly rumours but carry on your good, tireless work for the community.

We're on the same side, you and I. All I want is to confirm the description of a suspected killer, that's all.'

'I want a solicitor.'

With the speed of a man half his age, Meadows slashed his right hand across the desk, casting his blue folder and a glass of water to the floor. Patrick looked amongst the debris and saw that every sheet of 'evidence' in Meadows' file was blank. The Inspector slammed his palms down on the desk and, for a moment, Patrick thought he was going to lunge for him. Judging from the look on Mary's face, she did too.

Meadows stared deep into the teacher's eyes before moving to the black box between them and turning off the machine. He spoke in a controlled whisper so quiet Patrick had to lean in to hear him.

'I *know* you killed him.'

Patrick was desperate to wipe that superior look off the Inspector's face. Meadows was wrong – a sixteen-year-old girl had killed Denis.

Behind the Inspector the door clicked open and an unfamiliar cop entered. The mess on the floor caused him no alarm, as he'd obviously been watching the show through the one-way mirror, and he circumnavigated it to bend and whisper something into Meadows' ear; the Inspector continued to glare at Patrick.

'When was this?' Meadows asked after a long pause.

The man's murmured reply was lost to Patrick.

Meadows looked crestfallen. Eventually he snapped, 'Okay, fine, you can go.' He couldn't look Patrick in the eye.

Mary opened the door and a nonplussed Patrick trudged towards it.

'Mr Owen,' Meadows called after him. 'Don't go too far will you?' Yet another question. 'I doubt we're done with you yet.'

The reporters were outside, in force. They surged forwards when they saw Patrick, blinding him with cameras, questions.

'What do you make of this new revelation, Mr Owen?'

'Isn't your job untenable now?'

'Who killed Denis Roberts, in your opinion?'

He barged through, knowing better than to put his foot in it by talking to the press. He would do as he'd threatened to do in his interview with Meadows. He would hire a good solicitor.

One member of the press, very young, black, jogged alongside him. He asked, 'What do you plan to do now, Mr Owen? Are you going to resign?' Patrick assumed he was a college kid desperate for his breakthrough scoop, from pirate radio maybe. There was something remarkably unprofessional but honest about his hooded top, the Jesus swinging around his neck, the way he kept pace.

A black cab rounded the end of the street and Patrick stuck out an arm to hail it kerbside.

The taxi braked violently and he wrenched open the heavy door, jumped in. He was aware of other figures in the back as the young reporter dived in behind him and spat, 'Drive.' In no time at all the 'reporter' had produced a thin blade and pressed it against Patrick's left kidney. Another figure, bandana concealing his features, jumped up from his supine position on the floor.

And in the back seat, curled up as if to avoid detection by the outside world, was a woman wearing the grey office clothes he'd seen her in earlier, the remnants of a blonde streak almost completely grown out of hair sagging above screaming eyes.

'Sarah...'

The driver cracked his foot against the accelerator and, with a tobacco-wet cackle, raced them away from the police station.

TWO

'That's where I grew up,' the driver sneered, nodding towards darkness beneath the dual carriageway at the end of the estate.

Within, Patrick made out a flickering bonfire and a huddle of tents. A figure was slumped, immobile, against a concrete support. Judging by the foetal curl of his torso, he was injecting. Three children in torn clothing, no older than ten, kicked an airless football against graffiti and smoked cigarettes.

The scene was no sooner glimpsed than it was gone, and the taxi scythed on.

'Not like your gaff I bet, sir,' the youth who'd sprung up from the floor voiced.

Patrick tried to search the eyes above the mask for some hint of which Highfields child might be addressing him, but it was too dark. He could make out a similar rectangle of dead eyes in the rearview mirror, and liked the expression of their chauffeur even less.

'Where are we going?' Patrick asked. 'What do you want with us?'

Sarah's hand found his. Both were oily with sweat.

'Relax, man,' the black kid soothed, his knife remaining in place. 'We're just going for a ride, innit.'

The taxi weaved in and out of Union City, past a hundred versions of Sarah's block. Every now and again they saw groups of kids on stairways, flaking swings and roundabouts, the hoods of cars. One group consisted of about twenty, all chugging from beer cans, and the masked kidnapper slid down his nearside window to gob at them as the taxi cut past. A dozen half-empty cans were lobbed at their vehicle, striking the rear windscreen with a heavy thud, beer spraying across the glass.

'Northsiders,' the kid explained, rolling the window back up.

Nothing else was said for a time, until Patrick felt the need to act assertively in front of Sarah. 'So what do you want?'

'Chill, sir.'

'Who are you, calling me sir?'

'The name's N-Kid.' The boy made a sign with his hand across his chest, forefinger crooked, index out, the thumb jabbed straight, pinkie erect. 'This is Shanker.' He indicated the black kid, who also made the gang sign. 'And our driver's Dazz-Boy.' Dazz-Boy kept his hands on the wheel.

Patrick couldn't shake off the image of those shanty town kids under the carriageway, the evening diesel roaring above. He'd been involved in several classroom wars in the past but had seldom seen it as a class war. And yet, it had so clearly always been the case. He remembered Denis mocking him because he'd been to university, laughing at the very thought of it.

'You know why you were released?' It was N-Kid who spoke, mouth chewing his bandana. He sported a variety of vaguely Celtic shapes razored into close-cropped hair.

'No.'

'Want to know why?'

A mobile was passed to Patrick as a video began playing, the sound a few seconds ahead of the images. He heard Highfields name-checked against a black screen. 'Accusations.' 'Member of staff.'

And then he saw Jenna.

Sarah gasped and rejected Patrick's hand, grabbing the mobile.

The low quality of the speakers muddied whatever was

said, but Patrick could make out Jenna's school photo with her name captioned underneath. There followed a shot of the street in which Denis was killed, a police cordon flickering amid long diffused winds, and then Patrick appeared onscreen, in politico mode at the press conference. Finally, a reporter appeared, standing outside the same police station Patrick had just been released from, and an awkward, camera-hawking pause was broken when someone in the mixing room cut back to the studio.

'What is this?' Sarah asked. 'I couldn't hear a bloody thing.'

Shanker snatched the phone back, pulled the knife up, casually inspecting its point. 'Apparently your daughter made up the story about Mr Owen punching Denis because she was trying to make him sound "cool".'

Patrick rubbed his bruised eye. So, Jenna had stepped forward and announced the 'punch' as a fabrication of her own design? It was worse than feeble.

'Why?' she asked.

'She says she's in love with him.' The boy laughed.

And yet its lack of sophistication lent the announcement some credibility. Patrick hoped she hadn't followed through on his unforgivable, desperate plan to frame the innocent Matthew Keane by replanting the gun, having done something far simpler and ultimately more ingenious to shake Meadows off. It wasn't, however, something that would go any distance towards shrugging off those paedophile slurs.

He reached for Sarah's hand again but it was nowhere to be found. Perhaps that was part of Jenna's plan too.

'This explains why I was released from custody so abruptly.'

'Problem is, what the fuck's it got to do with Jenna?' N-Kid asked.

'Don't ask me.'

'I *am* asking you.' The knife was returned to Patrick's side.

'Patrick, what's going on?' Sarah demanded.

Patrick felt a twinge of remorse for accusing Jenna of involvement with this lot. It was clear they weren't part of any intricate plot against him, that they didn't have a clue who killed Denis. But they wanted honour. Revenge. The Union Souljas considered the police worse than fools and were taking matters into their own hands. That they were just boys made them doubly dangerous.

'How did you get a taxi?' he asked.

'We can get anything,' Dazz-Boy boasted from the driver's seat. 'We own this place. We picked you up outside the fucking police station, man.'

'And how did these gentlemen convince you to come along for the ride, Sarah?'

She turned from the window, knuckles white in her lap. 'They said you'd sent a car for me. They said…'

'Alright. That's enough.' N-Kid rephrased his question. 'Why is Jenna Moris sticking up for you?'

'Maybe what she said is true. Maybe she has a crush on me.'

From her recoiling body language, Patrick knew this hadn't impressed Sarah. It didn't impress his kidnappers much either.

'Don't fuck about with us. Jenna's not in the Souljas so she doesn't have protection, you get me? Don't make us go and ask her what's going on. She won't thank you for it.'

'Why *don't* you ask her? What's it got to do with me?'

'She means nothing to you? Fair enough. And what about her mother?' N-Kid grabbed Sarah's hair, twisting her head back against the headrest as Shanker leaned across Patrick and calmly placed the knife at her rippling throat.

'No one knows what happened to Denis, okay?' Patrick yelped. 'Let's not get ourselves all worked up.' He attempted, fruitlessly, to play the senior, to turn the back seats of the stolen taxi into his classroom. 'I'm the one who's been at the police station and, between you and me, they don't have many leads to go on. They don't know. Believe me, I had nothing to do with the death of Denis, but I do, as you're obviously aware, have connections to Jenna's family.' He indicated Sarah, quietly hyperventilating next to him. 'Those connections are no doubt the reason Jenna's backing me up. She's doing it for her mother. Please leave the pair of them out of this.'

The knife returned to Patrick's kidney as Sarah massaged her neck, shaking with anger.

They were no longer in the estate. From the window, Patrick could make out the new 'riverbank' apartments, an estate adjacent to the reservoir, glaring under the cold sun and, behind, the Shard's silver incisor standing to attention some distance from the older constructions of St Paul's and the BT Tower. London's changed skyline had long ceased to represent the vista of promise The Forsaken chose for the cover of their debut album.

Shanker asked. '*Did* you hit D-Man?'

The three gang members looked at him in silence.

'You weren't... there, were you?' he asked.

'Weren't where?' asked Shanker.

'Nothing. Forget it.'

'Listen, man. Hitting someone ain't killing them. You get me? But someone who goes around telling people they didn't hit no one when they did ain't exactly gonna be believed when they start saying they ain't killed no one either.'

'I really don't...'

'We ain't the police. You know, we respect *you* more than we respect the police, and that's saying something. You don't have to pretend, man. Not to us. We're *inner circle*.'

'Fine, I hit him.'

'We know. We was there.'

Patrick tried to react coolly to this, as one might try to react coolly when the volcano on the horizon starts to rumble. But any facade of composure was shattered as the taxi abruptly turned left, then braked hard.

'This is where you live, I believe,' Dazz-Boy said, tapping the wheel.

Patrick looked through the window to see The Heights. It was testament to Jenna's announcement that no members of the press bothered to wait outside.

'We'll give you...' N-Kid looked at his watch. '...two hours. Either you or Jenna has to take the blame. Understand?' The knife was sheathed into Shanker's pocket before he reached over and opened the door.

'Why are you doing this?'

No answer. For sport. Boredom.

Patrick stepped out, followed by Sarah. 'How can I find you?' he asked.

'We'll find *you*,' Shanker replied. 'We want justice, yeah? Justice. That's all.'

The taxi skidded off in a black belch of exhaust fumes.

'Ring Jenna,' Patrick said. 'Right away.'

Sarah scrutinised Patrick as though looking at him for the first time, shook her head. When Patrick attempted to thread an arm towards her, she snatched it away.

'Jenna clams up every time your name's mentioned. And now this...' He watched Sarah's hands curl into fists. 'Maybe I should've guessed something was going on. I saw the two of you whispering in the estate earlier, thick as thieves while the world revolved around you. You didn't even see me.'

'That was perfectly innocent, Sarah. You can't possibly believe...'

'Yeah? What were you talking about then?' Traces of affection bled from Sarah's face; she was a bad cover version of someone he desired right now. '...And the TV's saying she has a crush on you. All this "She wanted Mr Owen to look cool, as cool as the gangs patrolling her estate" rubbish. And then these pricks with God-awful nicknames kidnap me and bang on about 'D-Man' and who killed him and...' The anger had almost doubled her over. 'Tell me what the hell's going on, Patrick.'

'I can't.'

'Why not?'

'Because it's more serious than you realise.'

She stepped away from him. 'It *is* connected to Denis's death, isn't it? Why is Jenna saying what she's saying?'

'She's covering for me.'

Her face opened in horror. 'Why?'

'Because I'm covering for her.' He was close to shouting. 'Ring your daughter. Ring her *now*.'

Sarah's flat was empty. Patrick watched her slump on Jenna's deserted bed and ring Izzy, who suggested she try Marie, who suggested she call Uche, who suggested she try Izzy again. She hung up and stared at the phone as though it had failed her. On their journey over, Patrick had explained everything and she looked up at him now with the blank dispassion of a fresh mourner.

'If you go to the police, the gang'll kill her,' she stated.

He gazed out the window at the starless, orange aurora over London. 'Going to the police doesn't feel like an option any longer. No one'll believe Jenna's self-defence story after all this.'

'Even if the gang don't kill her, it's prison for sure.' Detachment peeled from her, inaction giving way to the fires of injustice. 'I'm going to go out and look for her,' she resolved. 'I can't just hang around here.'

Patrick walked back to her lounge and wilted onto the sofa. 'They gave me two hours.' He checked the numerals behind the shattered glass of his wristwatch. 'That was thirty minutes ago. I think they've already got her.'

'Got her? Where?'

'I don't know, but my time's running out. Unless I tell the gang the truth they'll kill me. I'm pretty certain of that.'

'And if you *do* tell them the truth they'll…' She was at the door, desperation in every rabid aspect of her movement. 'I don't know what to do. You go and look for her.'

He didn't move from the sofa. 'No.'

'What do you mean, "No"?'

Patrick could no longer contain himself. 'Look at my feet. They're fucking blue. Oh, and you know what? I woke up this morning to find I'd been suspended from work because the press are after my blood. But *that* was the best my day got because then I ended up being interrogated by the police and KIDNAPPED. You know, I'm actually beginning to miss the days when I was merely smeared as a child molester. And all of this – all of it – is because of your bitch daughter. No, I'm sorry, Sarah, but I've done my favours for that girl. I'm not bailing her out any longer.'

Sarah walked slowly towards him. He felt the heat of her anger swell.

'You should've left us the hell alone, Patrick. You should've left *me* the hell alone.' She then strode to the front door, slamming it shut behind her and slapping forward the photograph of Millie on the mantelpiece. It fell to the ground with a sharp crack of glass.

He consulted his broken watch again, then fixed his eyes on the front door she'd just departed through.

After a few minutes, an unlikely change began to take place within Patrick. Deadlines had been set, sinister ultimatums drawn up – and yet his fear, quite tangibly, started to dissipate. His very isolation handed him an advantage.

Something Jenna told him earlier gave him hope. She wasn't part of the gang but evidently knew enough about its inner politics to appreciate that it was possible to leave the Union Souljas. Patrick doubted 'leaving' meant walking away – getting shot in the back was probably the easiest way to resign, or joining a rival crew – yet those notions of internal dissent certainly made the gang less intimidating. Maybe he was thinking too much like an adult, placing rationality above appearances, but even his kidnappers earlier had talked about 'inner circles', suggesting bosses and underlings, Denises and Matthews. The gang put up a united front but didn't think with a unified mind. And

Patrick knew full well how differing opinions could divide and sway even the closest of allies.

After all, he'd belonged to a gang once.

Lights and sound, building to a throbbing crescendo. Drugged by the power at his fingertips, he'd gazed down into a sea of mortal, adoring faces.

To his left, Adam had been drunk and off-track, making up verses and slipping over rhyme, but the band had been strong enough to bring him back to safety. Even in the electric thrill of the moment, when things could have gone disastrously awry, no one had been troubled by Adam's messianic wanderings into scat-poetry and the problems in the Middle East. This was their encore at the Reading Festival, the zenith of their career. Nothing had been able to stop them.

Patrick had winked at a girl in the crowd as he disengaged himself from his instrument to the cheers of pissed kids celebrating GCSE results. Years later, Key Stage Four pupils would be shouting altogether less appreciative comments in response to his Art. The band had vanished into the crowds and slipped back into anonymity, but the buzz remained like an amphetamine in their collective system. Adam told him he loved him that night, high as the North Star, his pupils like the points of sharpened pencils. Three weeks later, Patrick was sleeping with his girlfriend.

It was cruel how his memories of that night – arguably the moment he felt most alive – were kidnapped by injunctions into the then-future. The degeneration into teaching. The best friend turned love-rival. No single snapshot in time was pure, he'd learned; regrets worm their way even into paradise.

But there was one aspect of his Reading performance no lost lover or career change could taint.

The night after the gig, his father had called to remind him to send his mother a birthday card. This was how it had always worked; Patrick had never written down birthdays, or addresses, and relied on his father's steel mind to jog his memory over family matters. They'd talked about nothing in particular, as fathers and sons do, but just before his father wound up the customarily brief call he'd said, 'I was watching you on TV last night.'

Patrick had made a self-deprecatory grunt. His father had some interest in early rock and roll but Patrick could never claim to have been educated, musically, by him and had never been able to rely on his tastes as any great barometer of quality. Elvis was commonly regarded as influential, as was Buddy Holly, but no one wrote any musicals on Clyde Hankins or Jimmy Torres as far as Patrick was aware.

'I thought you were... alright, son.'

Never had his father flattered him before, or expressed even a sniff of much longed-for pride in his son until this occasion. Dumbstruck by such mutiny in protocol, however meagre, Patrick had only managed a smile as the disconnected purr segued into the sing-song squeal of the telephone exchange's reminder tone.

The turn of Sarah's key snapped him from his memories and it took a few seconds to swim back to reality. Torrents of expletives were launched at him before he had a chance to fully acclimatise.

'I was trying to protect you. I'm sorry.'

'Protect me?' she yelled. 'Or get into my knickers? I thought I trusted you, Patrick, but it turns out I don't even know you. What kind of a person are you, to do something like this...?'

Patrick stared at his hands. 'I don't know...'

She looked over him with a kind of abstract curiosity. 'Why are you still here?'

He gazed up at her, as though seeing her for the first time. 'Where should I go?'

Reluctantly, Sarah walked forward and sat beside him in a stunned silence. Patrick looked at his watch again.

'I need a moment,' he said after a while, standing and crossing to the bathroom.

Inside, he took out his phone and called Ana.

'Hi, it's me.'

'Patrick, what the hell's going on?'

'Can you put Danny on, please?'

There was a short pause, followed by a squeaky voice exclaiming, 'Hello Daddy!'

'Hey Danny, what you up to?'

'I'm playing at the hotel. Mummy bought me a superhero and you can take the legs of Iron Man off and put the arms of Hulk on and take the head of Hulk off and put the head of Doctor Doom on.'

Patrick gulped back tears. 'That sounds amazing. Danny, you know I love you, don't you?'

'Silly Daddy.'

'It's true. I don't want you to ever forget that.'

'I won't.'

'More than I can ever say.'

'You just said it.'

'Yes, but *more* than I just said.'

'That's stupid.'

'Whatever. Just remember though, yeah? I have to go now. Goodbye, Danny.'

'Bye Bye Daddy!'

He waited for Ana to take the phone.

'Well?' she asked, suspicious.

Strength returned to his voice. 'I'm sorry. I love you too. I always have.'

Silence. When she next spoke, she sounded genuinely scared. 'What's going on?'

He let the arm holding his phone drop, squeezed his eyes tight. The voice continued, 'I could hear what you were saying to Danny, Patrick. What in God's name is happening? You're scaring us.'

He pulled the phone back to his ear. 'I just wanted to…'

'To what?'

Patrick swayed on the bathroom mat, avoided his own eyes in the mirrored cabinet. 'I don't know what I'm mixed up in here. I don't know when I'll next see you again. I'm going to do my best to stay safe but it means more to me, right now, that you're both alright. Look after him, won't you?'

'Patrick Richard Owen!' She was screaming now. He could hear Danny crying in the background. 'What are you playing at?'

'I have so much I want to say to him. I tried to write him a song but…'

'You're not making any sense.'

'You know "Find the Ocean"?'

There was a confounded pause. 'Of course I do.'

'Just play him that one day. It will tell him pretty much everything.'

'Patrick!' she screamed. 'Patrick…!'

He hung up just as Sarah's doorbell tolled. With extreme hesitance, he left the bathroom.

Sarah was standing in the hallway, her hunched body bracing itself, and they walked into the front room to see a series of shadows gathered outside. The endgame was coming.

'Open it.'

Trembling, she unlatched the door and pulled it inwards.

'Oh my God!' She lunged forwards to embrace her daughter.

Jenna seemed to hang still and lifeless in Sarah's arms, her eyes downcast, as ten or so masked individuals, some maybe as old as twenty, others as young as fourteen, stepped past the pair of them and strode to find their marks between the door and Patrick. He recognised the three from the taxi, near the front.

'Good news,' Dazz-Boy said. He was one of the older ones, the tip of a spiky tattoo crawling from his neckline. His eyes were green, sharp, dangerous, and Patrick felt sure he'd done time at least once. 'She's joined the Souljas.'

From Jenna's expression, no one would have thought this good news at all.

'So we all know now, don't we?' Shanker spat. 'About D-Man. About what happened?'

'Do we?' Patrick asked, targeting Jenna with the question.

'Now she's in the gang she's protected, right?' Sarah asked. 'You said she wasn't safe before.'

Shanker nodded, an exaggerated, half-dance of a nod, his shoulders dropping slowly. 'That's right.'

So that was her fate. Her protection. The Souljas would cover for her, provide an alibi if necessary, but, now a member, she'd no doubt find it hard to leave or defect without risking death. The expression 'ride or die' came back to him from somewhere and then, lurking at the back of the group, he spotted a boy with an external fixator on his arm, a smile of ingratiating stupidity adorning his face. He wore his paint-smattered shoes. One by one, the Souljas claimed the vulnerable and stupid. Or the vulnerable and stupid joined for protection.

'What was all this talk about justice earlier?' Patrick asked. 'Is this it?'

'This is it,' N-Kid confirmed. The whole gang seemed to grin. 'Over. We all know where we stand. No need to bother the police, innit.'

Sarah's daughter still wasn't looking anywhere except her shoes. Slowly, she put her hand out for Patrick to shake. 'Nice knowing you, sir,' she said, as her gang fell about in laughter. This macabre parody of sociability was clearly part of her initiation. Any remaining sense of authority, or hope of fair-play from the gang, left Patrick.

Jenna retracted her limp hand and, one by one, her crew turned to depart. Impassive, Jenna swivelled to leave with them.

'Jenna?' It was Sarah who spoke.

Her daughter looked at her, then Patrick. 'I'm sorry,' she said, and it sounded like she genuinely meant it.

245

The last to exit was Matthew, who lingered to sneer pathetically, as if the whole caper might have been his brainwave. His head was raised and his shoulders rolled in a simian hunch. Sarah didn't close the door after him.

For a long time the pair stared into the black void outside.

'They said she was safe. They said it was over. Patrick... What the hell just happened?'

What had been the threat issued in the taxi? *One of you has to take the blame.*

'She's safe.'

'Do you think she told the truth?'

'If I was in her shoes, I wouldn't have.'

Sarah squinted into the night. She looked older somehow. Her skin was dry and her eyes brittle. 'What... What will you do now?'

He shrugged an imperceptible itch of his shoulders. He didn't know what he was going to do. He recalled the screams of Ana and Danny, how close he'd already come to losing them. Though he felt compelled to go to his family, the danger, absurd as it sounded, was surely only just beginning.

'I need to get out of London, quickly,' he mumbled. 'But there are a few loose ends I have to tie up first.'

He looked back at her silhouette in the doorway, then stepped onto the cold walkway, spied immediately the gang at the far side of Bateman. Drinking. Jeering. Being teenagers. The taxi was there with its lights on, playing an abrasive wail of bad music through its speakers and casting indistinct spotlights on the floor. Jenna, bottle of beer in hand, was being spoken at by Matthew and was the only person looking Patrick's way.

'Patrick...' Sarah whispered. 'Be careful.'

The teacher made off, fast.

Keep walking. Don't look back. Show no fear. Keep walking. Keep walking.

Keep walking.

With twenty metres to go before he left the block, the car stereo was muted. He didn't even need to look over his shoulder to confirm every pair of eyes watched him, and as he stole through puddles of shivering water, and his own image shivered with them, he felt the rain of pure hatred upon his back and his quickening footsteps echoed off the walls like gunfire.

THREE

When the school was woken into boisterousness by the lesson changeover bell, Patrick strode to his door. He was amused to find pupils' conversations stopping as eyes took him in with the mystery of a new species, a Victorian freak show. He'd returned unclean and deformed from his ordeal and people behaved peculiarly around him; Harriet had even dropped a mug of tea at her feet as his phantom skulked in that morning. Although she and Charlotte were gracious in his defeat, said the right things about how awful the last few days must have been, there seemed to exist the common feeling that he was damaged goods, that he deserved his ignominy. Weren't there, they surely felt, just too many stories circulating to be ignored?

Patrick had gone to work to find he'd been replaced indefinitely by a supply teacher called Mr Beal who sported cream swirls of psoriasis at his temples and seemed the only person genuinely pleased to see him, on account of his Sevens falling silently into line, cattle-prodded by Mr Owen's infamy. While Mr Beal's lesson was in progress, Patrick disappeared into the kiln room and sought out Jenna's clay head from the collection of Year Eleven sculptures.

It had dried now and one of her grey eyelids had fallen off due to a clumsy application of slip. He raised it above his head and hurled it to the floor, where it exploded to reveal the gun in the centre of a radiating star of powder and facial shards. Patrick plucked the murder weapon up, then stuffed it into his belt and buttoned his jacket over it. There was no way to get it out the school without setting off the scanners at the main entrance, and the exit behind the canteen was now also replete with the devices, thanks to the breaking and entering skills of his favourite journalist.

He walked back into the classroom and, for the last time, speculated on how conducive to creativity the view from his window might have been. The very name Highfields conjured up visions of windswept pastures, golf courses or country valleys, making this vision of a heavyweight estate lurking in mist something of an insult. Above Union City, the sky was a flat smudge of charcoal.

Mr Owen left his classroom for the last time, then entered the office to retrieve his guitar.

Christophe was teaching his Eights when Patrick entered.

'Morning, sir,' Patrick said, pretending not to see the Ofsted inspector sitting in the corner.

Observing the guitar poking over Patrick's shoulder, Christophe attempted an insincere smile. 'Hello.' He instructed his class to read through page forty-two in their textbooks then found refuge under his postcard of François-Noël Babeuf. He said to Patrick, in a quieter voice, 'Been a strange few days, no?'

'Strange is an understatement. I got punched by a boxing champion, accused of being a paedophile, and a child beater, and a murderer. The police tore my flat to pieces, poked about under loose tiles, inside the cushions of my sofa. I got dumped by the first person I've liked in years. Oh, and a local gang want me dead.' Christophe looked uncomfortable but Patrick didn't care; hadn't his colleague been the one who warned him nothing good would come from romancing the mother of one of his pupils?

'Apart from that, everything rosy?' Christophe attempted to sound bullish. A few of the kids strained to listen in but the whole room, teachers included, were talking in whispers and the resultant blanket of white noise drowned any juicy details. 'Do you think we could, maybe, talk later?'

'That Homicide Inspector really had it in for me, you know,' Patrick said. 'Did you tell him about the video we watched on Matthew's phone?'

'I thought it might've been relevant.' Curt. Defensive. 'Perhaps, I thought, there were clues about the gangs in there after all…'

'Yeah, well, he got all Batman on my arse in the interview room. Worked me into a state just to show up again with some bogus testimonies and fool me into a big reveal…'

'Patrick, I'm in the *middle of a lesson*…' The Ofsted inspector in the corner was shaking his head, scratching mysterious numbers onto his observation sheet.

'Meadows asked you to inform me that a description of Denis's killer was doing the rounds, didn't he? Well, it wasn't. He hoped I'd provide some information that tied me to the scene.' An interviewed resident must have reported a hurrying, gold-trainered figure, but that was all Meadows had. 'Unfortunately, you couldn't leave it at that, could you?'

'I don't know what…'

'Stop bullshitting me,' Patrick whispered. 'You told Meadows about me hitting Denis, probably palming it off as "rumour" because you were too interested in smoking that grass.' Though his supplier's stash had gone up in smoke, Patrick was pleased to note Christophe's face betrayed no pain and his arthritic digits refused to hang gnarled or wizened by his sides; Denis's cannabis was still in safe hands.

'He was very persuasive,' Christophe justified. He looked at the floor the way Jenna had done the night before. 'Call it a professional judgement.'

'I bloody knew it.'

'I'm sorry. Really. I'm gutless. I don't know how the press found out though. That wasn't me.'

He could hardly blame Christophe for the convergence of events which had led them to this conversation. Patrick alone had put those unfamiliar clothes on, groped in the bleeding dark for murder weapons. Christophe had suspected Patrick of killing Denis, perhaps still did, and he wasn't the only one.

'Same reason they find out about everything else, I imagine. A leak. A link in the chain you thought you could trust.'

Patrick turned and swept from the Frenchman's classroom.

Outside the gymnasium a sign announced, 'Silence Please. Mock Exams in Progress'.

Patrick pushed open the door and Mr North, head of Year Eleven, looked him up and down without a smile then hurried to the other side of the gym, despite being in the only place on Earth, apart from gravesides and the London underground, where a conversation was impracticable anyway. A whiteboard revealed the test had thirty minutes left to run.

The students scratched in booklets as sun coursed through tiny triangular rips in old black curtains, sprinkling dust particles amongst the ancient woods and brickwork while teachers strolled the aisles, their shoes an unwelcome tick-tock in arrhythm with the large clock at the front. Patrick saw Hosam Mohammad gawping at the pair of legs beneath Kate Richardson's desk. Sally Handley reapplied her nail varnish with Tip Ex.

Matthew was over by the wall bars, reading his test paper under a cloud of disdain. The boy inclined his head towards the teacher's presence, wordless, still scripted by the silence of the gymnasium.

And there was Jenna. For a moment she and Patrick looked at one another, their complicity screaming in the electric stillness, their respective uniforms unkempt, unironed. He wondered if her peers turned from her the way his did from him, whether she heard the rumours repeated back in their silence. Patrick had experienced his fair share of abuse over the years so he fancied he knew what Jenna was going through, but to be called 'a lying, time-wasting, adolescent fantasist' by the very newspaper baying for his own blood twenty-four hours beforehand couldn't have been pleasant. She, like him, had returned to school too soon. They both played the innocence game.

He walked swiftly across the polished parquet flooring and stopped at her side, aware of the phallic heaviness of the gun in his belt, the guitar strap across his chest. 'Did you tell them it was me, Jenna?' His voice was soft but whipcracked through the hall nonetheless.

Certainly the gang had passed on the opportunity to kill him in the estate the night before, but had they only decided against it because of the risk of witnesses? Because Sarah had been there? He searched for an answer in Jenna's face, saw nothing but the eyes of an automaton avoiding his.

'Patrick!' snapped a voice behind him.

It was the first time Mr Hutchinson had used his first name. Colin, Patrick thought his headteacher's forename might have been. Or Charles. Never before had he seen a face quiver with such fury.

Patrick marched towards him, splitting the sparkle of light behind climbing bars. 'I resign,' he announced.

'Accepted,' Mr Hutchinson growled, tugging him from the gymnasium into the main foyer.

PC Thomas was reading a *Fantastic Four* comic in his little cubicle behind reception.

'Patrick's leaving,' the headteacher announced into sound holes drilled through protective Perspex.

It took the policeman a pretentiously long time to place the reading matter to one side. 'Probably for the best,' he said, without venom, emerging from his booth. 'Let's have a look at that guitar.'

Patrick handed over his Les Paul. 'It's been gathering dust in the office,' he justified. 'I thought I should leave the place as tidy as possible.' The pistol burned at his hip.

'Cost you a fair bit, I daresay?' The Constable placed his fingers in the A major bar chord, strummed. 'It's out of tune,' he said, twisting at the tuning pegs. Patrick explained that he hadn't played the instrument for a long time.

Mr Hutchinson, incensed, ripped the guitar off PC Thomas and handed it back to its owner, who threaded the guitar strap over his shoulder.

'See you around, gentlemen.'

Patrick walked through reception, passing into the security scanners. The alarm ripped throughout the foyer like the keening of some maligned robot.

'Hold on,' PC Thomas shouted.

The ex-teacher stopped. 'Steel frets,' he explained, then turned towards the door.

Patrick Owen left Highfields Secondary School for the last time, his heart in his throat, security alarms screaming all around him.

He placed the guitar in the armchair opposite and the gun on the coffee table, then sat looking between the two objects for a long time. The foam in his cushions spilled out where the police had poked about for justice.

Losing his job caused him little distress. Getting into education in the first place had been a premature idea at best, a lazy response to his degree and rudderless existence after being forsaken by The Forsaken, and he could hardly be expected to carry on patrolling the same playground as Jenna any longer, or teach his GCSE class with Denis's name scratched out in the register. What hurt most was losing his first meaningful human relationship since Ana hitched up her skirts and expatriated to Latin America.

Before he'd realised what he was doing, Patrick had snatched up the gun and rammed it in his mouth. It tasted like blood, dental fillings.

For some while he sat with the weapon against the roof of his mouth, finger on the trigger, daring himself to play the dangerous odds that separated life and death. He had no idea if a bullet sat in the chamber or if the gun would even fire any longer but it didn't matter: the suggestion of suicide hypnotised him with its sheer simplicity. Escape was an intoxicating gamble.

He looked around the living room, over the black blur of the gun. This was the life he had built for himself, the summary of his time on Earth. A cactus sagged on the windowsill. The tomes on art theory were fifteen years past their relevance date. The deskbound Waterman pen had never signed an autograph. The room was a poor suicide note.

He wondered how many days of unanswered phone calls from Ana or his mother it would take for him to be discovered with the murder weapon in his mouth. If that didn't close the Denis Roberts case, nothing would.

At this thought, the firearm slid from his mouth and Patrick wrenched it towards a sofa cushion, pressing the trigger. It didn't even click; the entire firing mechanism had melted. He cast the gun to his side, drowsy but in control again.

Taking out his mobile, he rang Sarah's number. The answer-phone kicked in after one and a half trills.

'Hi, it's me. I don't know what to say. I can't remember whether I told you *why* I helped your daughter conceal the evidence. I might have told you I helped her out of compassion. You asked me to look out for her, remember? But the truth is she blackmailed me. Anyway… If only we'd met under different circumstances, huh? I'm kind of confused at the moment and I've known you such a little amount of time but… I guess what I'm trying to say is… You got under my skin, in spite of everything.' He cleared his throat, then continued: 'The last time I saw you, things… If you'd like to meet, to talk, even if it's just to say goodbye, I'll be at a pub called The Old Ale Emporium tonight. I'm meeting an old friend, but… maybe we could talk after. If you want.'

He exhaled, aware he was rambling. Glancing at the melted firearm at his side, his purpose was suddenly clear. 'You asked me that time if I was for real, remember? Well, I was. I was. Goodbye, Sarah.'

He hung up, then fetched a small screwdriver.

It wasn't easy disassembling the weapon. The kiln had chewed it up well and the magazine was only removed from the butt after jacking this way and that. After the magazine fell out, Patrick clawed at what might have once been clasps on the top of the gun and succeeded in sliding the top back to peer inside the chamber. There was a single bullet within. After prising amid congealed metal, something that might have been the barrel came loose, followed by a large spring, a spoke of steel the length of a matchstick and what Patrick assumed to be the firing pin. He took the screwdriver to the handle and eventually succeeded in separating the two halves, then over the course of his afternoon hacksawed the remains until nothing remotely resembled the external casing of a handgun.

He stuffed his pockets with the larger remains of the gun, pieces which couldn't be destroyed easily or flushed into the drain like the rest of the metal particles, clips and assorted off-cuts, then packed a few days' worth of clothes into a rucksack and tossed it over his shoulder alongside his guitar. He let himself out of his flat and locked the door.

Patrick took the tube to Leicester Square, via a route so circuitous he couldn't possibly have been followed, then walked straight to the spot in which he'd waited for Sarah at the start of his Christmas holiday and dropped a section of the barrel in a litter bin.

Next, he took the short journey to the Coliseum on St Martin's Lane, where he and Sarah had seen Madame Butterfly. He removed the bullet from his pocket and threaded it into one of the holes in a wall-mounted cigarette disposal unit outside. It made a dull clink as it nestled itself amongst ash and filter tips.

After some searching, he found the restaurant they'd eaten in. He went in and ordered a light meal but couldn't eat it, instead favouring the frenetic view of London out the window, the blur of legs and shopping bags. Before he left, he ducked into the toilet and dumped the gun's trigger in the cistern.

Afterwards, he hopped back on the tube and journeyed west, jumping off the carriage just before the door slid closed to make sure he was the last to depart. Booking himself in for one night at the Lionswater Hotel, he asked specifically for the same room he and Sarah had shared. He didn't hang around any longer than it took to press the recoil spring, which had fused into one unbreakable lozenge in the fires of the Art department's kiln, into the wet soil of the cyclamen.

He walked back in the direction of The Old Ale Emporium to meet Adam, disposing of a portion of the slide, which still partially displayed the weapon's serial number, in a recycling bank outside the police station. He cast a look around. Still, he was alone.

Darkness gathered. In the distance, the inky night seemed to be emanating from the estate itself.

The Old Ale Emporium wasn't a pub Patrick frequented often. A mob of tobacco-writhed alcoholics festooned the exterior seating, their glum dogs tethered to a rotting chalkboard which proudly advertised, in writing long ago smudged by London rains, the delights of Sky Sports.

Inside felt more salubrious, and warm. A middle-aged barman in a Doors T-shirt looked at Patrick as he approached, as though his customer were in the wrong place, an out-of-towner, and he himself barely recognised his reflection in the mirror behind the rack of spirits as he ordered a pint before settling into a windowed booth. Two men at a neighbouring table sucked down English barley and a boy and a girl, perhaps university students, lounged in a corner, skin as clear as their eyes, clothes fashionably twenty years out of date. It made sense to Patrick that youth imitated the generation before the generation before; they didn't want to stand shoulder-to-shoulder with their immediate elders. The pair ignored the jukebox, which crooned something older than they were, and their eyes never left one another. They weren't lovers, but they soon would be.

Through misting eyes, Patrick attempted to read a broadsheet's front page. Despite the accompanying graphics of financial markets, red lines zigzagging downwards with an almost cartoon zeal, he just couldn't engage his brain fully enough to determine what the article was about. He began flicking through the rest of the paper, saw himself on page five, put it to one side, then drank quickly and peered at the darkness beyond the grimy window for hooded youths.

'Oi! Shithead!'

Patrick jumped, turned.

His old frontman was recognisable only from his seventies' rockstar fashion sense. Black leather jacket. Corduroy flares. Adam looked twenty years older than he'd been when Patrick last saw him. His mop-top was thinning at the crown and there were flecks of white in his scraggly goatee. Excess had written unflattering lines either side of his mouth and his eyes were low-lidded, kohled by irreversible tiredness. He smiled as he approached.

'You look awful,' he told Patrick.

'You too.' Patrick held up his empty glass. 'Buy us another.'

Once the customaries were out the way, Adam enquired about Patrick's recent adventures and Patrick regaled him with the story, save that which would put him in prison. Very little of his tale, therefore, was accurate.

'I guess you're better off without this Sarah, huh? I mean, her daughter sounds like a right bitch.'

Adam was sober and sensible, if not exactly erudite, and dispensed his wisdom in small aphorisms. There being 'plenty more fish in the sea' had never sounded better than when delivered with a Mancunian accent. But there was no avoiding the conversation. Patrick took a deep draught of beer.

'Ana left me.'

'I'm sorry.'

'No. It's me who should be sorry.'

'I know you'd always fancied Ana.'

It was true: her Spanish skin and Bourneville eyes had marked her out as a natural beauty but, better than that, her awkwardness always seemed strangely irreverent in rock-star-wannabe company. 'The fact that she was your girlfriend was a problem, but…'

'No kidding,' Adam spluttered. His eyes kept sliding enviously across to Patrick's guitar.

'…I hope you don't mind me being honest here, Adam. I adored Ana so much I think I'd have tried to steal her off anyone.'

'You really don't need to…'

'I think I do. Bear with me. Neither of us felt particularly thrilled to be double-crossing someone we both cared for. Assuming you'd kill the pair of us, we found ourselves faced with two choices. We could admit everything, or cut short our affair. We decided to cut it short, but…'

'The Lionswater.'

'Exactly. It was supposed to be the perfect one-night-stand. I remember walking through the hotel reception the next morning, the sound of Miles Davis ringing from the bar's speakers, and thinking to myself "I want to be with this woman for ever but…" She was *yours*. She was yours. I had no right. And then we saw you, slouched on the sofa by the entrance. Remember? You had about twenty fags crushed out in a large glass ashtray next to you. You looked at us totally without surprise…'

He wore the same look, eight years later. 'You and Ana had always flirted, and then… one day your flirting suddenly stopped. It didn't go unnoticed.'

'And then you punched me.'

Adam smiled. 'Words didn't come easily to me in those days. Are you saying it was my fault, for finding out about the pair of you?'

'I think I'm saying that it was no one's fault.'

Adam sighed, swigged. 'Our second fucking album had only been out six days.'

'I know…'

The pair of them stared into their pints' eyes, drummed softly on the table with forefingers, tore at sodden coasters.

Released from Ana's spell, the pair were free to discuss their memories of gigs, both good and bad, and the time when Adam started a brawl by launching a drumstick into a predominantly biker audience. Such conversation led, inevitably, to talk of the band's restoration.

Adam was enthusiastic about the idea and his teenage fervour was a tonic for Patrick. That someone could be so contented by the thought of retracing their steps was natural enough – at the heart of every mid-life crisis is the misconception that innocence can be regained by rewinding a clock – but Patrick was unsure how the band's reunion could work, whether the old songs had aged well enough.

'Well, let's get out there and see if our crowd's still waiting,' Adam suggested. '*Everybody's* reforming these days.'

Patrick sat back in what appeared to be an old church pew. Someone had deemed it necessary to scratch 'John's got a big prick' into the wood and had even provided a telephone number for, presumably, verification purposes. 'You think they are?'

The young couple in the corner looked like they were preparing to leave. Adam hollered to them.

'Hey, you two, you'd be well chuffed to hear The Forsaken were gonna get back together, wouldn't you?'

The girl managed to frown without a single line spoiling her face. The boy asked, 'The *who*?'

'No, The Forsaken.'

'I don't know what you're talking about.'

Patrick watched the young couple exit into the cold, boisterous street.

'Too young,' Adam sighed. 'Too young.'

'I think you lost them at "chuffed", to be honest. But you're hardly *ancient*. Did you really mean what you said on the phone? About being too old to die young?'

'Fuck yeah. I always assumed I'd cork it at the age of rock 'n' roll death. I'm already way past Cobain, Morrison, Hendrix.' Looking at him, anyone would be forgiven for thinking he still chased that particular dream. 'Even Jesus died at thirty-three and I'm a few past that poor sod too.'

Patrick inspected his glass. 'Then what's the point of getting The Forsaken back on the road? There's no glamour in choking on your own vomit at our age.'

'Are you kidding? There's plenty of glamour in it. Is this the voice of reason I hear, the voice that persuaded you it would be a great idea to become a secondary school teacher? Look how that ended up.' Adam indicated Patrick's rucksack, next to his guitar. 'By the way, what's with the bag?'

'I'm leaving town.' Patrick fished in a pocket for his keys. 'I was going to ask a favour. In a couple of days, could you collect some stuff from my flat? I've got all I need in the short term but I'll want some more clothes and bits soon…'

'Where you going?'

Patrick shrugged.

Adam leaned back on his chair and assumed full-on crucifixion pose, spread his arms out along the backrest, straightened and crossed his legs. He really did believe he could yet outdo Christ. 'Here's a crazy idea…'

Patrick knew what was coming. It might have been the beer, but even their old telepathy seemed to be returning.

'…Come kip at mine for a bit. You've got your guitar. We'll get some beers in and just jam, like we used to. It'll be great. What do you think?'

Patrick shouldn't really have needed to give this any consideration. He wanted so desperately to time-travel with this old friend, to regroup, to escape London's gangs, his Plan B life. Instead, he found himself contemplating Adam's bloated, ageing appearance, and seeing the mirror of his own graceless maturation, not least in his delusional infatuations with the past. Furthermore, Adam's lonely, single lifestyle brought to mind painful thoughts of Ana and Danny, how terribly he missed having family around, the opportunity to be the father to Danny he himself had never had. Rejoining The Forsaken might not necessarily have represented roadblocks to this, but, right now, it hardly symbolised moving forward.

And, lest he forget, he was a wanted man.

'That's a tempting offer..., but I need to be on my own for a while. I think it's... safer that way.'

Adam squinted at the guitar once more. 'So... Why'd you bring that with you? I kind of thought, you know, you were keen to... *Get Back*.' He sung the words in McCartney's voice but couldn't disguise his hurt.

Patrick reached for the Les Paul.

'It's for you. I can't write any more, not really, but I expect you still can. You're the guy who wrote "Find the Ocean", after all.'

Adam, for once, was speechless. 'I thought you hated that song,' he finally said.

'So did I.'

Adam's eyes were watering. 'Ah, man, I... I don't know what to say...'

'You don't need to say anything. Just take it. It's going to a better home.'

As Adam reached to accept the guitar Patrick was passing, the window behind him exploded, rained to the carpet in a curtain of tiny glass beads, and two loud bangs, as though cars had collided at high speed, seemed to make Adam cry out in pain and grab his chest just below the left collarbone. There came a surge of muffled screams before both sound and sight diluted. Patrick thought he saw a kid running from the pub to dive into a black cab which powered away with a familiar urgency, and then the world was on its side as carpet fell upon him, those beads of glass razor-sharp against his cheek. Blurring hands and faces and darkness crowded for supremacy above him, and his last memory before darkness won was of sketching a guitar for his father at the age of seven and his father nodding indifferently at the drawing before suggesting he go and show it to his mother.

FOUR

Again, that nauseating, curdling smell – once experienced, never forgotten. Except, this time, the heavy scent of death was his own.

The shock partly blocked the pain, just as the plastic mask hastily clipped over his mouth and nose obscured his view of the blood. Men in white. Men in blue. Voices, urgent.

Then vision stormed into darkness.

A pair of polyethylene fingers peeled back an eyelid and burst his brain with a sweeping torchlight. 'Tell me your name,' intoned the scraping, deep voice of a calm god.

Patrick said nothing. It couldn't have been him they were addressing. He let his head fall and saw the window of the pub was missing, save for a few glass spiders' webs along the bottom of the frame. He made out an overturned table and chair, saturated in glass, and an idle ambulance outside, the shoal of voyeurs already gathering.

His eyes filled with red pain.

'What've we got?'

'One dead, sir. And one injured. Sir.'

Patrick's senses fired awake. He looked around frantically.

'Some help over here please!' someone bellowed, very close. Above him, a bag of blood hung on a thin sliver. 'Quick. He's critical.' Tubes threaded crimson liquid.

Paramedics obscured Patrick's view. Pain too.

An outline of a body in white tape next to the jukebox. A black body bag. Blood soaking up the glass. Glass soaking up the blood.

'Looks like a drive-by,' someone announced, as Patrick caught a gust of cheap aftershave.

'Hospital. Now.' Another god.

Strong hands held him. 'This may hurt,' a voice warned. But he felt nothing as he was lifted and powered into the night past a bloodied guitar, his backpack, half-drunk pints of ale.

The darkness swept him as faces parted in the crowd. And a familiar woman running towards him. 'Patrick!' she shouted. 'Patrick!'

Sarah.

His body split by agony, he couldn't be sure if anything was real. A silent, throbbing scream greeted Sarah's haunting expression of... was it disappointment? No, it was surely grief and shock. Patrick tried to speak but his lungs weren't behind the effort, and he could only fold back into a hazy world of agony as the bright, white belly of the ambulance claimed him.

'Mate, I've seen *hundreds* of dead bodies but they still mess with my head.'

'Same.'

There was a jolt as the ambulance turned. The lights burned through Patrick's closed lids. He felt light, peaceful.

'Sometimes it's like they even speak. You know, the body's last gasps for air and that? Like a discharge of... I don't know. Memories? It's bloody sinister. To tell the truth, I don't like to get too close to them.'

'I know what you mean. In case they somehow infect you with their... *oblivion*. Silly isn't it? You never get used to it.'

Someone zipped something closed.

'Poor bugger. At least he would've died pretty much instantly.'

Even through the painkillers, Patrick brought sounds forth from his chest that weren't human. They took another corner. The siren tore the night.

'This one's going into cardiac arrest,' one of the gods said, panic raising the timbre of his voice, rendering him mortal.

And then, smiling faces. Christmas morning. Danny not even crawling yet, dressed in an elf Babygro. Ana under the mistletoe. His mother, her first Christmas without her husband, holding her grandson on her lap as they both slept peacefully. Peacefully.

And then nothing.

When Patrick woke some time later it was with the curious sense that he'd already woken a dozen times without ever regaining consciousness. He was in no physical pain, but couldn't move the lower half of his body and his mouth was parched and glued.

He was in a ward with three other beds, all exposed save for one in the far corner whose lilac curtain was pulled closed but couldn't mask the sound of coughing from within. The man to his immediate left was only visible because he was sitting out in his chair, wincing in a red dressing down, his dark but clumpy hair matted from sleeping in his own sweat. He stared ahead of him as though barely awake. The man opposite was unshaven, the hair on his head grown out into a tight brush. He was sour-faced but strangely resigned, contemptuous of everyone and everything, as though he'd been in the hospital some time.

Cold light screamed through the large window to Patrick's right but the view was only of the roof of another part of the hospital, the large grey fans of air conditioning units spinning disconsolately. The sky was as white as a bandage and a few birds wheeled underneath it.

The morphine machine next to Patrick shrilled, to alert him to the fact that he could self-administer, and he stabbed at the button near his right hand and released a fresh shot.

A female nurse hurried over from an unseen work station.

'How are you feeling?' She looked barely fifteen and her hair was back, her uniform so white it showed up a long, stray dark hair on her chest. She unhoused his stats from a clipboard mounted at the foot of the bed and pored over the notes without waiting for a reply. It had been, of course, a plainly ridiculous question.

'Can you pass me some water?'

She did so and Patrick drank a deep draught of room-temperature liquid, then threw up over himself. The curtain was pulled closed and his clothes and bedding changed, his body inert and embarrassed under her professional hands.

Afterwards, the surgeon paid him a visit and told him how lucky he was. He was accompanied by another two doctors and they peeled off the bandages from his side, then very painfully removed the plasters from the wound to check whether it had healed properly. Patrick self-administered another morphine shot as he was informed about the risks of infection, and the possibility of blood clots. The surgeon scratched at Patrick's toes.

'Feel that?'

'Yes,' Patrick lied.

'Can you wiggle them for me?'

He could not.

'You've had major trauma. Not many people get shot in the chest and live to tell the tale.'

Patrick jabbed at the morphine button but it wasn't ready to release yet. He was improbably high and the whole experience was like something from a bad sketch show.

'You won't be walking for a while, I'm afraid,' he stated. 'But... You're alive. Someone from Physio will come and see you later, and bring you a wheelchair so you'll be able to get yourself about as soon as possible. Have you got any questions?'

'How's Adam?'

'Who's Adam?'

'The guy I was drinking with when…'

'Get some rest,' he suggested, moving off.

The nurse returned and gave him an anticoagulant shot in the stomach, then took his blood pressure and temperature.

'Take these,' she said, placing a cardboard thimble of pills beside him.

'What is it?'

'Vodka Martini, shaken not stirred,' she joked, beginning to tourniquet his arm and sinking another needle in, sucking out a syringeful of blood.

'Where are my belongings?' Patrick asked.

'The police have them.'

'Does my wife know where I am?'

'I expect so.'

She showed him how to raise the bed so he could sit up, told him two days had passed since the shooting. He had vague memories of arriving at the hospital, drunk on the gas and air mix they kept shoving over his nose, waiting, parked in a bay for the medical team to assess him, for the X-rays to be taken. He remembered the shiny white ceilings passing overhead, the changing faces of nurses and medical staff. He remembered his underpants being cut off before he was wheeled towards the operating theatre and the smell of rubber as the anaesthetic was pressed across his face. He remembered being scared and alone, so far from his son, and wondering whether or not a religious persuasion would have made him a stronger person at that moment in time, and whether it was really too late to convert.

A shadow at his side barred the light, its back to him, pulling at wires, switches. The curtain was drawn.

'What time is it, doctor?' he asked.

The shadow yelped.

'Sarah…?' he asked.

She spun round and flashed a smile. 'You're awake! How are you feeling?'

He stabbed the morphine button.

'That bad, huh?'

Patrick grimaced.

'I wanted to see how you were. Terrible thing. Terrible. Have they found the person who did this?'

'No idea.'

'No. I don't suppose you'd know, would you? What happened?'

He repeated his previous answer. 'I think I'm going to throw up.'

Sarah rapidly handed Patrick a kidney bowl, then retreated as though having pulled the pin from a grenade, but he wasn't able to vomit under such scrutiny and dry heaved once, twice, then placed it back on the bedside locker himself. His side ached after that, and he could feel the ribs within twisted, jarred, saw the image of them under X-ray in his mind's eye, misaligned and cracked. Blood had seeped through the bandages and turned them brown where the bullet had entered and the surgeon had gone in to wash and clean out the wound.

'Thank God you're alright. I came as soon as I heard.'

He vaguely recalled her dreamlike appearance outside the pub. 'You came straight here?'

'Yeah. Like I said. As soon as I heard.'

'I think Adam's dead. I saw a body bag.'

'I'm sorry.'

'It was supposed to be me.'

'Shh. Don't think about it now.'

A nurse swept through the curtain and the rigmarole of body temperature and blood pressure takings was restarted. Sarah stepped outside while he had to piss into a bottle. The urine was so dark it looked like stout, but at least the catheter was out.

'You've got a temperature,' she told him, wandering off.

Sarah returned. 'Do you need anything? Some food? Something to read? There's a pretty good shop downstairs.'

'Thank you for coming,' he said again.

She smiled, but it was defeated, worrisome. He must have looked awful.

'It's not over,' he said. 'They won't stop. I was going to run away but I left it too late. They won't stop until I'm dead.'

The nurse reappeared through the curtain with a frowning doctor, and asked the usual questions. He was given codeine again and he peeled off the dressing on his side, painfully ripping away the last of the hair to study for infection. He seemed happy there was no pus but ordered the nurse to take a swab. The stitches were blue and huge, numbering, in that middle area alone, about twenty-five. The ward felt intensely hot and the prodding fingers of his nurse impossibly cold.

'Does this hurt?' she asked in response to Patrick's prehistoric language of anguish.

'For Christ's sake, warm your hands first.'

Tiredness lay heavily upon him still. The sleep he'd managed had been anaesthetic-induced and now he was just as artificially awake. The morphine machine was beeping, not because he was eligible for a fresh injection, but because the bag obviously needed changing. The two cannulas in his wrist chafed and he barely had the energy to give the surrounding skin even the most casual of scratches.

'Are you… out of the woods?' Sarah asked him when the medics retired again.

He took a long look at her. 'I hope so. I came… close. How the hell did I get mixed up in this?'

She was silent.

'You know, every time I close my eyes, I still see that window shattering, hear that gunshot. I smell death all the time.'

'Don't…' she said, horrified. She put her hand over her nose, as though the scent came back to her too. It was a small gesture, but it confirmed something within Patrick. And underneath everything, her same, disillusioned facial expression.

'At least I would've died in the pub,' he joked. 'Not that horrible place where Denis ended up.'

They looked at each other without mirth.

'Red meat. Burnt hair. Shit. That's what Denis's body smelt like.'

'Stop it,' she said.

'Sarah, what were you doing when I woke up?'

'Nothing. What do you mean?'

'You were trying to turn off my machines. I'm afraid it's not that simple. I'm no longer linked up to life support. Sorry. All you turned off was my morphine dispenser.'

'What?'

'You were at the pub. I saw you. Why did you tell me you came straight here?'

'What does it matter?'

'Why did you come? For confirmation that I was actually dead?'

'Are you…?'

'Your face, Sarah. I remember. You made this same face when I saw you as I was being lifted into the ambulance. You weren't upset, you were *disappointed*.'

'Patrick…'

'It's funny. Maybe it's all these drugs, but I'm clear headed for the first time in ages… Sarah, your precious fucking daughter is fine. The same people who tried to kill me will protect her.'

She spoke so quietly he could barely hear her. 'You don't know that.'

'Well, it's not guaranteed I suppose. Not while I'm alive and can tell them the truth.'

She didn't say anything.

'You were the only person who knew I was going to be at that pub. You tipped them off. You must have done.'

She looked around her, more desperate now.

'Patrick…'

'You fucking bitch. Jenna was always protected by the

gang, wasn't she? That punch I gave Denis really was my death warrant.'

She dragged her chair closer. Her face had bleached.

'We just needed your help Patrick, that's all.'

We?

The air in the ward was replaced by something viscous and bile-tasting. 'Oh my God… Just *how* long have I been duped for? You were in it all along.'

Sarah drew even closer, her face impossibly sad.

She whispered, so quietly it was almost imperceptible. 'I wasn't *in* it. I *did* it.'

It was Patrick's turn to be speechless as Sarah's mouth almost touched his ear.

'I think you know why I did it, don't you?' Her voice was cracking. 'That… boy… had assaulted Jenna before. I came to speak to you when the… abuse began again, remember? I mean, the plan was in its early stages then but… Over Christmas, Denis assaulted her again. He… raped…' She could hardly say the word. 'Despite your so-called "advice" to him.'

Patrick recalled the promises he'd made Sarah in his classroom that evening. He hadn't done a thing.

She couldn't look at him. 'Once we found out about the punch, I knew the plan couldn't fail. Frankly, after Jenna told me about your confrontation with Denis at the front of your classroom before Christmas, it was solid enough, but *that*…? That was… Well, let's just say it helped.'

Patrick croaked, 'When you say you *did it*…?'

Sarah's forehead was on his. To all the world, it would have looked a tender moment. 'Jenna arranged to meet Denis, in secret. Except… I was the one waiting there. I hid in the dark in the fur coat she sometimes borrowed off me. You must have noticed we look alike? The same physique, height…'

'And you…?'

'I shot him in the head.' She said it so offhand, like it was nothing. 'Then went back home and pretended to be asleep

271

while you cleaned up the evidence for us. We'd brought you in, as the risk taker, but had to make sure you kept quiet. It worked better than I thought. Jenna's bribe couldn't really fail, could it? You even visited the flat after the murder was announced, asked us not to say anything about the grass which you'd taken great pains to show me under Jenna's bed. In the end, the sniffer dogs found out about the drugs, but you'd already taken them off us by then. I admit I was nervous, but you kept your mouth shut. You probably weren't going to stay silent forever though, so...'

'So you gave me your body.'

She looked away. 'I used you, yes. And Jenna's performance was exemplary, though much of it wasn't an act. She felt it, poor girl, even though I was the one who pulled the trigger.'

'You let her take the blame. What kind of a mother does that?' He tried to pull himself away, but she held him by the shoulder and he lacked the strength to escape her.

'I got rid of him for her. *That's* the kind of mother I am,' she cried in a voice garrotted by sorrow. 'I knew the gangs would exact a revenge. But... but...'

'But on *me*.' Patrick felt redness march across his eyesight. Dizzy, he reached for water.

She grabbed his wrist. In her eyes, he saw madness, apology, desperation. 'Jenna said nothing at the police station, as we agreed. But Meadows suspected you. The sooner you were... killed... the better, frankly, before you ruined everything.'

Patrick was about to vomit when he felt the single, wet tear which had crossed from her cheek to his.

'It was hard to keep up the pretence, for both Jenna and myself, but I had to trust her. She didn't want me locked away, any more than I wanted to lose her. I *couldn't* lose another daughter, Patrick.' The tear was not for him. 'Then you started to wobble. You confronted Jenna in the estate, and were so close to working it all out, accusing her of

272

Denis's premeditated murder… But you seemed genuinely unstable and she was worried you would come clean in the interview room…'

'I wish I had.'

'We hadn't been expecting news of you hitting Denis to leak. And, to be honest, we didn't know if the gang would try anything after that… But Jenna put them off the scent – that was my idea – to take police pressure off you. To leave you only to the gangs… But then we were kidnapped. I admit, I thought it had all gone very wrong then. I didn't bank on the gang having such a strong code of honour. But I carried on with the act. What else could I do?'

Almost every part of Patrick's body hurt. 'Did Jenna tell them I killed Denis?'

Her lips were trembling. 'What do you think? By then the final piece had fallen into place: you let me know exactly where you were going to be that evening. And Jenna told the Souljas.'

The image of Jenna's automaton's eyes in the exam hall came back to him. Her mother was controlling her. She obviously didn't want to lose her mother, the sole remaining member of her family, yet neither did she want to be attacked by Denis again. He wondered how complicit Jenna really was, whether she regretted ever telling her mother about Denis in the first place, and how often their arguments, such as the one in the school playground after the press conference, threatened to derail the plot against him. Maybe she, too, had spent the last few weeks wondering how the hell she'd got involved in those dangerous games, why she'd spent so long cosying up to her attacker just so her mother could gun him down and drag her through weeks of lies and risk. Had Denis terrified her that much, to go to such extreme lengths?

Patrick remembered the encounter in the alley, the glint of the blade pushed up against his throat, Denis's acrid breath. Of course he had.

His heart was thumping faster than he'd ever known.

She looked at him with the same nervously calculating eyes she'd looked at him with after their aborted Lionswater encounter, as though begging herself for the confidence to carry out her plan to its end, then cupped the back of his head, stroked his cheek. There was something lovingly final about it, as there might be moments before the bloodletting in the abattoir.

'Forgive me for coming on strong at the parents' evening, but after your midnight Dear John I needed to... keep you on the hook. And, I admit, I *was* startled by a face outside my window that night after the press conference, but sleeping with you was...'

'Collateral damage,' he rasped.

'Oh, Patrick...' She tried to smile but it was one of utter desolation. 'You thought I was falling for the great rock star?'

He laughed without mirth. 'You make it all sound so easy.'

She put her mouth up to his ear. Her breath was warm, sweet.

'Believe me, it wasn't. *It isn't.*'

Their eyes met, though in truth they could barely see each other through the swelling tears.

'I'm sorry,' she whispered.

Then, before he knew what she was doing, Sarah whipped out the pillow from beneath his head and, in one fluid move, pressed it over his face.

He couldn't move his legs, couldn't kick out. She seemed to be bearing down on him in several places. His head. His wound. He was weak and, by degrees, could feel his breath failing as she ebbed the panicked squall from his chest, filled his mouth with NHS cotton. His silent words bubbled like blood. Harder and harder the pillow pressed and deeper and deeper he felt the pull of a sleep which he knew would be his last. All that separated his quiet murder from the trained staff who might save him was a thin, drawn lilac curtain.

Finally, it seemed, his lungs burst.

A terrifying scream, dredged from hell, pierced his remaining senses and he tasted and then gulped at syrupy air as the pillow relaxed. With some difficulty, Patrick shook the pillow to the floor and saw Ana with her hands round Sarah's middle, as though performing a particularly violent Heimlich. The words which shrieked from both women were guttural and inaudible, more so when Sarah clawed a long scratch along Ana's right arm, drawing blood, and forced the release. Sarah spun round and, like a woman possessed, lunged for Ana's throat as ward staff sprang through the curtain and attempted to pull the scrabbling pair apart.

Wide-eyed faces of curious patients peered through the curtains. Finally, Sarah was peeled from Ana. Giant wracking heaves sobbed out of her as she was bundled back and her arms pressed roughly behind her back. She screamed in pure, vivid anguish and the ward almost shook with the force of it.

'Even look at my husband and I'll break your neck, bitch,' Ana spat.

'Call the police,' Patrick gasped.

The young nurse saw his distress, ran to his side.

Patrick massaged his exploding chest, winced. 'She tried to kill me.'

'Which one?'

When Patrick nodded at Sarah, Ana was released.

'It's okay,' Patrick told everyone, with a slight smile. 'This is my wife.'

Ana rushed towards him.

'I told you I didn't trust her.'

'You were right not to. She murdered Denis,' Patrick told her. 'Don't let her get away,' he called after security as they escorted Sarah out.

If she was looking at him as she was led into the corridor, Patrick never saw. He was watching the gauzed sky change to onyx outside, the creeping shadows chasing dusk across the hospital roof. What looked like a murmuration of starlings swept across the rooftops, but it might also have been the codeine casting spectral stains across his tired retinae.

'Visiting hours are over,' the nurse told Ana.

She sat next to her husband and croaked out a laugh. It was the first time they'd shared a bed in roughly a year and it was the first time she'd laughed in one in even longer.

'Where's Danny?' Patrick asked her.

She took his hand and squeezed it. 'At your mother's. I didn't want him seeing you like this.'

'Adam's dead. I'm sorry.'

He looked into her eyes, waiting for the information to bed itself in.

'I know.'

They remained there in silence for some time. The medical staff repaired the damage to his small section of the ward, checked him over, plumped up the pillow he'd almost been suffocated by. The morphine machine restarted its shrill beeping.

'You scared me, on the phone.'

'Sorry.'

'I knew it was serious when you told me you loved me. It was the first time you'd said that in a long time.'

He turned to his wife, perplexed. 'It was? I thought I was always telling you?'

She shook her head, a rueful smile barely concealed. 'Oh Patrick. What the hell did you get involved in? Why couldn't you let me help you?'

He sighed. It hurt. 'Things escalated quickly.'

'You can say that again. Are you safe now?'

He looked over his wounded body, the drips and machines being reset by his nurse. 'For now, I suppose.' He felt impossibly tired. The Souljas would just have to take his hospitalisation, and months of physio, as downpayment for Denis's death, until the truth came out, as it surely would, at Sarah's trial.

'So what happens now?'

'Well, I'm never going back to teaching.'

She experimented with a modest laugh. 'No, I meant...' The ward hummed. The wheels of a trolley scraped somewhere. '...I don't have to take this job offer, you know.'

Patrick half-turned. 'What do you mean?'

'You need to recuperate, and it sounds like you're better off out of London for a time too, so... I don't know. Maybe you could come back with us to Argentina? Danny needs you, Patrick. He's missed you more than you could possibly imagine. And, maybe... I'm not saying it won't be difficult, but... We could see how it goes. It could be a chance for a fresh start, for all of us...'

Patrick gazed at his wife in mute, drugged wonder. He wouldn't be leaving this hospital for some time but the thought of heading faraway with his son, with Ana, was morphine itself. He could only nod in quiet shock.

They both became aware of a clicking pair of feet along the ward, growing louder before they slowed.

When Meadows appeared, his dour face registered a brief surprise then, unthinkably, a degree of amusement. Though he couldn't possibly have known what had occurred in the last hour, there was something in the older man's bearing which tried desperately hard, Patrick recognised now, to foster the pretence that he was one step ahead of everyone. Meadows stopped with a sharp snap at the foot of the hospital bed, his lined head tilted to one side as he eyeballed the bedridden Art teacher and his unfamiliar visitor. The customary notebook was already in his hand.

Patrick propped himself up onto one elbow, gritted his teeth against the violent pain in his side.

'Detective Chief Inspector, I'm prepared to revise my statement.'

ACKNOWLEDGEMENTS

Since the title of this book was announced, several people have been in touch asking whether its contents are autobiographical. They are not. During the majority of the time I spent teaching in England, I was privileged to work at an outstanding secondary school in leafy North London, championed by a management team and hard-working colleagues far removed from the characters depicted in *The Art Teacher*. None of the incidents described within these pages occurred (to my knowledge) and there's good reason why this book is fictional: bureaucracy rarely makes for a riveting read.

I've been careful not to name any of my characters after real people for fear of causing offence but if I erroneously borrowed someone's name it's because my memory is terrible and more than two-thousand different pupils passed through my various classrooms during the years I worked part-time, desperately trying to make a go of my soppy, unlikely dream of getting published. Either that, or I just thought you had a cool name.

Highfields too, does not exist, though it should be said that schools with similar problems do, schools where staff feel undervalued and under-supported and their pupils fail to receive the attention or edification they deserve. Like Patrick, I'd make a lousy politician but it's clear to me that we marginalise issues relating to, and reduce the funding for, the education system at our peril.

There are several people I need to thank.

Early advice, which was justifiably scathing, and incredibly helpful, came from Matt Thorne. Likewise, feedback from Harriett Gilbert guided me toward newer directions. To anyone who's ever read my work, in whatever form, and offered either honest or dishonest reviews, I thank you, principally the members of my London City MA programme and Tony Hayles and Matthew Strawson. Thanks to the APS team for laughs and spicy chicken in my carnivorous days. And to Mum, for a lifelong love of reading. Sorry about all the swearing.

To all at Legend Press: you are. Legends. Tom, Lauren, Lucy, Lottie, Jessica: thank you so much. Special thanks must go to Rob whose editorial sagacity has transformed this book in subtly powerful ways too numerous to mention here.

My agent, Louise Greenberg, deserves particular praise for patience and wisdom beyond measure.

Most of all, thank you Patricia, for putting up with closed doors and wishful thinking, for being the designated driver far too often and for giving me two beautiful children under bluer skies. The people above all helped in some way along the line, but I couldn't have done any of this without you.

We hope you enjoyed Paul's brilliant debut, *The Art Teacher*.

Paul's second novel, *Blame*, centres around a man called Lucas. He has a good job in pharmaceuticals, plenty of casual friends and the conviction that whatever ill-advised habits he may have are well under control. When the father he's hated for most of his life dies in perplexing circumstances, Lucas impulsively accompanies a girlfriend on her visit home, instead of heading to his. A long-forgotten diary soon plunges him back into the events leading to his family's collapse.

Here's a sample of *Blame*:

The three of us trudge to the summit with heads bowed, the north wind twisting the long grass flat under our feet. Our midday sun is a ghost behind clouds pregnant with snow, and nothing in this beautiful, hostile place has a shadow.

Mum holds the box. It's made of thick purple cardboard, about the same shape and size as a child's shoebox, and is bound by an unpretentious elastic band. Suddenly, she slows.

'Here. This is the place.'

The view rises to meet us as we scale the crown. Fifty unspoilt miles of the south coast unfurl with jutting piers, undulating shores and wind-lashed hawthorns. At the horizon, the sky becomes the land becomes the sea. My eyes smart with the cold.

'He loved this place,' Mum confirms for the hundredth time, this recently retired woman who used to dress for any occasion but today wears tired jeans and a shapeless brown jumper. The weather has made an unruly thatch of her hair.

She slides the lid off and the three of us peer inside.

My brother's reaction is as I'd expected, but I take no pleasure from the vaguely harrowed expression he wears. He's not a man of science and had been expecting the grey ashes of television drama. What he sees is an exercise in simple physics: the pulverised dry bone fragments from a cremulator risen, via convection, through the lighter granules after ten years of sitting in the corner of Mum's bedroom.

'It looks like…' he begins.

'I know,' Mum says.

A middle-aged man approaches from a worn path below, his waterproofs vacuum-sealed against his torso by the swirling wind. A black Labrador leads the way, sniffing expertly at the sparse hedgerows. I look to the others.

'Shall we wait?'

They both nod. We've waited a decade; another two minutes won't hurt.

'We should turn our backs,' my brother suggests, pointing across the green-grey, 'so he's taken across the Downs, that way.'

He's.

We turn away from the wind, though it seems to make little difference.

The approaching man quickens, as if he knows we're waiting for him. His eyes are apologetic. In his wake, clouds break and snow begins to spiral in small flakes, black against the white sky.

It's Good Friday and this must surely be one of the last truly cold weekends of the year – the ground under us is frozen and I can see the snow beginning to settle already – but it's an important anniversary, and we've managed to all meet up, so this is the day it has to happen. I was opposed to the idea, at first, but my brother's right: those fragile, shell-like bone particles are *him*. This is more than a gesture. This is a disposal. We have arrived at an ending.

Mum begins to pour as she walks along the brow of the hill, leaving a little trail of fragments behind her. As the larger granules run out, the smaller particles are released, catch the wind and disperse in a thousand different directions. My brother reels, having caught some in the eye. We laugh. My mother hands the box to me and I empty a little more. The ash diffuses through the wind in a spectral curtain of swirls and eddies. I can taste it on my teeth. Mum stands back at some distance, lost in thought, eyeballing the view. I hand the box to my brother and he shakes out the remainder, his eyes red from the cold and the ash. Then, it is over.

We stand there, cinders in our mouths, our hair, upon our coats, watching the snow mingle with the dust, float back down to Earth a part of it, and with every blink I see a fresh tableau within the churning sky. Candlelit lovers caught unaware through a thin gap in a door. A phone call announcing a murder. The beginning of love above the New York skyline. Blood leading to the closed doors of an ambulance. All times are here and now and one and the same, condensed, with this moment, into a single journey. And it all seems like yesterday.

We fall into a group hug and stare out over the whitening view. I'm the first to speak.

'Bye Dad.'

Time travel. It's an easy, forgiving process. It takes nothing to go back, to rewrite.

It's often said that history is scripted by the winners. Personally, I think 'survivors' would be a better word. I've been several people in my time, and my return visits to those others' pasts are unreliable at best and complete fabrications at worst. I have survived myself, but only just.

Don't believe a word I tell you. Take it from me.

We return to the car park, our shoes creaking across the compacting snow.

I can see my wife reading a book in the back of the Cherokee. Our son is upright in his Mamas and Papas car seat beside her, in a sleep that could, and does, survive fireworks and thunderstorms but cannot cope with the imperceptible tread of a parent's footstep. Sure enough, he stirs, then turns a slow, accusatory head towards me. This extra sensory perception, in turn, alerts his mother to my presence. She counters her smile immediately, assuming it's inappropriate. I beam back, but this only serves to make her uneasy. She knows the full range of my smiles, and this one didn't fool her at all.

She stuffs her book out of sight and winds the window down. Her eyes, pink and watery, focus on the empty box Mum carries.

We all get in without another word. My brother in the back. My mother next to me. I turn the engine and it stutters, hesitates, then starts. I know it's just my imagination, but the snow slowing the wipers seems grittier than usual. The analogue clock mounted to the Jeep's dashboard shows it's much later than I realised. Once again, time ran away from us.

'Will the snow cause problems for the car?' Mum asks.

I reassure her that it won't.

On the way to the restaurant, I attempt to close my mind around the memories and feelings we've just thrown into the air. I can't rationalise or order those lonely fragments of time. All I can do, as the chatter around me grows in its geniality and my son – quite rightly – steals the conversation away from the darkness, is watch the narrow roads unlace in the rear-view mirror, my thoughts whirling with the bone particles, hunting for answers, for chronology, trying to get back, right back, to a beginning of sorts.

And then I hit the ice. The Jeep bucks, jolts out of my control. I try to do as you're told to do in the circumstances and steer into the skid but the steering locks beneath my hands and we glide, in slow motion yet at thirty miles an hour, into an oncoming van, its driver's horrified face nothing but an open mouth screaming towards us.

COME AND VISIT US AT
WWW.LEGENDPRESS.CO.UK

FOLLOW US
@LEGEND_PRESS